ILLICIT ARTIFACTS

Visit us at www.boldstrokesbooks.com

By the Author

UnCatholic Conduct

Illicit Artifacts

ILLICIT ARTIFACTS

by

Stevie Mikayne

2015

ILLICIT ARTIFACTS

© 2015 By Stevie Mikayne. All Rights Reserved.

ISBN 13: 978-1-62639-472-8

This Trade Paperback Original Is Published By
Bold Strokes Books, Inc.
P.O. Box 249
Valley Falls, NY 12185

First Edition: November 2015

This is a work of fiction. Names, characters, places, and incidents are the product of the author's imagination or are used fictitiously. Any resemblance to actual persons, living or dead, business establishments, events, or locales is entirely coincidental.

This book, or parts thereof, may not be reproduced in any form without permission.

Credits
Editor: Cindy Cresap
Production Design: Susan Ramundo
Cover Design By Jeanine Henning

Dedication

To the fabulous staff at the Carp Chiropractic Clinic. Thanks for letting me crash your space to get some writing done and for folding me into your crazy crew. (And yes, I do know you've been passing around a copy of *UnCatholic Conduct*, giggling to yourselves!) You're inspiring, uplifting, and downright hilarious. Cheers to all the times—good, bad, and complicated.

With love,
Stevie

CHAPTER ONE

Jil stood in Elise's forbidden library, staring for a moment at the old mahogany desk. The warm, spicy scent of old tobacco candles mixed with the lingering trace of Elise's perfume that still clung to the heavy drapes. Smells triggered memories, right?

That's why she felt like she'd just run into the broad side of a truck.

Elise's essence wafted from the rich carpet that covered most of the floor—Jil felt like if she looked up into the loft, she'd find her sitting there in a pair of pince-nez, leafing through first edition volumes.

She put her hand to her chest as it constricted. She'd forgotten how physical grief could be. For the past three days, since Padraig had called to say Elise had died, she'd avoided this place—avoided coming home to find the house empty.

The silence in this space was tangible. She never would have come home if she didn't have a funeral to prepare for.

She could wait to say good-bye.

A big part of her was rebelling against that as well. Screw the rituals. Screw the viewings and the hymns and the burials and the prayers. Elise would never be more missing to her than she was in her library at home.

Maybe if she let herself cry, the elephant on her chest would get the hell off and leave her in peace. Jil sat on the bottom step of the staircase and closed her eyes, letting the memories flash through her mind instead of pushing them under.

They would fade over time, like the smell of this room.

She would sell this house and someone else would live here.

She'd move on with her life and look back fondly on the woman who'd given her a home when she needed one and stayed with her long after the system said they should be separated.

She looked over to the two-story bookshelf—pristine, as usual.

The last time Jil was home, Elise had lent her materials from her precious collection to use on a case, and had insisted on talking about her will. Her impending death had been no surprise.

Then why did it seem so sudden?

Jil got up and paced the room. She felt a restless energy she usually only felt when she was about to crack a case. Only this time it was personal. She had to read Elise's final directives—make a move toward laying her to rest.

She ran her fingers along the desk's smooth wooden face panel, feeling for the spring that would unlatch the secret compartment. The panel shifted under her hand, popping up slightly, and Jil slid her hand in to recover the slender folder that contained Elise's instructions.

She found a list containing the names and numbers of everyone she'd need to contact, including the lawyer whose name was sticky-noted to the front of the envelope marked "Will."

Jil shuffled that envelope to the back. She didn't want to see it.

The funeral home had called this morning, wanting to know if she would be bringing an outfit. They had the body and nothing to dress it with. Nobody else had keys, so she'd had to come over. Jil was as close to family as Elise had. Now the house would have to be sold. And the gutter was still falling off outside, as it had been on her last visit.

Maybe she could call the handyman before the lawyer listed the house…

The tile hallways echoed with the sound of her boot heels as she made her way upstairs to Elise's bedroom, the folder in hand. The house still smelled as if Elise had just been in the kitchen cooking. She breathed in slowly, drinking in home for the last time.

Her phone buzzed. Jess. *How's it going? Need help?*
Almost done, she texted back. *Be home soon.*

She walked into the bathroom, which gleamed with ornate fixtures and white marble. How had Elise had time to keep her bathroom this clean? The shower in particular was a blazing white that looked startling, even for Elise's level of cleanliness.

Was she lonely?

Trying to keep busy?

Scrubbing every inch of this house so Jil wouldn't have to do it?

She sat for a second on the edge of the Roman tub, swallowing down tears. How could she be gone?

In the blue ceramic trash bin sat a bottle of cleaning solution. Jil took it out. It was unlike Elise not to recycle. Further evidence that she was tired. Not herself. "Sparkling white, then out of sight. Goes on strong and evaporates for a glistening shine!"

She caught herself mindlessly reading the directions: *Mix one capful to a quart and spray on!* and gave her head a shake. She had many more important things to be reading.

Garbage day wasn't until next week. She put the cleaning solution back in the empty trash bin and turned the light off.

In the walk-in closet, she found a dry-cleaning bag hanging on the back of the door, a sticky note penned in Elise's hand stuck to the front. *For the funeral.*

Jil grabbed the bag and the little makeup case next to it, into which Elise had packed some lipstick, a strand of pearls, and an ornate butterfly brooch she wanted to wear.

"Don't you worry about grave robbers?" Jil had asked.

Elise laughed. "It's costume jewelry. Not worth anything. Make sure to take off my emerald ring, though. That's for you. And please remember my lipstick. I don't want to look like a clown laid out in funeral makeup."

As Jil packed up the last few items the funeral home needed, she heard the front door opening.

"Hello!" she called.

A slight young woman with dark strawberry blond hair and very pale skin stood in the foyer, clutching a bag with a medical emblem.

"Hello." She smiled tentatively.

"Hi." Jil landed on the last step. "Can I help you?"

"I'm Anastasia. The visiting aide? I'm here to help Elise with her shower and meal preparation." Her brow creased as she looked beyond Jil without seeing Elise.

Jil stared at her for a second. "I'm…sorry," she stammered at last. "Elise is dead."

"Dead?" Anastasia said. "Oh dear. Oh, I didn't know…nobody phoned me…I feel a right idiot coming here like this. I'm very sorry for your loss. You…you're Jil?"

"Yes. I'm sorry. I had no idea Elise even had a visiting aide. I suppose it would have been up to me to make phone calls. Sorry for wasting your time."

"That's no problem. It's terrible for me to show up like this. I'll let the agency know."

Jil looked down at the white emblem on the navy background of her bag, which matched the one on her coat. She never could figure out what snakes and medicine had to do with one another.

"I just have a few medical supplies in a box in Elise's room. I leave them here between visits. You know, to prevent spreading germs from one patient to another. Can I just fetch that back, and I'll be out of your hair?"

Jil gestured toward the stairs. "Help yourself. I'll be in the kitchen."

The aide passed her, then tiptoed noiselessly up the stairs, and Jil turned her attention to the kettle in the kitchen.

She took down the tin of Irish breakfast tea—the tea she and Elise had loved to share. As she set it on the counter, the tin rattled.

Why?

Frowning, she shook the tin and heard something clatter inside. She opened the lid and sifted through the tea leaves. A sliver of silver glinted back at her from the bottom, and she pulled it out—a key.

If Elise had put a key in this tin, it could only have been meant for her.

So what did it open?

As the kettle whistled, Anastasia popped her head around the swinging door. She held a small cardboard box half-full of medical miscellanea. "Got it. Thanks for letting me in."

"No trouble," said Jil, turning to fill the teapot. "Would you like a cup?"

Anastasia hesitated, then put the cardboard box down and sat at the table, still wearing her coat.

Jil passed the milk and sugar and poured a cup of steaming black tea into Anastasia's cup.

"She spoke of you often," Anastasia said, stirring sugar in slowly. "You meant a lot to her."

"I guess I should have been around a little more," Jil returned. "Then I might have known she needed a visiting aide."

"Only in the past few weeks. And only every few days. End of life can be a little…"

Jil set down her mug. "Gross?" Being terse seemed to displace the ache in her chest. She hoped she didn't come across as unfeeling.

"Well, for lack of a better phrase…"

Jil noticed that Anastasia fidgeted with the gold bangle around her wrist. She probably made her nervous.

"Where will you go now?" she asked, trying to be kind. "More patients?"

"No. She was my last one for today." Anastasia finished her tea. "Do let me know if there's anything I can do."

Jil tried to smile. "Thanks."

Just then, the doorbell rang.

"That'll be the neighbors," Anastasia said, standing and slinging her purse over her shoulder.

Jil looked at her quizzically. "Were you expecting someone?"

"No. But that's what happens when somebody dies, I'm afraid. You're bombarded with Bundt cakes and casseroles. I see it all the time." She picked up her cup and carried it over to the sink. "I'll leave you to your guests."

"Great," Jil muttered.

They walked to the front door, and as Jil opened it, Anastasia slipped past Mrs. Walowitz—the neighbor across the way—who held out a foil-wrapped dish.

"Jillienne darling, I'm so sorry," Mrs. Walowitz cried. She wrapped Jil into a suffocating embrace with one arm and balanced the large casserole dish in the other. "Let me come in and make you some tea. Mrs. Franks will be over in a few minutes with a lovely banana bread she's been making. We can all sit down and have a chat."

Jil cringed inwardly but led the way to the kitchen. Just as she sat down, the doorbell rang again.

❖

Jil hurried into the funeral home, turning down the stairs to avoid the visitation going on in the next room. The pungent scent of flowers hung thick in the air, mixed with the fine dust wafting from the formal furniture.

"I'm sorry to be late. Every neighbor on the block dropped by!"

The young funeral director looked up from her desk and smiled. Her blond hair was pulled back in a severe bun, but her red lipstick—a shade that came close to bordering on crimson—chafed against her navy uniform. A free spirit?

Her nameplate read *Karrie*.

"Hello. How can I help you?"

Jil held out her hand. "I'm Jillienne Kidd. I'm here to make the arrangements for Elise Fitzgerald."

Karrie frowned. For a moment, she seemed frozen to her chair. Then she came around the desk to shake hands. "You're Jil? I'm so sorry to be rude, but can you prove it?"

Jil took a step back but fished out her PI license and flashed it. "Didn't know I needed ID."

Karrie's face had blanched, and she leaned back against the desk.

"What's the matter?" Jil asked. "Why do you look like you've seen a ghost?"

"Can you please excuse me for a moment?" Karrie pushed off the desk and rushed to the door. Jil heard muttered voices in the hallway, and moments later, Karrie reappeared, making an effort to compose herself.

"Jil, please sit down."

Jil felt her stomach drop. "I'll stand, thanks. What's the problem?"

Karrie exhaled slowly. "I'm very sorry to have to tell you this, and I take full responsibility for the mistake I've made, but... Mrs. Fitzgerald left an heirloom meant for you in my care, and I've accidentally given it to someone else."

"Who?" Jil demanded. "And what was it?"

"An emerald ring, I'm afraid. And the thing is…I thought I gave it to you."

Jil raised her eyebrows. "Well, clearly you didn't give it to me."

Karrie pushed her hand through her hair, undoing part of her carefully arranged bun. "The Jil Kidd I met looked almost exactly like you."

"When did she get here?"

"Not half an hour ago. I only had time to give her the envelope, and she said she'd be back to make the final arrangements."

Jil's stomach plummeted. Someone was impersonating her. Why? "But I'm here instead."

"Unfortunately, yes…um—that's not what I meant."

Jil felt her mouth twitch, but suppressed the urge to smile. "It's okay. This is obviously not your fault."

"Nothing like this has ever happened to me before."

"Really? Consider yourself lucky." Jil bit her tongue. "Sorry. It's a bit shocking to find out someone is pretending to be me. And just to get a ring?"

Karrie slid into her chair. "I'm so sorry. And worse, I have no idea how I'll get it back for you."

"Well, luckily for you, I'm a private investigator, so I'll take care of that part."

"Oh. Oh! That's the best news I've had all day. My boss is just about ready to give me the axe. If we had a police investigation and the cops were here, he'd absolutely fire me. I'm pretty sure he'd kill me, actually. I'm not sure what to say, except once again, I'm so sorry."

Jil shook her head. "You know what? It doesn't matter. I will figure this out as soon as I have time. For now, my priority is this funeral. After that, I find out about my doppelganger."

"I'll admit, I'll be glad to see this finished."

"Was Elise that bad?"

"No, of course not. She was on a schedule, and the pathology report messed it up. I've done my best to get things back on track, but…" she trailed off.

"Elise had a pathology report?"

Karrie swallowed hard. "God, I'm really putting my foot in it today, aren't I?"

"Tell me more about it."

"It's standard, normally, when a patient dies at home."

"Even when they're terminally ill?"

Karrie tilted her head from side to side, seeming to weigh her answer. "Not always, but often enough. I didn't think much of it, honestly. My dad was actually the medical examiner in this case. He didn't say anything to me about any unusual findings. I just figured they were back-logged."

"Do you think I could see the report?"

Karrie hesitated. "Normally, I wouldn't be allowed to show you…but seeing as I've totally screwed up delivering your ring and have been the worst possible funeral director today, I guess I could accidentally leave it on the desk for a few minutes and go to the bathroom."

Jil winked. "A few minutes is all I'll need."

"Great." Karrie took a file from her desk and set it on the table, then walked to the door.

As soon as she'd gone, Jil jumped up from her ornate wooden seat and grabbed the report, scanning it quickly. Most of it, she didn't understand. Then she spied the industrial-sized photocopier in the corner.

Bingo.

In record time, she'd copied the whole thing and tucked the hot pages into her bag. She replaced the file on the table just as Karrie came back in.

"All right, let's get down to the rest," Karrie said. "The good news is that, despite the long delay, there isn't much to do, so you'll only be here a few minutes. Everything was pre-planned."

"Of course it was."

Karrie winked.

"Let me guess. She chose everything from the music to the thank-you notes."

"That's about the size of it, yes."

"I guessed that when I found out she'd given me specific instructions about the lipstick." Jil handed over the tube of iced mauve.

"Oh yes, I got them too." Karrie's eyes danced. "Right at the top of the list, and with at least four sticky notes. Open casket and good makeup. She was quite clear."

"Remember the brooch, okay? And the shoes, even though I know you can't see the feet." Jil's breath caught as she pictured Elise, lying in her navy suit in a mahogany casket, her hands clasped lightly around a rose.

Her phone buzzed and she picked it up to turn off the volume, catching sight of a text from Padraig. "Sorry, excuse me."

You're not at home. I'm here.

Damn. She'd forgotten about his visit today.

"I'm sorry, but I have to leave right away."

"No problem. Everything's basically done. All you have to do is show up for the viewing tomorrow."

"I'll be here." She pushed the makeup case toward Karrie, then turned and hurried out to the parking lot.

❖

As she pulled into the visitors' parking section at her flat, she spotted Padraig's SUV. She pulled up beside him in the tiny lot and got out. "What's up, old man? Want me to put the coffee on?"

He opened his window. "No time today. I'm already on my way to the airport." His Irish accent seemed to have thickened since he'd announced he had to go back to Ireland for family business.

"Flight moved up?"

"Yeah. Good thing I'd already packed."

Jil peeked in the back. "I thought you were going for a few weeks? Are you bringing your whole house with you?"

Padraig fixed her with a glare. "You know, that old adage about men needing only a change of britches is completely false. I like to look good abroad. I need at least three suits—"

"Okay, I'm sorry. Jeez Louise."

"Anyway, I'm sorry for the shite timing." Padraig sighed and handed Jil a set of keys. "I don't trust the boys to balance the books and keep the lights on while I'm gone."

"No, of course not. They'd turn the place into a frat house." She frowned. She knew she should tell Padraig about the impersonator and her ring being stolen but something else was bothering her more.

"What is it?" Padraig knew her too well.

"Nothing. Probably nothing. I'm not even a medical examiner."

"But you're a pretty damn good detective, so…what gives, Kidd?"

Jil squinted—a bad habit that was starting to produce unattractive lines across the bridge of her nose. "I talked to Karrie today at the funeral home, and she said something to me that I'm not allowed to repeat. But do you think it's odd that Elise's autopsy took an extra day? I didn't even think about it, but now I'm wondering."

"Wait, what are you saying?"

"Why did they perform an autopsy on her anyway?"

"Did you ask?"

"Yes. Karrie said it was because she died at home."

"But you're skeptical?"

Jil's shoulders slumped. "I don't know. I don't know! Should I be skeptical? Should I just be glad someone cared enough to make sure she did in fact die of natural causes?"

"She *did* die of natural causes, Jil. I found her myself. In bed. She looked like she'd just gone to sleep there—peacefully. Wrapped in her duvet cover, comfortable."

She breathed out slowly.

"I know. You don't need the details."

"It's not that," she whispered. "It's just that I didn't...I didn't get to say good-bye to her."

He looked at her, hard. "That's not the time to say good-bye. The time to say good-bye is when you were going home at night and you gave her a kiss and said 'See you next week.' That was all the good-bye she needed from you."

Jil looked skyward.

He leaned closer, frowning. "What is it?"

Jil sighed and shrugged. She suddenly felt tired. "I knew she was going to die. I knew it would be soon. It just seems *too* soon, you know?"

He shrugged, sitting back in his seat. "Did you think that maybe you're looking for a reason?"

Jil looked away. "I had considered the possibility. I know it's probably nothing. It's just that I have this feeling..."

Padraig frowned. "Have you told anyone else?"

"No."

"Do you plan to investigate this?"

"I don't know yet. I don't even know if there's anything to investigate. I'd feel stupid bringing it up with the police if it were nothing."

"Aye." He sighed. "I wish I could stay to help you with this. And I wanted to be here for Elise's funeral."

"I know. She'd understand."

"She was a good foster mother to you, and I'm sorry you've lost her."

His frankness made tears well up in Jil's eyes, and she fingered the handle of the driver's side door, avoiding his gaze as she swallowed down the feelings she'd been certain she'd dodge by preparing as much as possible for Elise's death.

"Don't get me started, Padraig. I still have to get through the funeral and wake and all the other horrible processes people insist on."

"Jess going with you?"

Jil looked up to her third floor flat and imagined Jessica inside, apron on, moving efficiently around the kitchen, stirring garlic and onions, and—

"She can't. It's in the middle of the workday. She has a school to run. Besides, she can't exactly pen 'funeral with girlfriend' into her St. Marguerite's calendar."

"Give it some time." Padraig clapped a rough, calloused hand over Jil's and gave it a small squeeze.

"No choice." Jil hitched her bag up higher on her shoulder. "See you when you get back. Don't hold up your plane."

He tipped his hat to her and shifted the car into gear. "I'll see you in a few weeks. Keep the boys on a tight leash while I'm away!"

She watched him pull around the corner before entering the main lobby of her building, a painful lump forming at the base of her throat. He had family business to attend to. He had to go.

But as he left, she couldn't help feeling like he'd ditched her.

CHAPTER TWO

H i," Jess said.
     Jil kicked off her brown leather boots and dropped her scarf and hat on the side table next to the door.

She wore Jil's old black apron and held a wooden spoon in her hand, stirring something that smelled delicious. Exactly as Jil had pictured her. Just like she'd found her every night since Elise had died.

"What is that?"

"Leek and mushroom risotto."

From the corner, Zeus raised his massive head, then snuggled back down onto his bed.

"Don't bother getting up," Jil said. "Lazy beast."

"Don't blame him. He had a good long run and he's tired."

Jil slid onto a stool at the island bar and accepted a glass of white wine that Jess held out.

"I hope you like it. It's Riesling, to go with our theme this evening."

"Which is?"

"I'll let you guess." The kitchen light reflected off Jess's dark green irises and made her look even more dangerous and sexy than usual.

Jil felt a pull in the pit of her stomach—a magnetic force that drew her to Jess, even though she knew so many things about this relationship just couldn't work...

"Do you want to talk about your day?" Jess slid a plate across the island—parmesan cups with something smoky and salty in the middle and topped with sweet fig compote.

Jil closed her eyes as the crispy cheese melted slightly on her tongue and savored it a moment longer before swallowing. "No, not really. You?"

Jess pulled on mitts and reached into the oven. "I wouldn't know where to start." She smiled ruefully, and Jil noticed the faint lines of fatigue around her eyes and mouth as she turned and poked the contents of the flat roasting pan, then slid it back into the oven. "All I can say is 'Thank God it's Friday.'"

Jil grinned. "That means even less to PIs than it does to principals."

"This is me, attempting a weekend. I'm trying to take a more traditional approach to my work."

"Really? Traditional at the Catholic Board?"

"Can it. I'm still cleaning up the mess you made at my school." Jess winked and slowly circled the island until she stood within arm's reach.

Jil smiled as Jess reached up and touched her cheek, running her fingers lightly across her temple and through her dark hair.

She felt the familiar resistance—the mental barrier that never fully crumbled. Jess was the principal at the Catholic Board. She lived in the biggest, most soundproof closet ever created.

She almost didn't reach back.

But Jess's hand slid down her arm, and the smell of her—sweet raspberry and the garlic clinging to her ribbed turtleneck—managed to break through.

Jil circled her arms around Jess's waist, and drew her in until she stood between her thighs. "Hi."

"Hi." Jess dipped down and captured Jil's mouth, and she slipped her tongue inside, warm and soft.

"I missed you," she murmured on her lips.

Jil's stomach lurched. "Me too." She slipped her hands into the back pockets of Jess's dark jeans, and pulled her in until they were pressed together as one.

"It's okay to miss her, even if you expected it," Jess whispered.

Instead of answering, Jil tilted her head back to take more of Jess into her mouth, biting her lower lip gently in the way that made Jess sigh.

Jess gently pulled away. "Um, I think if we keep going like this, my dinner is going to be burned."

"Yeah. I kind of have the same feeling. Maybe I'll go grab a shower while you're finishing up…"

"Yes. Good. Go." Playfully, Jess slapped her ass and pointed her toward the bedroom. "Don't be too long."

❖

Jil woke up cold, her neck twisted at an unnatural angle, and reached down to pull up the duvet, but found only a throw blanket. Shit. She hadn't meant to fall asleep on the couch.

The Italian food, and the two—three?—glasses of wine, and the fire, and Jess's warm hands massaging her feet…yeah, she'd fallen asleep.

Zeus snored by the balcony door in the kitchen, yipping occasionally as if dreaming of catching something. That's probably what had woken her.

The clock on the HD box read 2:45.

Not again.

Jil sighed and rolled off the couch onto the floor. As her ass hit the ground, Zeus raised his head.

He slowly pushed to his feet and shook his ears, making a sound like elephant fans flapping in the breeze, then shuffled over to her. He shoved his great head under her arm, almost lifting her off the ground.

"Zeus, for God's sake!" She couldn't help laughing as he lay down, jowls in her lap. "Sorry to wake you, buddy. Did Jess go home?"

Zeus rumbled as Jil's fingers worked the fur around his ears, and he buried his chin even deeper into her leg.

Jil listened hard. She heard the humming of the refrigerator, the low buzz of the central heating, and Zeus's sighs and groans, but couldn't tell whether Jess slept in the room next door. She leaned back against the couch and grabbed the knitted throw to wrap around herself.

The cream cable-knit blanket had been her mother's. It had lain at the foot of her bed when she was a child, and she'd dragged it through every foster home until she'd come to a stop at Elise's—the only place she'd ever had her own room.

Maybe that's why she'd been dreaming of her childhood—again. It seemed like every night this week she'd been back, revisiting the journey that had brought her to Elise.

❖

She sat hunched over in the refrigerator box at the back of the train station, freezing and blowing hot air into her hands. She couldn't really sit up, but lying down on the street seemed like such a final decision—like she'd joined a rank in society she would never be able to escape. She wrapped her blanket more tightly around her, over her parka, but the cold had seeped into her organs, her bones, her blood. And now she had to pee.

She couldn't leave her box though. Night had set in, and with it, the city's landscape had changed from vaguely sinister to downright dangerous. Grown men, hardened by lives of poverty and addiction, got shoved around and maimed, and even murdered. She was a sixteen-year-old girl. What chance did she stand if someone found her?

She'd pushed one end of the box against a Dumpster and sat facing the exposed end. In one hand, she held a picture of her mom; in the other, a dull switchblade she'd snagged from one of the other kids in her last foster home, before she'd run off.

And the snow had started to fall.

Tears crept silently down her face, and she swiped her nose with the back of her hand.

At the Hendricksons', five foster kids would be sitting down to spaghetti or boxed pizza. Her stomach growled. She imagined pouring milk into her glass, taking a bite of pepperoni—Nicole, the mom, telling everyone to slow down or they'd choke. She was all right, some of the time, when she looked up from her computer long enough to notice any of them.

Nicole was fine mostly, but Rob was a creep.

He wanted to crawl into bed with her and hold her. He'd lie there for an hour—sometimes longer—the weight of his arm crushing her small breasts as he breathed hot and damp on her neck. Sometimes he murmured in his half-sleep. Sometimes she got the feeling that he was just waiting, waiting for something...

At every noise and creak in the house, she'd pray that someone would open the door—find him there—and in the next breath, pray that nobody ever saw.

As if responding to some clock chime that only he could hear, he'd pull back the covers, and, as quietly as he'd come in, slip out of bed and leave. Heady wisps of his Dark Leather shampoo and musky aftershave clung to her pillow and kept her awake.

Two weeks passed, and she started falling asleep at school. Once, at the kitchen table.

One morning as she unloaded the dishwasher, she heard a low voice behind her. "Soon he's going to want to watch you shower." She whirled around to find Hani, who was seventeen and had been living with the Hendricksons for two years already. Her dark eyes had always held deep secrets. Jil could never tell how deep.

"He'll come in after you're already in. He'll wait til you're washing your hair, and your hands are stretched up, then he'll sit down on the step to the bathtub and make you finish your shower."

Jil stared at her. "Then what?"

Hani lowered her eyes. "Just watch out."

The clock now read 3:02. The wine pressed heavily on her bladder, and Zeus's head wasn't helping. She gently eased herself out from under him and walked through the door in the hall into her en suite. She took a long time washing her hands, letting the water run hot over her forearms.

That morning, just as she'd lathered shampoo into her hair, the doorknob turned...

Maybe she should have had some warm milk. Chances were stacked against falling back asleep, even though it was pitch-dark outside. She shook her head, physically dispelling the memories.

When she emerged, using the door that led to her bedroom, she squinted hard at the lump in the bed. Jess hadn't gone home after all.

She warred with her feelings—gratitude that Jess had stayed; frustration that she hadn't asked; desire to get into bed and hold her and run her hands over Jess's bare skin until she woke up, and she could kiss her and touch her and erase any feeling of her old life, when she didn't know who she was or what she wanted...

Jil carefully drew back the covers and slipped between the sheets, her freezing feet making contact with Jess's warm toes.

She stirred and sighed softly. "You're finally here?"

Jil let out the breath she'd been holding, trying not to wake Jess. "Sorry to disturb you."

"Couch was cold I take it?" She turned over and slipped her arm around Jil's waist, pulling her in.

The sudden heat of Jess's body made her even more aware of her own cold limbs, and she began to shiver.

"Geez, you're freezing." Jess pulled her in even tighter, wrapping a leg around Jil's thigh and pressing her breasts tight against Jil's.

Jil gasped, her nipples hardening.

Jess laughed under her breath. "Sorry."

"S'okay." Jil tilted Jess's chin up and kissed her gently on the lips. "I thought you'd gone home."

Jess pulled back, her eyes dark pools, lit only by the sliver of moonlight coming in the window. "Did you want me to?"

Did she?

"No. No. I'm glad you're here." Jil cupped the back of her head and kissed her again, fitting herself snugly against Jess's warm, soft body, barely covered by a dark blue negligee.

Jess snaked one arm under Jil's T-shirt and gently squeezed her breast. "Let me make myself useful then."

Jil felt heat flare where Jess touched her, lighting a sparkling trail that blazed along every nerve in her body. She sighed, on the edge of a moan, as Jess pulled her shirt higher and put her hot mouth where her fingers had been, sucking Jil's nipple into her mouth.

Warmth filled the space between them, a space that seemed so wide. "I want you closer," Jil whispered.

Jess slid down in the bed, pulling Jil's jeans down with her as Jil pulled her own shirt over her head. Naked and shivering, she reached for Jess and pulled her back up to kiss her.

"Why are you still dressed? I want to feel your skin."

Jess grinned in the half-dark and shucked the silk.

Her skin was almost as supple and smooth as the negligee, and Jil ran her hands over every inch she could reach—rich and sweet and...like home.

She loved watching Jess's body writhe as she touched her, played every inch of her like a delicate harp, drawing sighs and moans and cries from every cell in her body. She knew already when to draw back, to give Jess's reluctant joints the chance to catch up with her eager nerves.

The very definition of coupling. Knowing without being told.

Jess rocked against Jil's hands and mouth, climbing steadily, beautifully, to the peak.

Then shattering.

Jil almost shattered too, watching her, and Jess barely had to touch her before she felt the first pulls and waves clenching her lower belly. She thrust her hips up to meet Jess's every touch... submerging, surrendering.

God!

After, Jil captured Jess's mouth once more, running her hands over her back and pulling her in, closer, closer. Their bodies fit tightly, like puzzle pieces locking. Jess's breasts filled the hollow just below her own, her chin rested against her breastbone, their legs and thighs intertwined.

She couldn't get close enough.

❖

Padraig found her, of course.

"No daughter of Aimee's is going to be sleeping in a cardboard box," he said.

She was so relieved to see him, she almost threw her arms around his neck. Almost.

"What the hell took you so long?"

He chuckled. "Didn't know you were so unhappy there. Why didn't you tell me?"

"You're the private eye. Why didn't you know?"

He bundled her into the car, where the heat from the air vents blasting icy air still seemed warm to Jil. She pulled her knees up to her chest in the passenger's seat, just trying to stop shaking so she could fasten her seat belt.

She didn't even ask where they were going.

At the Second Cup, she ducked into the bathroom. Her back felt like the frost had bitten her skin from the hips to the ribs, and when she peed, it burned. She must have let the hot water run for five minutes or more. When she emerged, Padraig sat at the corner table, drinking a large coffee, and on the table next to him sat a tall cup of hot chocolate with whipped cream.

"Thanks," Jil muttered, sliding in across from him.

"Ye've obviously lost my number," Padraig said darkly and handed her a small stack of business cards, one of which he tucked into her bag. "Consider memorizing it."

Jil cracked a small smile.

"Why did you run away?"

She took a sip of her hot chocolate and declined to answer.

"You're sixteen now, Kidd. You know placements are going to get tougher to find."

"I could be on my own."

Padraig scowled. "You're still a child. You'd never survive. You need looking after."

Jil looked through him. She'd never asked him and never would—why she couldn't live with him.

"I'm not going back there. Rob is a perv."

Padraig winced, then leaned forward, his face hard. "Did he touch you? Did he hurt you? I'll kill him."

Jil shook her head slightly. "No. Not yet."

Padraig cursed softly. "Right then. Somewhere else."

The fist in her stomach unclenched a little.

"Come back to my office with me. You can sleep there tonight. Tomorrow, I'll think of something."

CHAPTER THREE

As the first rays of wan sunlight pooled onto the dark hardwood, Jil left Jess sleeping. She pulled on her running gear in the bathroom, then grabbed her iPod and beckoned to Zeus.

"Can you keep up with me, lazy bones, or will I have to tie you to a tree while I run the trails?"

Zeus whined and leaped off his bed as Jil laced her runners.

December and the streets were cold but free of snow. A miracle in Ontario in the weeks before Christmas. Wreaths hung on every door of her building, and someone had planted giant urns with birch branches and evergreen boughs that glittered unnaturally with enhancements purchased at Michael's.

Zeus shied away from a homeless person dressed as Santa Claus as Jil pulled him down the street and headed for the park overlooking the water.

When had Elise told her about her illness? *Had* she even told her?

Jil shook her head, trying to remember. It seemed so long ago but had only been a few months. It had been a shadow over her shoulder that had followed them both for years. She would dip in and out of illness, into remission and back again.

And then, this past year, something shifted and they both knew she wouldn't make it back.

But had she actually said it out loud? Had she actually said, "I won't be here for Christmas this year?"

The river had frozen over partially, the deeper water still lapping around the fragile outer rim of ice that jutted out about ten feet from the shoreline. Icy air swept her hair back, and she pulled her running scarf up over her nose. A few minutes of breathing that air and she'd be gasping for breath, unable to run. Forget it.

After stretching and walking a few meters, she took off slowly. Zeus pulled his attention away from the seagulls and loped beside her. A few minutes—that's all she needed to clear her head and concentrate on the order of the day. Swimming through memories of her teenage years was not how she'd planned to spend the rest of this year.

The wake was Monday. The funeral, the day after. Though why they bothered to call it a funeral, she couldn't imagine. Elise wouldn't be buried until March because of the frozen ground.

Good. That would give her some more time.

She gave herself a mental kick. Time for what? To demand another autopsy?

Elise should be laid to rest, not warehoused in a mausoleum like a science experiment cooling on ice.

But Karrie's words still needled her. Why the delay with the autopsy? Elise had been sick. Dying. She'd died of cancer—hadn't she? Why did she want to look deeper?

Three kilometers in, and she felt every step in her joints and back.

"What do you think, buddy? Should we pack it in?"

Zeus bounced.

Her cell buzzed and she stopped to grab it.

Chet. *Sorry to bug you, but the computers are down in the office.*

Jil swore. *Take a weekend, why don't you?* She texted back. But she'd already turned toward home.

Padraig was right. His family business *did* have shite timing.

❖

Jess turned her office phone to Do Not Disturb and powered off her computer. The hand on the clock read 1:56. Four more minutes and the wake would start. Right now, people would be coming into the vestibule, taking off their boots and coats with self-conscious precision. Smoothing their hair. Stopping to sign the guest book.

She'd imagined this ritual as many times as she'd imagined the phone call that would eventually come from the hospital, telling her Mitch had finally died.

Jess took her rosary out of the top drawer and fingered it.

There were years past where she would have prayed a decade for Elise's soul, but now the prayers felt hollow and cold. Their magic had left her.

When had this happened? When had she started to feel so excluded from her faith that she could no longer find comfort in its most basic rituals?

Maybe when she realized those rituals were chaining her to a life she didn't want anymore. The holy rites were beginning to feel like holy traps.

She held the tiny cool pearls in her aching fingers and instead said a simple prayer for Jil.

I'm so sorry I can't be with you.

Then she laid her rosary back in its case in her top drawer.

A prayer should never end with an apology.

❖

"All set?" Karrie straightened an errant flower from one of the standing arrangements and turned to face Jil.

"You're going to open that now?"

Karrie nodded. "As long as you're ready."

Jil breathed out slowly, then nodded. "Okay." She watched as Karrie reached over and pulled the upper half of the casket open, like the lid on a suitcase.

She remembered how, at her mother's funeral, she thought Aimee had been cut in half, because her legs and feet had been hidden by the lower part of the casket.

In movies, the casket lid always lifted in one piece, revealing the entire body. She hadn't been prepared for the reality of half-measures.

"Does the bottom open too?" Jil asked in a hushed voice.

Karrie smiled. "Why? Does it creep you out too? The no legs thing?"

"Yeah."

Padraig led her by the hand to the edge of the casket. "You kneel here. You can say a prayer if you like, or just talk to her."

She didn't want to kneel. Then she couldn't see her mother.

Aimee's dark, lush curls framed her face and fell to her shoulders—even as she lay sleeping. Jil reached a hand out to touch her mother's fingers, which clasped a small bouquet of roses. They felt like cold, soft wax. She brushed her fingertips along Aimee's knuckles gently.

Padraig didn't stop her.

"I'll leave you to have a moment alone," Karrie said. Her full ruby lips made every vowel sound slightly over-pronounced.

Jil forced herself away from her memories and into the present moment. She looked at Elise's white hair, coiffed into perfect curls. Her face, in death, looked younger, as the wrinkles and stress lines she'd formed in more recent years had relaxed.

Jil reached out and straightened a crease in her scarf, her hand brushing over Elise's old Fauxbergé brooch. "Got to make it look good, eh, Elise?" she said softly.

Karrie pretended to be busy with something in the corner—setting out a guest book or something. Another man in a dark blue suit appeared in the doorway to the visitation room and gestured almost imperceptibly. Jil caught his movement out of the corner of her eye, and Karrie nodded, glancing at the large clock on the wall.

One fifty-nine.

She caught Jil's gaze. "No need to rush. It's two now, so the guests will start to arrive soon." She stepped two paces toward the casket, beside the door. "When you're ready, you can come stand with me here. We're the receiving line."

A receiving line of two. But she felt gladder than she could say of Karrie's company. She didn't think she could hold up a receiving line all by herself.

"This is only until four, right?"

"Yes. Then again from seven to nine. Mrs. Fitzgerald chose the shortest time slots possible because she didn't want you to have to greet people for days. She said if they wanted to see her in her finery then they'd get up and make it out."

Jil fell into place beside Karrie, glancing down at her simple Oxfords that looked like something out of an English boarding school, the dark black tights with tiny pulls, as if worn three times too often. And her funky turquoise glasses—so out of place, but so fitting on her young face.

"How does someone in her twenties decide to become a funeral director?" she asked.

Karrie shrugged. "My dad, mostly. I used to go to work with him sometimes, you know, after school or in the evening if he couldn't get a sitter for me. My mom died when I was young. I grew up with just my dad. Anyway, I always used to wonder what happened to the bodies after Dad finished doing the autopsies. When the guys with the long white cube vans came to pick up the bodies, where did they go? Who dressed them up and made them look good for their funerals?"

"So how did you find out?"

"In high school, they had this 'bring your kid to work day' thing. I always went to work with my dad, so I wasn't that excited about it, but then I found out that he'd asked one of the prep guys at the funeral home if I could shadow him and his partner for the day. They said yes, and I got the inside scoop. Totally fascinating."

Jil smiled. Everyone had to have a passion, right?

Out in the hall, she heard the noises of people removing their coats and boots, pausing outside to pick up a memorial card and get a cup of coffee from the room across the hall.

"That's where I started, you know, after getting my papers. I had a job downstairs, preparing the bodies, doing the makeup."

"Seriously?"

"Yeah. Shelly from *My Girl* was totally my hero."

Jil grinned. "Jamie what's-her-name?"

"Yeah."

The first wave appeared at the door.

"Ready?" Karrie put on a professional smile—Jil recognized it, just like Jess—and subtly ushered the crowd toward the casket.

She caught herself looking around, scanning the crowd for Jess. But of course, she wasn't there.

Around dinner hour, the crowd started filtering out.

"You're free until seven. You can go for dinner, or whatever you need to do, then be back for seven."

Jil snorted. "What the hell am I going to do for three hours? Go to a movie?"

Karrie smiled wanly, but in the absence of her professional duties, seemed to struggle to meet her eye.

"What?"

She startled. "Nothing. Nothing at all."

"Bullshit. You know something. What is it?"

Karrie sighed. "I'm a terrible secret keeper. But this really isn't the right moment."

"There's rarely a right moment, I've noticed."

"Yes, but there are definitely some wrong moments, and it's hard enough to meet and greet lines of mourners without this kind of news."

Jil stood up straighter. "Give it to me."

With a sigh, Karrie drew Jil into the bay window. "I asked my dad about the autopsy—about why it took so long."

"And?"

"And he said 'nothing was traceable.'"

"Those were his words?"

"Yes."

"Did you ask him what he meant?"

Karrie blew the bangs off her face. "I did. He said there were some...irregularities. But nothing conclusive. So it could be nothing. Which is why he did conclude natural causes in the end."

"But he suspects something."

She bit her lower lip. "Just between us, he considered some sort of toxin, but without any evidence at the cr—" She paused. "At the scene where she died, he didn't have enough information to test further."

"Could it have been some meds she took for her illness?"

"Well, certain medications you take at the end of life could cause those irregularities, and those would have to be excluded. But her medical records arrived with her body. Everything she'd been prescribed was listed..."

"And I've looked in the medicine cabinet. Most of what she took was still there."

"Could she have been taking something not prescribed?" Karrie asked softly.

"What, like a street drug?"

"Or something homeopathic, maybe?"

"It seems unlikely. Elise wasn't really into shark tooth powder or anything like that. But I can't say for certain I knew everything she took."

Karrie shrugged, her eyes full of sympathy. "Sometimes it's better just to let things go, Jil. Especially if there's no way to know and looking will just drive you crazy."

"But if someone poisoned her—and that's what we're saying, right? Someone could have poisoned her?"

"I guess. But is it likely? Why would they?"

Jil straightened up again as someone walked toward them. She plastered on a fake smile, but between her gritted teeth said, "That's what I need to know."

❖

Jess checked her phone.

Nothing.

The wake should have ended by now.

She sighed and got in her car, then pulled up to the loft in the dark. Streetlights glowed off the snowbanks, casting a watery sheen on the pavement. She parked on the street. Jil only had one parking spot. When they got their own place, it would be with two parking spaces.

She gave her head a shake. A nice thought, but not exactly practical.

How would they move in together, exactly?

What did she plan to do with her house? How could she invite any of her family and friends over? Not to mention—how could she go about divorcing Mitch and keeping her job?

Nope. Parking on the street looked to be in the cards for a while.

When she got inside, Zeus greeted her at the door, and she grabbed his leash to take him out.

This was as close to domestic bliss as they were going to get.

CHAPTER FOUR

The deep clanging of the tower bells reverberated through Jil's breastbone as she stood on the old flagstone path in front of the church. Mourners had gathered, and Jil had been roped into several rounds of small talk with neighbors and friends of Elise she'd met only a few times—most of them years ago.

She stood apart now, willing everyone to leave her alone. This is why Padraig should have been here—to protect her from having to talk to people. She vowed to give him shit when he got home.

Who said the deepest loneliness was being surrounded by others?

She would have talked to Jess, of course, had Jess been able to come. That would have raised too many questions, of course, so she'd had to stay away. Go to work. Be a principal in a board where she could never be free and open and happy.

The tall oak doors, heavily gilded with wrought iron, were pulled open as the hearse pulled into the circle. It glided smoothly, with no sound, almost like an electric car. Fitting for the formality of the occasion.

Karrie got out of the passenger side and came to Jil. Her navy trench coat whipped around her ankles as the wind gusted over the parking lot, and she pulled on dark leather gloves as she walked. "We're all ready, if you are."

Jil glanced over as the pallbearers loaded the casket onto the portable trolley. Such a compact box for such a dynamic person.

"What will happen to her after the ceremony?" Jil asked. "Until she can be buried?" She hadn't thought that far ahead. Each step seemed to require her full concentration, and she didn't have the energy for advanced planning.

"Well, she'll be going back to the mausoleum until the spring, when we can start burying again."

Jil nodded. "Right. And where's that?" It seemed important to know where Elise was going—that she wouldn't be disappearing, out of sight.

"The mausoleum we use is at Beechgrove Cemetery. There's a large building there on the north side where the deceased are held until burial." Karrie looked straight at her while she talked, not shying away from any details. Jil admired her for that.

"But she will be buried here? At her own church?"

"Yes, that's right. She has a plot here already. This cemetery is just too small to accommodate a mausoleum."

Jil sniffed. Right. Okay. She realized that people were watching her—that they were waiting for her to be ready. As she steeled her shoulders, she caught sight of a petite woman in a blue trench coat slip into the church. She looked familiar.

Was that Anastasia? The home health care aide? Nice of her to come to a funeral.

She didn't have time to say hello before the bells began to ring.

She looked once more at the casket, then up to the heavy oaken doors. Once again, she faced the crucifixes and kneeling—this time for Elise and not because Padraig had assigned her here.

Why did the love in her life always come veiled in the impenetrable cloak of Catholic incense?

What was she doing? Sitting here staring at the clock, ignoring her job? She should be at Jil's side today.

She'd considered every possible excuse for ducking out of school and hurrying to the funeral, but then what?

How could she sit through a Mass, mouthing the words and kneeling, genuflecting, responding in all the right places? All the while knowing God and all the other parishioners could see right through her?

She couldn't sit in the back row and watch. Seeing Jil crying and not being able to put her arms around her would be worse than staying away.

And after every sin they'd committed since they'd been together—some of them in this very room—how could she possibly take communion?

People would recognize her. If she stayed seated, there would be talk. What sin could have been so great she hadn't received absolution and confession? And if she took it anyway—

No, she'd never be able to take Mass lightly.

Best to stay away altogether.

❖

After the service ended and the hearse had driven away, Jil walked through the cemetery, hard packed from the early winter. Snow buried many tombstones, and she stopped to brush off a few of the smaller ones as she took the long road from one end of the cemetery to another. In the garden of angels, she read a few epitaphs.

What would she put on Elise's?

Had Elise chosen her own?

Probably.

The walk took her an hour, and at the end, her nose had turned numb with the cold, and the salt from her tears had dried on her cheeks, leaving it feeling cracked. She felt cast adrift in a way she'd never expected. Orphaned by Elise's death. Betrayed by all the questions she'd left behind. But orphaning could really only happen once, and it had happened when she was a little girl.

She crossed the center garden with the wooden benches and brushed her hand against the water fountain that sat inert for the winter months.

So why did she feel so alone now? Motherless for the second time in twenty years.

There, on the hill, would be Elise's final burial spot. She trudged up and sat on the cold stone bench that would face the headstone that would eventually be placed there.

"You think I'm going to come talk to you?" she muttered.

Well, she wasn't entirely wrong.

❖

The handyman's truck idled in the driveway when Jil arrived, and she found him around the side of the house.

"Hi, Ben," she called. He waved back, and she noticed he'd gone a little gray around the temples under the white painter's hat he always wore.

"Should have come by earlier," Ben said. "But I wasn't sure you'd want to see me."

Jil gave him a shove on the shoulder. He'd been Elise's handyman for as long as she'd lived here. "Don't be ridiculous. Of course I would have been glad to see you. Especially if this gutter had actually fallen off the house."

"It's loose all right, and looks terrible hanging off like that."

"No kidding." Jil laughed. "I'm supposed to get the house ready to sell."

Ben sighed deeply. The lines around his mouth had deepened, and his eyes held a heavy sorrow. "Your foster mother was one hell of a woman. It's a real shame she's gone."

Jil swallowed hard. "Do you want to come in for some coffee? We can make a list of the must-dos."

"Sure. That'd be nice."

Jil opened the door to the house and stiffened. The alarm didn't go off. She looked at the panel on the wall and noticed a green light. Had she forgotten to turn it on? Something else felt wrong. The house seemed too cold. A draft came from somewhere near the back, and the scent of baked muffins and potpourri had dulled, as if carried away on the unwelcome gust.

Ben stopped behind her, and Jil pushed over the threshold, saying nothing. She kept her short brown leather boots on and strode through the hallway to the kitchen, Ben following close behind her.

"Let me just get things started. Why don't you have a seat?" Stalling, she sliced up one of three chocolate Bundt cakes still remaining and set it on a tray while the coffee machine started up.

"Will you excuse me for a moment, Ben? I just have to grab some paper."

Ben settled himself into a chair at the table as Jil ducked out of the kitchen, heading straight for Elise's library.

The mood had changed. The familiar smell had been replaced with something colder—fresher. She scanned the room. Something felt off in here. The antique Spode mug that held her pens faced the wrong direction. The files on the bottom shelf were in the correct order, but they leaned slightly to one side instead of vertically.

You're being paranoid.

Jil absently fingered a gold leaf bracelet that lay on the side table next to the door. Elise had loved to collect rare artifacts, particularly if they were well crafted. She'd spent months tracking down this Anglo-Saxon jewelry.

As an art history professor, nothing delighted her more than history in the flesh. And in the absence of the real thing, convincing replications of history.

Jil backed down the hallway and turned up the staircase. The draft seemed to be coming from up there. Ben emerged from the kitchen, a piece of half-eaten Bundt cake in his hand.

"Do you feel a draft?" she asked him.

"Upstairs window's open a crack," he said helpfully. "Saw it from the driveway."

Jil jogged up the rest of the stairs, crossed the space to Elise's bedroom, and found the window slightly open.

She stared at it for a second, thinking back. The neighbors had bombarded her for hours. She'd come upstairs to get a few minutes of peace...

Did I forget to close it?

She paused. *Did I even open it?*

She jammed down the windowpane. Instantly, the air around her felt warmer.

In the hallway, she stopped to look at her favorite painting—the huge Monet replica Elise had loved. Every time the front door closed, the exquisite oak frame shifted one inch up on the left, and every time she passed it, since she'd been sixteen years old, she pulled it back into line. She knew this painting as well as she knew the faded lavender wallpaper in her own bedroom.

And something about it looked strange…

Ten years ago, Jil had tripped over the vacuum and accidentally knocked the painting off the wall, producing a three-inch splinter along the right side of the frame. Which was still there.

"Of course I'm not going to let you buy me a new frame." Elise had scoffed. *"This splinter proves you've been here. It's part of the painting's new history."*

It hung the same crooked way. But something about the overall palette looked slightly darker. The signature at the bottom right looked a shade lighter than she remembered. When was the last time she'd really looked at it closely?

She backed up to examine it, blinked, and stared again. Something in her gut flipped, and she knew with a certainty she couldn't put her finger on: This painting was not the same.

CHAPTER FIVE

The glowering detective looked through the whole house, paying particular attention to the doors and windows. "I see no sign of forced entry," he said, striding back into the kitchen. "Or of anything being stolen."

Jil took in his dark blond hair and two-day-old scruff. His open shirt collar and fitted jeans lent a certain casualness to his appearance that his navy blazer couldn't completely offset. Boots—not dress shoes. Not even sort-of dress shoes.

And he seemed to be taking this case about as seriously as he took his footwear.

"How can you tell if I can't? Elise had hundreds of artifacts. And if I didn't disengage the alarm system, who did? Someone broke in here, Detective. I want to know who."

"You say you found the upstairs bedroom window open?" He leaned against the counter, fixing her with his dark blue eyes. In another life, she might have found him attractive. She felt certain other women did. A good-looking man in his late thirties with that confidence and that swagger probably attracted lots of trophy wives.

But she wasn't the trophy wife type.

"Yes, the back window, leading in from the balcony," she said.

"And you can't remember whether you opened it or not?" His voice held just the faintest bit of condescension, which she supposed she deserved.

"Detective Fraser—"

"I think we can skip right to first names, don't you? Call me Nicolas, or if you're feeling particularly brave, you can try Nic."

"Jil," she muttered, extending her hand.

He shook it firmly. "So tell me about this painting."

"It's a Monet replica. Been here as long as I have," Jil said. "She bought it at an antique sale in Montreal, from what I remember."

"I've never seen anything like it, actually. I'm not familiar with that piece."

Jil remained silent. She had looked online the night before, but couldn't find *Evening River Seine* mentioned in any of the catalogues she'd searched. Most of Monet's pieces were in museums or private galleries, but this one hadn't been listed at all.

"Okay, Jil, here's the deal. You say nobody forced their way in?"

"No."

"You say you can't identify anything that's actually missing?"

She sighed heavily and shook her head. She knew how this looked.

"And you say that you may or may not have opened the window yourself while you were here the other day, being bombarded with neighbors and casseroles?"

"It's possible, but I don't think so."

Fraser leaned forward. "I've looked through the whole house—every room. I don't see any sign that this place was robbed. There's a gold bracelet lying on the table downstairs. That Gorham vanity alone is worth looting the place. Not to mention the silver mirror, the seven antique watches, the earring tree, the beautiful—and I mean *beautiful*—necklaces."

She looked away. "Most of those things are costume jewelry."

"But not all."

Jil shook her head. "No, not all."

"And the Monet replica is still hanging upstairs."

A different replica. But she could hardly say that out loud. It seemed ludicrous, even to her.

"You were upset. You weren't thinking clearly. Isn't it possible you simply forgot to turn on the alarm system? That you left the window open yourself? It's natural for everything to feel suspicious and strange after a death."

Jil looked back at him, his eyes searching hers for an explanation—a dismissal. "Detective Fraser, I've lived in this house since I was sixteen years old. My foster mother was a very gentle woman, but she had one rule in this house—to protect her collection. Her artifacts meant the world to her. Even pieces of clay pots spoke to her in a way that normal people will never understand. They reminded her of her travels and her adventures. She relished them as mementos, but they were also extremely valuable. Never in my life have I left the house without turning on the alarm system. I know someone was here."

Fraser nodded, then closed his notebook. "I understand your point of view. But try to understand mine. There's no way I can make a case of this. We just can't dedicate resources to a scene of no crime."

Jil leaned forward. He was getting the better of her at every turn and it pissed her off.

"I understand completely. But understand me—I am a PI, and when I smell a rat, something's usually rotting in the walls. I will find out what's gone on here, and when I do, I'll be sure to let every newspaper in the city know that Rockford Police dropped the ball and you were leading the investigation."

Fraser's face darkened. "Is that a challenge?"

Jil grimaced. "You bet your ass."

Fraser's jaw twitched as he opened his notebook again. "Is there anything you can tell me—anything at all—that will help me make this a viable case?"

Yeah. Someone impersonated me at the funeral home and took my emerald ring.

But she'd promised Karrie she wouldn't report it to the police. She couldn't have that girl's job on her conscience.

Fraser looked at her oddly. "Did anyone come by, anyone unusual? I mean, besides all the neighbors with the Bundt cakes."

Jil rolled her eyes. "No. Just the home health care aide."

"She came after your foster mother had died?"

Jil frowned. At the time, that hadn't seemed odd. "Yes."

"Did she go upstairs?"

To get supplies. "Yes."

"Can you describe her?"

"Five foot seven, one hundred and twenty-five pounds. Dark strawberry blond hair, medium length. Dark hazel eyes and a cupid's bow mouth, very pale skin, no jewelry. She wore navy scrub pants and a white scrub top, carried a navy coat with wooden toggles, and a black tote bag from the St. Augustine Agency."

The detective raised his eyebrows. "Shoes?"

"Black leather slip-ons with a half-inch heel."

"The color of the emblem?"

"White. Would you like me to draw it for you?"

Fraser lifted his chin. "No, thank you. I can find it online."

She tilted her chin to meet his eyes. "Good."

"One more question—is there any way she could have known the alarm code?"

Jil frowned. "I can't see Elise giving that out to her, but I suppose anything is possible. I didn't even know she had an aide, to be honest with you."

"Very well, Ms. Kidd. I will put this in the report. It's possible that the aide left the window open to air the room out, that you simply forgot to turn on the alarm, and that's the end of our mystery. I can't imagine many home health care workers double as cat burglars at night."

Jil didn't want to discourage the investigation, but she couldn't imagine how anyone could have climbed into that upstairs window either.

"Will you be staying here?" Fraser asked.

Jil frowned. "Maybe," she replied. "At least until I can sell the place."

"Not a bad idea," Fraser said. "I don't think you'll have any more trouble, but I don't want to make any promises."

"That's okay. I like to get up close and personal with my cat burglars. I'll probably find her before you do anyway."

Fraser narrowed his eyes. "Don't you have your own cases to be working on?"

"Yep."

"Then I'd advise you to stick to spying on cheating husbands and their lovers, and leave the real crimes to the real police."

Not the first time she'd heard that.

"I was the 'real police.' I get more done as a PI. And I will find our friend before you do. Guaranteed."

Fraser made a growling sound at the back of his throat, then stalked through the front door.

Jil locked it behind him, then jogged back upstairs to look at the Monet again. In the daylight, the difference looked clearer than ever. She stood staring at it for a full five minutes, examining every square inch of the canvas.

Someone had switched this painting, but why?

The only suspect she had at the moment was Anastasia, but even though her gut told her to be suspicious, she had a hard time imagining a person of her slight stature being able to switch out a painting of that size alone in the dead of night.

But maybe she hadn't been alone.

Chills shot up her back. How many people had been in her house?

At that moment, Zeus nudged her arm and she relaxed.

She didn't know a lot about art theft, but from what she did remember from her robbery courses, most thieves didn't bother with the frames. In really valuable paintings, they took the time to dismantle the frame and gently prise out the canvas. In other cases, or when pressed for time, the thief would cut out the painting with a knife, then roll the canvas into a tube and be on their way.

She examined the frame for any evidence of tampering, but it looked clean and crisp. So the thief had dismantled the frame, taken out the original gently, and replaced it with the new canvas. That would have taken hours, which meant she'd known she had plenty of time to work, uninterrupted.

❖

Back in the kitchen, Jil looked at Fraser's business card lying smugly on the table. His morning had probably already filled up with museum robberies and home invasions. He didn't even think she had a case. She'd solve it herself and save them both the unpleasantness of any further interactions.

As she considered the next step, her phone buzzed with a message.

This is Tamara Reynolds.

Wonderful—the lawyer for the will.

I'd like to set up an appointment with you at your earliest convenience.

Of course she would. If she could finish up her job, then she could get paid. Well, Jil wasn't in any rush.

She had taken Elise's folder home with her, refusing to open the envelope that said "Will." Elise had no other children or family. Her husband had died decades ago, and her only sister had died a few years back.

Jil already knew she was inheriting the house, which she would sell, then use the proceeds to set up a charity for a scholarship for foster kids. Maybe the lawyer could help her with that instead of wasting time with appointments for checking and rechecking the dates of Elise's final will and testament.

She deleted Tamara's message and slipped the phone back in her pocket as Ben's truck rumbled into the driveway. She ran down to meet him, repair list in hand.

❖

"Steal a replica? To replace it with another replica?" Jess poured her a glass of Bordeaux.

Jil leaned her elbows on the bar top counter and took a sip.

Jess took her own glass and settled on the window seat in the kitchen, tucking her feet up under a throw blanket. "That doesn't make any sense. Why do it?"

"There's something I'm missing here. I just don't know what it is yet."

"Well, it seems like a lot of trouble—to impersonate an aide to gain access to someone's house in the dead of night, to steal a replicated painting and replace it with another. Why bother?"

"I can't imagine." Not once had Jess suggested that maybe Jil was imagining things, and for that, she felt exceedingly grateful.

Jess hesitated. "Is it possible the first painting was original?"

Jil snorted. "Do you know how much a painting like that would cost, Jess?"

Jess returned her incredulous stare. "Well, yes, I do know something about art. If you'll remember, I dated an artist. Much as I might like to forget that."

"Sorry," Jil muttered. "I didn't mean to suggest…never mind, you know what I mean. Elise was a professor. She didn't have that kind of money. She'd have to have stolen the painting from the Louvre."

Jess looked into her glass.

"What?" Jil said.

"Nothing."

"Well, there's something."

Jess sighed. "I'm certainly not suggesting Elise stole a painting from the Louvre…"

"But?"

"But you should remember, she had a whole life before you met her, Jil. It's possible she has some secrets you don't know."

"Secrets like she was an art thief in her college days?"

Jess laughed softly. "Hardly. But it seems like you have some investigating to do."

Jil wondered where to start. First, find out what the goddamned lawyer wanted. Then get back to tracking down the art thief.

"I'm sorry," Jess said softly, folding her warm hand over Jil's. "I did want to be there with you."

Jil nodded and drained her glass as she stared out the window.

CHAPTER SIX

While the sun made a watery entrance into the cold gray sky, Jil took Zeus quickly around the block, grabbed a five-minute shower, and slipped into the closet. Jess turned over in bed but didn't wake up. Jil held her breath as she put on a pair of jeans and a black blazer, snatched up her wallet, and carried her shoes to the front door.

Why didn't she want to tell Jess where she planned to go?

Because she didn't know how to explain her hunch? Because she was afraid of that sympathetic "I'm sorry you lost Elise and I'll tolerate your conspiracy theories because I love you" look?

She couldn't tell her.

Instead, she ordered a large coffee from the Second Cup drive-thru, then followed the GPS's directions to the industrial area, where single-level buildings with large signs shared space across several lots. She squinted up and down the winding road, looking for a sign for St. Augustine Health Care Agency.

There—the third one on the left—a light blue sign with a white emblem.

She pulled into the lot and walked inside carrying a basket of muffins. The receptionist greeted her with a fake smile.

❖

Jess awoke to an empty bed. She stretched slowly, groaning as her muscles protested and spasmed. She flexed and bent her fingers, noticing that a few of the fingers on her right hand had gone completely numb. She shook her wrist, and ice shards shot down her pinkie.

Great.

She reached for her phone and checked it for text messages from Jil.

Nothing.

Where had Jil taken off to so early? Why hadn't she said good-bye? She considered sending a text, but something in her memory of Jil's closed face—her silent reproach—made her change her mind.

If Jil was upset with her for not being at her side during this whole ordeal, she could understand why.

In the shower, she let the water stream over her face and shoulders for a long time before attempting to wash her hair.

She hadn't felt this stiff and old in a long time.

A lead ball sat at the base of her throat, making it hard to breathe. When she thought of a full day of meetings ahead, the constricting feeling began to choke her. She breathed out with effort and clamped her eyes closed. She wanted nothing more than to crawl back into bed and let the day pass.

But of course, she couldn't.

She struggled into her suit, applied as much makeup as her stiff fingers would allow, and faltered out the door into her other life.

"Hi, my name is Jil Kidd. My foster mother was recently a patient with your agency." She put down the basket of muffins.

"Do you remember the name of your nurse?"

"Anastasia. Is she here? I wanted to say thank you."

The receptionist looked down at a list by her desk and then picked up the phone. "Annie, can you come to the front for a sec? Jil Kidd is here to see you."

Jil waited, her breath catching with every inhale. As she waited, her glance drifted through the lobby to the other side of the glass-enclosed vestibule, where people sat in chairs.

"Is that a doctor's office?"

The receptionist followed her gaze. "No, it's our outpatient nursing clinic."

When Jil still looked quizzical, she continued. "It's for the patients who can come in for care—you know, for wound checks or catheter changes, or whatever."

"Don't the nurses visit the home?"

"Yes, if the patient really needs them to, but this is more efficient and costs less. Cutbacks and all."

Jil sighed. She hated doctors' offices, and this waiting room closed in a little tightly for her liking.

In a moment, a slight young woman with strawberry blond hair and tortoiseshell glasses emerged from the back room and walked toward them. Jil watched her approach, her brain calculating all the ways she did not match the person she'd met. She got to the metal gate, swiped her pass, and walked through to the waiting area.

"Hello, I'm Annie." She held out her hand.

Jil shook it. "I'm Jil." She struggled with how to proceed and decided on the simplest explanation. "My foster mother, Elise Fitzgerald, should have been a patient of yours."

Annie frowned slightly. "I seem to remember having an Elise on my roster a few months ago, but I never did go out to see her. She cancelled the appointment, I think. She said she'd decided to go with another agency…"

Jil exhaled. A part of her hadn't wanted to believe it—that someone could have been deliberately targeting Elise—but it seemed she'd been right. Who had cancelled the appointment? Elise? Or fake-Anastasia?

"I thought you said you knew Annie?" The receptionist looked confused.

Jil turned to address them both. "Can you call your supervisor here please? I think we need to talk."

The receptionist frowned but turned to the phone and dialed. Meanwhile, Annie hovered by the desk, her forehead wrinkled with concern.

In a moment, a petite woman with black hair, wearing a navy blue skirt suit, appeared from a side office. She swiped her pass and the metal gate opened for her. "I'm Rochelle Townsend, the nurse in charge here. Would you like to step into my office?"

Jil nodded and gestured to Annie. "Please come with us. This involves you."

The door closed behind them with a shallow clunk, which gave the impression of closing the door to a playhouse. The walls seemed thin too, like they'd run out of building material and had to erect screens in between the offices instead of real walls.

Jil lowered her voice. "My foster mother was ill toward the end of her life. I didn't know she'd hired a nursing agency until I met her visiting nurse, Anastasia, a few days ago."

Annie raised her eyebrows. "But…but I've never met you before today."

"I know. An Anastasia who looks just like you came to Elise's house, wearing the coat you have on now and carrying a St. Augustine bag. I met her. By the look of things, she'd been there for several weeks."

Annie gasped. "Why would she do something like that?"

Rochelle's jaw tightened, and she sat down hard in her chair. "Someone was visiting your home, pretending to work for us?"

"Not only pretending to work for you, but pretending to *be* Annie. We have reason to believe she is an art thief, and I'm looking for her now."

"How could she gain access to patient information? We have very tight security."

Jil considered the door. Probably not as tight as she'd like to believe. "Annie, have you noticed anything unusual happening in your life lately? Anyone following you? Anything stolen?"

Annie put her hand to her chest. "My purse was stolen a few weeks ago. At the shopping mall. I slid it over my chair while I had lunch and when I got up, it had disappeared."

"What was in it?"

"Just some cash and my driver's license."

"Your nursing ID?"

Annie slid a glance toward her supervisor. "Yeah."

Rochelle raised her eyebrows. "They stole your ID badge?"

She nodded.

"And you didn't mention this to me?"

"I didn't think...I never considered..." she stammered. "I just reported it lost to HR and they retook my picture."

"And your driver's license?" Jil probed.

"I had that replaced too."

"Did you report it to the police?"

Annie shook her head. "I only had about twenty dollars in the purse. I didn't think they'd bother with me for that amount."

"Thank you, Annie." Rochelle dismissed her. After the door closed, she turned to Jil. "What else has been going on here without my knowledge?"

Jil had a sudden memory of Jess asking the same thing about her own school. Sometimes it seemed as if supervisors were the least informed members of any hierarchy. Everyone had a reason to hide something from them.

"I guess we're going to find that out. Do you have time for this right now? Can we dig a little deeper?"

"This just trumped everything else on my to-do list." Rochelle shook her head. "Someone has gained access to our client files, impersonated one of our nurses—someone who may not even be a nurse at all—and has gone into the home of a palliative care patient. And what did you say she stole? Artwork?"

"Sort of. I can explain in more detail later, but right now, I think we need to figure out how she got access to this information."

"Well, I'm pretty skeptical." Rochelle peered over her glasses. "The doors are locked after hours. We're only open from eight to five, so she couldn't have snuck in after that, or she would have set off the alarm. All nurses have to swipe their ID badges when they enter, even during the day. But even if the imposter had Annie's

ID, she would have to come in here to her filing cabinet. Someone would recognize her."

Not necessarily, Jil thought. Nobody liked to believe they were as oblivious to irregularities as they really were. Often, they needed proof. The trick was to show them something instead of telling them. That way it seemed less like an accusation. "Can I show you something?"

Rochelle nodded.

"Your computer, please?"

Rochelle flipped open her laptop and angled it toward Jil, across the desk.

Jil typed in a web address and waited for a video to load—a short clip of a basketball game—players in white T-shirts versus players in black T-shirts. "When this video starts playing, I need you to count the number of times the ball is passed from person to person. Keep a running total in your head, okay?"

Rochelle looked at her. "The number of times it's passed?"

"Yes." She pressed play, and the basketball players started dribbling the ball, passing it rapidly from player to player. Jil watched Rochelle's eyes dart back and forth across the bottom of the screen, and her lips moved silently as she counted the passes. Exactly what she'd done herself the first time she'd seen this video at the police academy.

The video ended and Rochelle looked up. "Forty-seven," she declared.

"You're sure?"

"Yes. I'm sure I counted forty-seven."

Jil nodded. "Why do you think you were able to keep track of all those ball passes?"

Rochelle leaned back in her chair. "Well, it's kind of like my regular workday." She laughed. "There are so many balls in the air around here that I have to keep track of. I guess I'm used to focusing hard."

"Do you think other people are like that around here? Focused?"

Rochelle nodded. "Yeah. I would. That's why I find it hard to believe that someone could sneak in here unnoticed."

Jil smiled wryly. "I know you find that hard to believe. But it happens all the time. Can you tell me, when you were watching the balls pass back and forth, did you see anything unusual happen on the basketball court?"

Rochelle frowned. "Not really, no."

"Watch again. This time, just watch. Don't count." Jil pressed Replay.

The game started again, with players passing the ball back and forth quickly. Twenty seconds in, a man in a gorilla suit walked into the middle of the court, waved his arms, and continued through. The video ended.

Rochelle stared at the screen, then up at Jil. "That's not the same video. It can't be."

Jil gave her a rueful look. "It is. Exactly the same video."

"How could I have missed that? A giant gorilla!"

Jil leaned across the desk. "Because you were focused on something else. Now, if you are focused on your work, as is everyone else, could someone looking exactly like Annie, with her coat, her bag, her swipe pass, walk straight through the office and to the back room?"

"That's incredible." Rochelle closed her eyes for a moment and shook her head. "I can't believe this."

Jil let her take a moment to collect herself. "Can I see the rest of the office now?"

Rochelle opened her eyes. Jil held her breath. "Yes. Absolutely. Let's find out how this person got in here."

Jil stood up. She knew exactly how she'd gotten in—through the front door. "Let's start at the lobby."

Rochelle led the way out the door and back to the front reception desk.

Flipping open her notebook, Jil followed her. Annie said her pass had been stolen three weeks ago. The imposter probably hadn't waited long to use it.

"This is Mandy," Rochelle said. "She is our full-time receptionist."

Mandy glanced up and pasted on a smile. Jil read the questioning look in her eyes. Was she in some sort of trouble?

"Hi, Mandy, I'm Jil. I'm a private investigator."

A frown crossed her face. "But I thought you were a client?"

"Someone's been impersonating one of our nurses," Rochelle broke in. "Anastasia, our nurse, was not the Anastasia who arrived to treat Jil's foster mother, Mrs. Fitzgerald. We're trying to find out how the imposter got in here."

"Someone was impersonating Annie?" Mandy's eyebrows shot up.

"And coming in the building with her swipe pass."

"No. There's no way. She'd have to walk right past me."

Jil looked at Rochelle, who took a deep breath. "It's not your fault," she said. Before the gorilla video, she might not have believed that statement, but now Jil saw plainly that Rochelle didn't blame Mandy at all.

Still, if a thief was trying to get by undetected, she would conceivably try to do it when she'd be least likely to get noticed.

"Have you been away during the past month?" Jil asked. "Holidays or anything?"

"No, I don't think so."

"What about illness? Have you called in sick?"

Mandy frowned. "A couple weeks ago, I caught strep throat. But I went to the clinic on a Saturday morning."

"Do you remember the date?"

Mandy pulled the desk calendar toward herself and pointed out the day to Jil. Two days after Anastasia's purse was stolen. Now, how could the imposter have known when she might be off work?

She glanced at the waiting room over the half-wall partition. "Did you talk about your sore throat at work? Mention it to anyone?"

"She mentioned it to me," Rochelle said. "Late in the afternoon on a Friday."

"Yeah, that's right," Mandy said. "Rochelle told me to get to the clinic if it didn't clear up because some of the nurses had been coming down with strep. Which is what I had."

Jil frowned. "Okay. So on Monday, you were back at work."

"Yes."

"And did you have any visitors?"

Mandy glanced at the calendar. "There's a blue dot on here, so that means we had a visit from a drug rep."

"The lemonade bar lady," Rochelle said.

"Lemonade bar?"

Rochelle rolled her eyes. "They're always bringing treats along with their samples. I guess they think we'll be more likely to choose their products if they feed us a little sugar."

Jil grinned. "Does that work?"

"No. We've got that system beat. We don't open the samples right away. We save them up and open them all at the same time. By then, all the chocolate bars are a blur!" She smiled, then her face closed up again as she remembered...

"This drug rep—did you know her?"

Mandy frowned. "She was new."

Rochelle met Jil's glance—fear flickering across her eyes. "I'd never seen her before either. You don't think..."

"Do you remember where she was from?" Jil interjected.

"Yeah. PharmaTek. It's a huge company. They send someone every time their company comes out with a new gauze or antibacterial salve for us to try."

"What did this drug rep bring this time?"

Mandy and Rochelle looked at each other. "I can't remember," Mandy said. "My throat was still sore and I was distracted by the lemonade bars."

"I think it might have been some sort of new non-stick bandage." Rochelle frowned. "She left a sample. I stored it in the back with all the others."

Mandy nodded. "Everything is put in a bucket on the shelf in the supplies cupboard. We keep it in the original bags so we can tell which samples come from which company."

"So you never open samples before the end of the month?"

"No. We have a potluck lunch on the last Friday and open all the bags. It's kind of fun." Mandy bit her lip. "At least, it always has been."

"Do you remember what she looked like?"

"She was young," Mandy said. "Platinum blond hair and lots of makeup."

"Tall?"

"Skinny and tall, yeah. Well, maybe it was just the heels."

"She wore tall heels?"

"Yeah, four inches at least. She had fabulous legs."

Jil smiled. "Good thing to notice."

Mandy blushed. "Sorry. She was really pretty. I'm not gay or anything, but I noticed."

"Not gay? That's too bad." She winked.

Mandy blushed even redder, and Rochelle laughed.

"One more question."

"Yes?" Rochelle leaned in.

"Who's in charge of supervising that clinic across the way? Do patients have to register?"

"Well, the nurse in charge changes every two days, but most of the patients are regulars."

"How busy is it there? Could a 'new patient' sneak in and sit for a while, unnoticed?"

Rochelle frowned. Jil could see the skepticism in her face, but after seeing the video, her perspective seemed to have changed about what was possible to miss. "It's a busy place. Sometimes the nurses see more than thirty or forty people before ten."

"Who might be in there? Patients and who else?"

"Family members bringing the patients in. Personal Support Workers or attendants from the accessible buses. Nurses. The doctor on call. Lots of people move in and out of there."

Jil sighed.

"What are you thinking?"

Jil leaned in. "Okay, this is my best guess. 'Anastasia' walked into the clinic either posing as a patient or as an aide of some sort. She sat in the waiting room to listen in to this side of the clinic. Who knows how many days she came—maybe two or three. She overheard Annie say she was going out for dinner and where. She overheard Mandy say she had a sore throat. She used this information to plan a strategy, and then when she thought Mandy might be away on the Monday after she got strep, she came in, impersonating a drug rep."

"But she didn't go inside."

"Doesn't matter," Jil said. "Seems to have been a reconnaissance mission. She wanted time to look around. How long did she stay?"

"She chatted quite a while," Mandy said ruefully. "She seemed pleasant and wanted some pointers about getting the nurses in here to like her."

"So she chatted you up about who liked which kind of chocolate bar?" Jil guessed.

Mandy nodded miserably.

Jil shook her head. "And all the time, she was probably watching people go in and out with their swipe pass, learning how it worked."

"There's a bit of a trick to it," Mandy agreed.

"Which would have tripped her up later," Jil added. "So after watching several attempts, she'd have a pretty good idea of what to do. So the next day, or the day after, while Annie was out on rounds, she dressed up as her, and walked straight through the front doors with her swipe pass, kept her head down, and raided the supply closet. Left with a bag, a uniform, a box of bandages, and whatever else she needed, including Elise's patient file."

Rochelle stared at her, white-faced. "I can't believe this."

Jil exhaled softly. "She's a professional, all right."

"We have to look in that bag." Rochelle strode quickly up the corridor, Jil close behind her. In the storage room, Rochelle riffled through the big plastic bin until she found a blue PharmaTek bag. She opened it and fished inside for the sample. "Gauze pads." She held up the box. "We got these same ones last month."

Jil took the box from her. "So if you had looked right away, she could have claimed to be new and not to have known you'd already received them. Clever."

"Not so clever." A triumphant smile lit Rochelle's face. "We have a security camera at the front door. I know exactly when this person was here, and now we can find her on our footage."

Jil nodded. It could be a good lead, but probably not as important as Rochelle thought. This woman was a chameleon. She and her disguises would be long gone by now.

CHAPTER SEVEN

Jil clicked replay and watched the imposter hold open the door for an elderly man who appeared to be coming in alone. This time, she had medium-length brunette hair and wore a skirt and blouse, low heels, and minimal makeup. Totally different from how Mandy had described her. One thing she couldn't hide, though, was the way she walked. This is how Jil had found her in the sea of video footage—three separate times.

The man smiled at her gratefully and accepted her arm when she offered it, helping him to a chair right next to the half-wall that divided the clinic from the nursing office.

She sat with him for half an hour, and when the nurse called his name, she waved good-bye to him, then turned and walked out the door. That was Wednesday.

Friday, she came again, this time dressed in a set of scrubs and sneakers, holding the door for a younger woman in a power chair. Had she waited for these people outside? Smoking a cigarette? Reading on the outdoor bench?

She'd seen someone alone and jumped up to help them, knowing nobody would ask any questions of a family member or personal support worker.

Monday, she appeared a third time, only now she wore a business suit, carried a trench coat, and had her blond hair tied up in a neat French braid.

She'd studied the footage for hours, getting a feel for how this woman looked, moved, talked, and smiled. She saw the distinctive crinkle at the side of her eyes, the way one corner of her mouth tilted up a little when she made initial contact. She was left-handed, had one leg slightly shorter than the other, producing a barely-discernible shift in her gait. Stripped from heels, she stood at five foot five. Her eyebrows were light, which meant her hair tended either toward a natural dirty blond or light brunette. And she had a tiny beauty mark above her lip.

As Mandy had said, she was exceptionally pretty, which meant she'd be used to people saying yes to her. Brazen didn't even begin to describe her...

She now had no trouble at all believing that this woman could pull a Catwoman, straight into the upstairs window of the house. Hell, she could probably scale a high-rise on a bungee cord.

Jil took several still shots from the video stream, uploaded them as image files, and blew them up as much as possible without distorting the clarity. She printed them off—three different "Anastasias"—and pinned them up over her desk.

After considering for a brief moment, she e-mailed Detective Fraser the images, with a favor request. "Please let me know if she appears in the criminal database. I'd like to know who she is."

Five minutes later, her phone rang.

"I thought you were going to leave the detecting to me," he said, his voice tight.

"Did you? Well, last I heard, you said I didn't have a case."

He sighed. "Is this your home health care aide?"

"Yes."

"How did you find her?"

"I have superpowers. So, is she in the database?"

"I don't know yet. I'm running a facial recognition now, but it will take some time. Would you care to explain to me what's going on in these photos?"

Jil sighed. "Right now all I know is that this woman likes to play dress-up. Clearly, that's not a crime, but it crosses the line if she's actually impersonating others, and that's what I'd like to know. Meet me for coffee when you find a match. I'll fill you in."

❖

When Jess entered the staff room, the chatter stopped. Teachers looked up from their tables, casting sideways looks at her as she moved past. Gradually, talk resumed, at a lower level. A few teachers left the room.

Of course the teachers were normally on their best behavior around her, but was this excessive? Was she overreacting or were they looking at her strangely?

"Morning, Jess." Rosie McMonahan strode past her into the kitchen, her gym whistle smacking against her chest. She reached to the highest shelf for a travel mug, then turned to Jess. "You want one?"

"Sure." Jess took the mug she offered and laid it down on the counter. "How are your outdoor ed courses going?"

Rosie shrugged. "I like the snow, personally, but my kids are cranky about cross-country skiing."

"Too bad."

"Yeah, that's what I said. I told them we were running out of gym space, and unless they wanted to take another science course to make up their credits, they were stuck with snowshoeing for at least one three-week cycle."

As Rosie reached into the fridge for the milk, Jess grabbed the handle of the coffee carafe. She pulled it from the hot plate, but the carafe slipped, thudding down onto the counter and splashing hot coffee everywhere. She leapt back, expecting it to fall to the floor and shatter, but it stopped just a quarter inch from the edge.

Rosie grabbed the dripping handle and moved the carafe back onto the hot plate while Jess grabbed a stack of paper towels. All eyes had turned to them. Someone muttered something at the back of the room.

Jess felt her cheeks flaming.

"You okay?" Rosie asked Jess.

"Yeah. Sorry."

Rosie took the paper towel from Jess and mopped up the mess on the floor, then filled both their mugs.

Jess muttered a thank you, then took her coffee—carefully this time—and headed back to her office.

Mary, her admin assistant, nodded to a package balancing on the edge of her desk, and Jess stopped to read the label—the store that sold equipment for students with developmental disabilities. A foam wedge or something that cost upwards of four hundred dollars.

It was barely Christmas and they were about to blow their entire annual budget.

"Call down to the D.E. classroom and have someone come pick that up, please."

"They just need your signature."

Jess looked at the receipt slips, considered the pen and trying to scrawl her name on the page while the entire office staff looked on, and felt her face beginning to flush again.

"Just use my signature stamp."

Mary looked surprised but didn't argue as Jess went into her office and closed the door.

❖

"I'm glad you could make it." Tamara stood up from her large walnut desk and extended a hand. The sleeves of her blazer stopped just below her elbows and cinched in at her waist, buttoned once across a perfect white camisole. Black curls bounced almost to her shoulders, and she smiled with her whole face—from her red-painted lips up to her dark hazel eyes.

She looked friendly, for a lawyer—not at all what Jil had expected.

"Nice to meet you as well." Jil dropped Elise's folder on the desk and sat in one of the plush wing chairs opposite the desk.

"You haven't looked at this?" Tamara seemed a little surprised.

"What's to look at? She's left me everything. I already know. She has no other heirs."

Tamara took a whalebone letter opener and slit the will folder neatly across the top. She put on a pair of dark blue glasses, then laid the two papers side by side. "Identical," she pronounced after several minutes.

"Unsurprising." Jil bit back any further remarks. The woman was only doing her job.

Tamara held her gaze for a moment before speaking. "It seems Elise sold all her investments and transferred them into cash accounts a few months ago, so that makes things a little easier. We still have to apply for probate before we can sell the house or transfer any of the assets."

Jil nodded absently. She let her gaze wander out the window to where snow covered the upper branches of a birch tree.

"What are you planning to do with the island in the Caribbean?" Tamara asked.

Jil looked back. "What island?"

"Just checking." A small smirk tugged at the corners of Tamara's mouth.

"Sorry. I am listening."

Tamara winked. "No problem. It's just that most clients hang on my every word, wondering if there's a hidden fortune their relative kept secret...I guess I'm just used to rapt attention."

"Elise wasn't my relative," Jil said. "She was a lovely older woman who was kind enough to get me out of a bad situation as a teenager. I don't deserve to inherit all her assets—whatever they may be."

Tamara raised her eyebrows. "Well, you're going to have to figure out how to accept her generosity, because her assets are pretty damn substantial."

Jil frowned. "How substantial?"

Tamara's face twitched, like she was trying to hold back a laugh. "Well, including the life insurance policy, about three point five million dollars substantial."

CHAPTER EIGHT

Jil leaned back in her chair and stared at the lawyer. "That's impossible," she managed finally.

"I've triple checked her financials. Believe me, they're accurate."

"Elise had a modest lifestyle. She owned her home, yes, but she worked up until a few years ago. She volunteered at the library, for Christ's sake! She only took a vacation once a year, if that. She couldn't have been worth three and a half million dollars."

Tamara shrugged. "Well, she didn't really have it all squandered away somewhere. That includes the value of her art and artifacts as well. And a policy she took out when you were seventeen. Not all of it's yours, but most."

"Who else is named?"

Tamara frowned. "Padraig O'Hannagan."

Jil nodded. "That makes sense. They were old friends."

"But you still get a pretty large portion of that, so…"

"I don't believe it."

Tamara held her gaze, something flickering behind her eyes— surprise? Indignation that Jil was questioning her?

"What the hell am I supposed to do with that kind of money?"

Tamara tilted her head. "Well, you could consider that island in the Caribbean."

Jil shot her a withering look. She knew Elise had collected a lot of valuable things, but God almighty.

"I'm sorry. I'm just going to need a minute here."

Jil bolted out of the lawyer's office, looking for a staircase to the roof. She found it and burst through the door onto the green terrace, or what would be a green terrace if it wasn't the middle of fucking winter. A brick, dusted lightly with snow, seemed to reside against the wall for the specific purpose of keeping the heavy fire door propped open, so she used it to keep the door slightly ajar.

Though maybe it wouldn't be such a bad thing to get locked out here for a few hours.

She pulled her coat around herself a little tighter. The wind up here ripped through her scarf and set her hair streaming behind her. She reached into the front breast pocket and extracted a package of Elise's vanilla honey cigars—which she only smoked socially, and even then, only when she'd had several glasses of full-bodied red wine.

Jil took out the intricate silver lighter Elise always kept with the cigars and flicked it until a flame roared. She inhaled the lit cigar, the smoke stinging her eyes until she turned around. Then her eyes continued to prick from the familiar smell rather than the scented smoke.

How could Elise keep such a secret from her? Whatever would she do with such a large sum of money? She couldn't possibly keep it. It didn't belong to her. How could it even have belonged to Elise?

Something else bothered her. Maybe Jess hadn't been that far off the mark. If Elise had that kind of cash, maybe that Monet *had* been real. Maybe Elise had only told everyone it was a replica so she wouldn't be robbed—a smart move.

So what else around the house posed as a replica but was secretly valued at a million dollars?

Jil took another long drag on her cigar, then took a seat on a stone bench, sheltered from the wind by a few evergreen trees and a rock face. She drew her knees up to her chest to keep warm as she smoked, breathing in Elise's comforting presence and letting it cling to her hair and her clothes like perfume.

❖

"Jil, I'd like you to meet Elise."

Jil stood on the threshold to the white house that looked like a large cottage. She took note of the red door, the clinging ivy, and the giant oak tree out front that looked like a great hiding spot, high up in its thick branches. This didn't look like any foster home she'd ever seen before, with worn climbing structures and minivans parked in the driveway.

She tried her best to look up to meet the gaze of the woman who would be her warden for the next two years, but felt like her eyelids were being magnetically pulled toward the stone porch upon which she stood.

"Lovely to meet you, Jil." Elise's accent sounded like Padraig's—soft and rich with the singing lilt of the Irish brogue.

Finally, Jil looked up and attempted a smile at the slight woman with graying curly hair and bright blue eyes.

Elise extended a small, warm hand, and as Jil shook it, she noticed the gold bangles that jingled on her wrist and smiled. "Do come in," said Elise.

Jil swallowed hard and crossed the threshold into the foyer. The smell of blueberry muffins and vanilla candles enveloped her.

"Let me put on some tea."

❖

She stubbed out her cigar butt against the stone wall and slipped back inside, down to Tamara's office.

"All right?" Tamara asked.

Jil attempted a smile, then sat down. "Can I ask you for a referral?"

"You need a tax lawyer?"

"No...Well, yes, probably, but more immediately I need an appraiser."

"You want a second opinion?"

"I always want to see for myself."

Tamara's eyes lit up. "I have just the gentleman for you."

"Another question, actually, if you have a sec."

"Sure."

"Elise left me this key. Do you have any idea what it's for?" She took out her keychain and showed Tamara the old silver key.

"Oh, that's where it went. Good."

"What is it?"

"It's a key to a vintage safety deposit box at the bank. I have one for you for the primary door, but this is for the antique box inside that."

Jil chuckled. Trust Elise to have a safety deposit box inside a safety deposit box. She accepted the utilitarian key from Tamara, added it to the chain, and left smiling.

❖

Mr. Hollands squinted at Jil's lighter through a tiny monocular, turning it side to side and making a small humming noise at the back of his throat. His balding head shone in the bright light from the overhead lamp. "Sterling silver," he announced. "Ireland, nineteen twenty-two."

Jil sat back in her chair. "Thank you," she said, though she hadn't asked him to appraise her cigarette lighter.

According to her background check, this man was sixty-three, had a PhD in art restoration, had authored two textbooks on historical artifacts, and had helped the FBI in the States track down several missing pieces. In short, a good referral from Tamara.

"No trouble, my dear. You say there are more pieces you wish me to examine?"

Jil sighed, unsure of how much to say. "Would it be at all possible for you to meet me at home? Well, not my home…um, my foster mother has died and left me some artifacts."

"Ah. And you'd like to determine their worth?"

"Yes, but more than that…I'd like to determine which of them are replicas, and which, if any, are real."

"Genuine artifacts?"

"Some art as well, if you could help me with that."

Mr. Hollands rose from his desk. He couldn't have been more than five feet two inches tall. "What kind of art?"

Jil thought about all the artwork that hung in Elise's place. She had to have thirty pieces.

"She was an art history professor. A wide variety of things interested her, and I'm afraid I'm not quite sure how to describe her collection."

"Ah. An eclectic collector," Mr. Hollands said. His thin lips stretched into a genuine smile, and he pushed his round tortoise-shell glasses a little farther up his nose.

Jil nodded. "She liked Fabergé," she said, glad to be able to contribute something.

Mr. Hollands nodded, and she noticed a flicker of doubt cross his eyes. She realized hardly anyone outside of a museum or a millionaire art curator would have a genuine Fabergé, but it seemed Elise belonged to the latter class after all.

"Tomorrow, around ten?" he said brightly.

She stood and shook his hand. "Yes, that would be fine. Thank you." Before leaving, she scribbled out her name and Elise's address. Bizarrely, she hoped she might have a few genuine artifacts to show him. He seemed like he'd be so excited to see them.

But if most of the artifacts at home were real, that only deepened the mystery she hesitated to solve.

❖

Jess closed the door to her office and sat on her small loveseat, coffee firmly in grip. She shook her head angrily at herself. When had she ever cared about idle gossip from the teachers?

When you started losing their respect.

The answer came as a jolt.

Had she lost their respect? When?

Could it be that gossip about her and Jil had filtered down into the rumor mill? She thought that when Jil's identity had been revealed—in a closed-door, not-to-leave-this-room staff meeting—that would put to rest any lingering whispers about their frequent tête-à-têtes.

But perhaps not.

A rap on the door made her jump, and a small trickle of coffee leaped over the edge of her mug and began sliding down the side. She swiped at it with the edge of her scarf. "Come in."

Rosie McMonahan stood at the door.

"Prep this morning?" Jess asked, gesturing her inside.

"Independent study. They're doing health in the library. Evan is supervising."

Evan Strauss was the head gym coach but would be retiring this year, with Rosie next in line for his position.

Rosie stepped inside and closed the door behind her. "I might be compromising my promotion by stepping out of line, but I came to check on you."

Jess gave her a sideways smile. "Take a seat. My door's always open."

Rosie sat in the opposite chair and put her elbows on her knees, leveling her gaze with Jess's. "Not lately."

Jess took a careful sip of her coffee. Her heart sped up a little. "You find me hard to reach?"

Rosie shrugged.

"It's okay, Rosie. Say whatever's on your mind. Life is easier that way." It would be even easier if she could follow her own advice.

"You're sure?"

"Of course. You wouldn't have come if it wasn't important."

"You're right. Ever since the—incident—it seems like you're only half here. I'm not the only one who's noticed. People are talking."

Jess felt a band constrict around her chest. So she hadn't been imagining it. But what were they talking about, specifically? She wanted to ask, of course—almost did—but how could she press for gossip and still be a respected leader? She couldn't.

"People always talk about their bosses, Rosie," she said and attempted to smile.

"It's not mean-spirited. The staff care about you, Jess. It's just that they need a leader too, and they're used to it being you."

Wow. She'd asked for a straight shot, but hadn't been prepared for how much it might stick.

She shook her head. An effective leader—what a joke. She'd been picked on purpose for her inexperience and her idealistic nature, set up in this school that was partly haunted and partly cursed, because the Old Boys needed a straw principal. She'd let the Sons of Adam funnel right through the bedrock of the school's foundation. A kid had died here this year, and her closest confidante and friend had turned out to be a private investigator sent to scrutinize her.

And then, she'd ended up sleeping with her.

Not to mention pursuing an ongoing relationship.

By some miracle—or curse, she didn't know which—she'd kept her job here and managed to hold the school together. But she'd hardly call herself a pillar of faith and leadership.

She couldn't even show her face at Mass.

How could she possibly lead a team?

Rosie's brow wrinkled, but she didn't look away. "Jess? What's going on?"

She could have said so much, if it had been Jil sitting here. But Jil was absorbed in her own problems, and—she gave herself a mental kick—she had never been here in the first place. She wasn't a teacher!

She'd known Rosie for years, ever since she'd been an upstart first-year teacher, with her shiny gym whistle and glowing smile. She'd protected Rosie when questions had come up about her relationship with Ivan.

But sharing her personal life with her staff had never been something that came easily to her. The less people knew the better. Still, she'd almost sloshed hot coffee all over Rosie this morning; she owed her something.

"I'm sorry I haven't been there for you, Rosie."

Rosie looked like she wanted to say something—*not just me*, probably—but kept silent, her brow still furrowed.

"Getting the school back together has been...it's been a challenge."

"Are you stressed out? Not sleeping?"

How had she guessed? Her question must have shown in her face because Rosie answered her.

"Because you have dark circles under your eyes and you look like you're walking through quicksand half the time."

"Not to mention I almost gave you a third-degree burn this morning." Jess smiled wryly.

"That too. It looked to me like you couldn't hold on to it."

Jess bit her lip. "Observant."

"I just want to help, Jess."

"I know." Jess set her coffee down on the side table, even though she knew it would leave a ring. "I would like to accept some help, believe me, but there's not much anyone can do."

"Are you sick? Got PTSD? What is it?"

"RA." Her hammering heart sped up even more. She'd never told anyone she worked with. How would they feel when they found out she was defective as well as distracted?

"What is that?"

"Rheumatoid arthritis. It's—complicated. Anyway, this morning when I woke up, my fingers were numb. Usually, it goes away within a few hours, but today, it's lasting longer. That's why—"

"Why you can't hold on to things."

"Yeah. That's right." She sat up straighter. She'd said as much as she possibly could with a teacher—even Rosie. The person she really wanted to talk to, of course, was Jil, but lately that seemed impossible.

CHAPTER NINE

The last bell had rung and the mass exodus had occurred in a record three minutes. Jess watched through the main office doors as students poured into the atrium and out onto the sidewalk, some of them lighting cigarettes between the double set of doors.

Her heart thudded faster in her chest.

It made her nervous when they congregated in swarms like that.

Some of them huddled against walls in cliques. What were they whispering?

Who had a secret that could undermine the life of another student—or teacher? Were small groups still meeting? Had other leaders for the Sons of Adam taken over? Or were the investigating teams doing a good enough job?

In her gut, she felt like it wasn't over, but waiting for the other shoe to drop would only make her paranoid.

She walked back into her office and shut the door. The department heads had submitted their monthly reports, and she had to review them all before leaving.

She wanted to be the last one out. To do her nightly tour of the school, making sure the classrooms were empty and the custodians were remembering to lock all the windows. Even in winter, some teachers liked to leave some windows open. Some of the upper rooms got so hot.

At four thirty, Jess set down the last report and gathered her coat.

The outer office was empty; outside, the sky had faded to a pink-streaked blue. Her own footsteps echoed back to her as she traveled through the atrium, past the religion department. She paused for the briefest second, looking in the window of where Jil's office used to be.

Twilight cast long shadows on the walls.

She walked down the hallway to the special needs corridor, the home studies classrooms, and the music rooms.

Dark.

Once she'd circled the auditorium, her hips were aching in protest, and she still had two more floors to go.

Why was this happening now? She'd always had a bit of stiffness, but never this bad. Never so bad that she couldn't walk her own school.

As she stood at the bottom of the staircase, Brian, the custodian, came bounding down, his ring of keys jangling. "Howdy, Jess. You on your tour?"

Jess looked at him and tried to smile. "Well, since you've beat me to it, I guess it's just the lower floor today." Thank God.

"All's good upstairs. The chess club just cleared out and they were the last today."

"Thank you, Brian."

"No problem. I'm just about to do one last check, then hand it over to the evening shift."

Jess nodded, and turned away to head back to her office. The evening shift came from five until eleven. She never saw them.

How well were they vetted? What did the hiring protocol for custodians look like? Did they have to have police checks? Were they supervised?

She'd thought briefly about this before, of course, but now she found herself wanting answers. Who came in the school when she left?

This job was getting to her. In more than one way.

Maybe tonight she'd talk to Jil. Get her take on things.

Maybe the two of them could plan a vacation after everything with Elise had died down. Just get out of town for a while. Could they?

❖

"It's only for a few days," Jil said as she opened a small suitcase onto the bed.

Zeus looked at her doubtfully, cocking his head to the side.

"You'll like it there. It has a nice yard for you to play in, and a park where we can walk."

At the W-word, Zeus's ears perked up.

"Sorry, I didn't mean now. Later."

He harrumphed and settled back down on the carpet to watch her pack.

She turned to the closet and riffled through for some pajamas and sweatshirts. This week, she'd had time off from work, but next week, she had to get back to the pile of cases on her desk, and Padraig's. Fraser had been right. She did indeed have a few cheating spouses to spy on.

As if in response to her thoughts, her phone buzzed with a text from Chet. *Greetings, fearless leader. Sorry to report the computer problem is not solved. Do you think you could drop everything and run over here with Daddy's credit card?*

She rolled her eyes. The boys were enjoying harassing her. No sympathy at all. She texted back. *Engage a tech specialist. Assuming you know how to use the Internet. If not, open a phone book. Get her to invoice me when she's finished.*

Too busy to see your friends? Chet joked.

Busy solving a case. What's your excuse?

Already solved all mine. Now I'm taking a nap.

How about beginning on Padraig's? Or are you on salary now?

She grinned as she tucked the phone back in her bag. It would be good to get back to work, especially to see the boys—and to take her mind off this mystery of Elise's she still wasn't sure she wanted to solve.

Just as she finished packing up her toiletries, the front door opened. She looked up.

"Hi," Jess said, standing in the bedroom doorway.

Jil's stomach flipped. "Hey. You're home early."

Jess looked from Jil's face to her suitcase. "Going somewhere?"

Jil swallowed hard. "No. Well, yes, to Elise's. Or rather, Zeus is going to Elise's, and I'm going to keep him company."

"Okay. For a while…?"

"I just need to keep an eye on things there."

Jess frowned. "Right."

Jil smiled wanly. She didn't feel like explaining. Why didn't she feel like explaining? *Jess, you were right. The painting was real. Now I'm afraid I'm leaving a whole lot of valuable artifacts unattended…*

Instead, she grabbed her coat from the back of the door and rolled her suitcase into the front hall. "Do you want a cup of coffee?" Jil asked.

Jess looked at her skeptically. "A cup of coffee? What, are we back to dating?"

Jil felt her temper flaring but worked hard to keep it in check. "No, but don't you feel like we're U-Hauling, just a bit?"

"Wow." Jess took a step back, her face flushed. "I'm sorry. I didn't mean to move in on your space." Her green eyes clouded, and she clenched her purse more tightly.

"Jess, it's not that—"

Jess put her hands up. "No, you're right. We never said we were exclusive. I shouldn't have assumed."

"Maybe not. I don't have a date or anything, if that's what you're thinking."

"Well, would you like to?"

Jil clenched her teeth. "I don't know. I haven't had much time to think about it."

"Because I've been hogging your bed and taking over your kitchen?" Jess snapped.

God, she was beautiful when she was angry. And so goddamned infuriating at the same time.

"I didn't say that."

"No, you're right. We shouldn't be moving so fast. We should take a beat, maybe branch out a bit."

"Jess, I didn't say I wanted to see other people."

"Well, it seems that you're continually surprised to see me. Like you might like to have someone else standing in your doorway."

"Maybe I'm just not quite sure when to expect you. You know—if you can squeeze me into the double life you seem so comfortable living."

Jess blanched. "That's not fair. You know this is new to me."

"Is it, though? You seem to have been lying to yourself and pretty much everyone around you for quite some time now. It's a bit difficult to be the partner who has to hide in the bathroom in case she might be recognized."

"Jil, that's not fair. You know it's temporary."

Jil swallowed hard. She would not cry. "Yeah, sure," she said softly.

Jess grabbed her bag. "I'm sorry I can't wave a flag, Jil. I thought you understood."

"Jess, c'mon."

But Jess had taken three more steps toward the door. "I agree. It's not fair to you. I'm sorry. Let's just leave it for a bit."

CHAPTER TEN

For a moment after the door closed, Jil considered following her—to try explaining—but something held her back. She felt stuck in place, in every way. A serious relationship needed energy and time and commitment, and she lacked all three at the moment.

Where Jess wanted to talk and comfort her, Jil wanted to scream and hit something until it screamed back. Jess was understanding, beautiful, complex, and Jil just couldn't handle her right now.

She also didn't see how they could conceivably make a life together when Jess's job made it impossible for them even to be seen in public. It was too risky, too complicated, and too delicate. What she wanted was a one-night stand. A series of one-night stands. She needed sex that made her feel alive and free and uninhibited, not roped in—gliding on eggshells—careful and slow and considerate. She wanted a good fuck that released her in every way and let her collapse, unconscious—something to make her forget.

❖

Jess hurried into the parking lot and slid into her car. She slammed the door behind her, the tears still falling—hot, rapid streams that burned her cheeks and stung her eyes. What had just happened? She thought they'd moved past this point.

Ever since Jil had confessed who she really was, they'd had a nice, swaying rhythm—long conversations, good meals, and late bedtimes. Getting to know each other as people instead of pushing against the roles they used to play.

And now Jil was ducking for cover. Why?

She blotted her eyes and wiped her nose before pulling out onto the main road. The tears were partially blinding her, but she made it home, not even remembering which lights were green and which were red. Then she moved slowly into the house, shut the door to her bedroom, and cried until her chest hurt.

A cramp in her lower back woke her just before midnight.

At home, alone in bed.

With a quiet groan, she rolled over and got up. How long had she slept? Outside her suburban townhouse, the moon shone high and bright—a mocking beacon. She wrenched the curtains closed and limped to the bathroom.

The door to Mitch's side of the vanity always hung slightly off its hinge, and tonight it had opened a bit, revealing shaving cream and cologne—years old. Of course she should have thrown those things away, or at least boxed them up.

But then what?

Where would she put it all? In storage? Along with a key she'd hand him in the envelope with the divorce papers?

A slim possibility remained that he'd wake up—and this house had belonged to them both.

Which is why she'd practically moved in to Jil's condo, even though it was smaller...

A fresh surge of tears overwhelmed her, and she sat down, shaking, on the toilet seat. How could she have misread the signs so spectacularly—for a second time?

And what business did she have being surprised and hurt that a relationship based on a fundamental lie could have ended badly?

Her stomach clenched until she wanted to throw up. *Had* it ended? Was it over?

She took a pain pill, limped back to bed, and lay awake for a long time, staring at the curtains covering the moon.

❖

Jil dumped her duffel in her old bedroom and kicked off her shoes. One of them flew into the closet, but she didn't bother to retrieve it. Something about being back here in this old life elicited a teenage sullenness she thought she'd outgrown. She grabbed a towel and stepped into the en suite bathroom, smiling as she remembered the first time she'd seen this place.

In one day, she'd gone from sharing a single toilet with five kids to having a whole attached bathroom to herself.

And the blessed silence that came with it.

She stripped off and turned the shower onto its hottest setting. She wanted to strip away the horrible words she and Jess had exchanged. Of course she hadn't meant half the things she'd said, but she'd never learned how to stop acting so irrational when she was hurt. Maybe a by-product of having spent so many of her childhood years among people who really didn't care. The best thing to do was to hurt them first so they left you alone.

And that strategy applied pretty much universally.

She'd hurt Jess. Jess had left her alone.

She leaned against the wall and let the water trickle down her face and over her shoulders. For a second, she wished Jess was standing there next to her, naked and soapy and...

Like a black wave, an image flashed through her mind—not what she had expected.

The unwelcome memory pricked at her.

In the bathroom of her old foster home.

She really didn't want to go there. Cursing, she turned off the stream, hopped out, and made up her mind to focus on this case.

❖

Jess pulled in to her parking space at six forty-five a.m. The lot was deserted, and she let go the breath she'd been holding. Every morning as she parked, the memory of Alyssa's dead body sprawled out on the pavement flashed briefly, like a Polaroid behind her eyes.

She'd blink and it would be gone.

But every day, she wondered what sort of minefield she'd have to maneuver. Would she see more taggings? More violence? More secrets exposed? Of course, the network still had influence. Of course, they still held meetings somewhere.

Even with help from the outside authorities intent on finding and disbanding the secret society that had operated at St. Marguerite's for years, kids were still at risk of coercion, bullying…everything. And sometimes—no, often—she felt like a straw principal, set up to run the illusion of a school, but blind to the darker underground dealings that stirred directly beneath her office.

"Morning, Jess." Brian, the custodian, nodded as she came into the room.

"Good morning."

"Weekly report is in your mail slot."

"Thank you."

Another change. The head custodian would normally have keys to every room in the school, including her office, but since the incident, she now had the only set of keys. No more reports left on her desk. Her office was hers and hers alone.

Her hands shook a little as she opened the door. She resisted the urge to look over her shoulder. This was her school. She had to be in charge here.

But so much had changed, and keeping track of all the moving parts was proving exhausting—a new vice principal, a new head of the religious department. The residence buildings overhauled, new dons appointed from outside the school. Today, an interim chaplain would arrive. Poor Maggie Reitman had been on stress leave since the incident. Buck had taken immediate retirement, of course. He could hardly come into the school, let alone hold a class.

The thought of burning the place to the ground and starting over occurred to her, and not for the first time.

She could transfer out too. But what kind of mess would that leave for the next person? And how would she cope with a new school? She could barely walk into this one.

God. What a fucking mess.

The phone flashed red in the dim light from her desktop lamp. She yanked open the blinds and sat down for messages. Her stomach lurched. Could one be from Jil?

Of course not. She shook her head. Why would she call her here?

For the fifteenth time, she checked her mobile. Nothing.

But as she took up a pen to scribble down notes from the messages, the breath she held began to strangle her. She was choking on the effort to keep it together. Despite her best efforts, tears leaked through her tightly squeezed eyes.

She remembered Jil pushed up against this wall, kissing her, linked by invisible magnetic threads as her deft fingers undid her buttons.

Stop. If she couldn't stop thinking about her, she'd never make it through the day.

She might not anyway.

Because underneath all the rapid-fire thoughts of meetings, hirings, briefings, and schedulings, one persistent thought kept gnawing at the base of her brain.

She squashed it down because she didn't know what it meant. Because she wasn't ready for the freefall that would come from acknowledging it.

I don't want to do this.

CHAPTER ELEVEN

Just as Jil and Zeus came in from their morning walk, she heard a car in the driveway. She glanced out the window to see Mr. Hollands alighting from a champagne-colored sedan.

"Good morning." She opened the door for him to come in. Zeus sniffed his hand and bunted under his arm, knocking the slight man off-balance.

"Hello there." Mr. Hollands chuckled and scratched Zeus behind the ears. Zeus leaned on him, and he stumbled against the door.

"Go lie down, please." Jil gave Zeus a shove.

Zeus grumbled in the back of his throat but shuffled off to the living room to sleep off his minimal exercise.

"Coffee?"

"No, thank you. I have another appointment after this, and I can't stay too long."

"Right then. Shall we leap straight in?"

Mr. Hollands removed his black leather overshoes and doffed his hat and coat. "Certainly."

"I'm afraid I don't know what exactly to show you. Would you just like to have a look around?"

"Yes, I would." He scanned the kitchen, his glance lighting on this small thing and that. "Do you have any objection to my moving things?"

"No. I have to categorize it all anyway, either for insurance or to sell."

Mr. Hollands looked at her. "You know, in many cases, art collectors do have substantial insurance on their items. Elise would have had to provide the insurer with a list of the items and their value, as well as pictures."

Of course, that made sense. But Tamara hadn't said anything about insurance on the collection. Only life insurance. "I have an inventory, if that helps you?"

"Yes, it would. Thank you. That way I'll be sure to see everything. But if I were you, I might contact the insurance company for those details."

Jil frowned. How did he know so much about this?

"I see this all the time," Mr. Hollands replied, as if reading her thoughts. "Usually, I'm called in to assess the value of items after a person has passed away. People generally aren't very organized with their final affairs."

But Elise had been organized with her final affairs. Down to the final detail. So where was this policy—if it existed at all?

"Thanks for letting me know. I'll follow up." The classic polite evasion.

Mr. Hollands smiled. "Let's go see your collection, then."

They followed the inventory like a treasure map, Jil leading the way around their home, and Mr. Hollands examining each piece in detail before discreetly assigning it a number value on the inventory itself.

"Do you know the name of my predecessor?" he asked. He looked over his glasses. "Though I imagine she could have appraised it herself, if it was only for the estate."

Jil frowned, trying to remember if Elise had ever mentioned anything about an appraiser. Funny how the details of their separate lives had never seemed important. They kept track of the big things: holidays, birthdays, life decisions and partnerships and illnesses and transitions—but not appointments or appraisals.

And now it seemed as if by not knowing these details, she was failing in the one thing Elise needed her to be: informed.

"I'm afraid I don't."

"Well, no matter." Mr. Hollands smiled. "He or she has done a fairly accurate job. Most of these artifacts are genuine, and many of the paintings are originals. I would have loved to have gone along with her as she collected some of these. They are exquisite and very valuable."

Jil exhaled quietly. *Like three and a half million dollars valuable?*

Jil led him up the staircase to the second floor. He climbed the steps carefully, slowly, like a man who didn't want to put too much pressure on his joints.

"At my age," he joked, "you never know when things are about to give out."

Jil smiled back. "I'm especially curious about this one."

"This one?" Mr. Hollands crested the final stair and turned to look at the Monet.

"Yes." Jil switched on all the lights in the upstairs hall to give him a better look.

He squinted at the painting. "My, my," he breathed.

Jil watched him. His eyes grew wide and his brows came up so high they almost disappeared into the washboard wrinkles on his forehead.

"It can't be the *Evening River Seine*," he said in a hushed voice.

"It's not," Jil said. "It's a replica."

"It is indeed a replica," Mr. Hollands said. "But a special replica."

"Why is that?"

"Well, Monet's painting style was very technical and would have been very difficult to copy. If ever anyone had the chance to do it. The original painting is a ghost." Mr. Hollands fixed her with a troubled stare.

"What do you mean, a ghost?"

He removed his spectacles and cleaned them, as if he wanted to see the painting with the clearest eyes possible. "It's a lost painting. One that was never documented or displayed. The rumor is that it belonged to a private collection until the estate was sold in 1975. It was set to arrive at the Louvre for display but was stolen before it ever got there. There are rumors of this painting and one faded photograph from the inventory sent to the Louvre with the remainder of the collection. I saw it in a book once. But I've never seen the actual thing."

Jil's gut plummeted. It had disappeared from the Louvre? She heard echoes of her conversation with Jess in her mind.

He stared past her, musing aloud. "I don't think it's even on the International Registry of Famous Stolen Paintings. It just vanished. But someone must have seen it."

"Why do you say that?"

He turned to her. "Because to get the amount of precision that's evidenced here, you'd have to be working with the real painting. Digital photographs are one thing, but to get the texture and nuance of a piece of art, you have to see it, touch it. To get a piece of this quality, the replicator would have had to be sitting in front of the original."

If this painting was a duplicate, could Jess have been right? Did Elise have the original here all along? Why would Elise have stolen artwork in her home? Did she even know it was real?

Stupid question—of course she knew it was real. What kind of art history professor would she be if she couldn't tell a real painting from a fake?

But wait.

Jil put her hand on the railing.

This might explain why she didn't have an insurance policy on her collection—because it was priceless. And stolen?

Mr. Hollands stared at the replica. "Is there…is there anything else you want me to see?" he asked, at last tearing his eyes away.

"One more room, please. The library downstairs."

He obliged her as she led the way to Elise's downstairs sanctuary.

Once inside, Mr. Hollands scanned the shelves of Elise's library curiously. With a frown, he darted forward, then looked back. "May I?" he gestured to a book on the shelf.

"Yes, please."

Mr. Hollands pulled the volume from the shelf and showed the cover to Jil. *Illicit Artifacts from the 1900s.* He flipped through it carefully, then handed the text to Jil.

There, in full color, was the *Evening River Seine.* Her heart skipped a beat. She'd recognize that piece anywhere. It had hung in their upstairs hallway since the day she'd moved in.

❖

After hesitating a few moments, Jil answered the ringing phone.

"Hello, Detective Fraser—sorry, Nic."

"Hi, Jil. I was hoping I could stop by."

"Okay, sure. You know where I live."

He chuckled. "I've opened a case, just so you're aware. And I have some information about the images you sent over."

Jil's breath caught. "Do you know who she is?"

"She doesn't have a criminal record, as far as I can tell. She doesn't appear in our database of known criminals."

"Which only really means she hasn't been caught," Jil finished.

"That's right. The fact that she's got so many distinct appearances definitely raises some red flags, but for now, we have no ID."

She exhaled slowly. Another roadblock. Well, nothing new there.

"You're still going to try to track her down, aren't you?" he said.

Was that annoyance or admiration in his voice?

She swallowed hard, determined not to reveal any more emotion. "You can come over tomorrow."

❖

Nic Fraser paced along her front step, chewing gum.

Jil opened the back door of the Jeep to let Zeus jump down, then greeted the detective with a wry smile. "Didn't expect you so soon."

He eyed Zeus a little warily. "I'm on my way home. Thought I'd drop by again and see if there were any new developments you'd like to discuss." He made a move to pat Zeus's head, but seemed to think twice. "He's awfully large, isn't he?"

Jil smiled. "I like big."

"Is he any good as a guard dog? I've heard Danes are big chickens."

Zeus's ears perked up, and Jil scratched his ears. "He does his duty. Let's just say I wouldn't be moving in here without him."

"You're moving in?"

Jil opened the front door of the Jeep and pulled out her larger suitcase, which she handed to Fraser, then leaned back in to retrieve Zeus's enormous bag of food.

"Since we have an art thief and all."

"An alleged art thief," Fraser said.

Jil heaved her weight against the front door to un-jam the lock so she could turn the key. The dead bolt squeaked indignantly, but did slide, and she opened the door. Fraser raised his eyebrows.

"Something else to add to the list of things to repair before I sell this place." A pile of mail lay scattered across the front hall, and she bent to pick up as much as she could. "Come in. I'll make some coffee."

"Are you always this hospitable?"

Jil turned. "No, frankly, I'm not. But Elise was, and this is her house. She'd want me to make you feel welcome, even if you aren't taking either me or my report seriously."

A flicker of a smile lit Fraser's eyes. "Point taken. Though I am helping you now."

"You're under duress. Your reputation is on the line."

"Yes, it is. But I happen to agree with you that there's a lot brewing under the surface of this case. I'm just not sure you need to go digging into it. In my experience, sometimes it's better for family not to know about the past lives of the people they love. Their memories shouldn't be tainted by things they were never meant to know."

Jil fixed him with a stare. "How do you take your coffee?"

He sighed and shook his head. "Black with a little cognac."

Jil raised her eyebrows. "How about Bailey's?"

Fraser shrugged, and this time he did smile. "Whatever works. Do you want me to get someone to drive by at night? Just to check on you?"

"Huh. So we've gone from a scene of no crime to a police detail?"

"Well, not quite. But I could arrange for a patrol car to cruise by."

"Thanks. I'll let you know if it happens again."

As the coffee brewed, Zeus settled down on his bed in the living room, clearly having decided he could keep an eye on things well enough from there, and Fraser settled into the chair Jil offered him, crossing his ankle over his knee.

"Tell me about Elise."

Jil reached for the Bailey's that Elise kept in the bar trolley and poured a generous amount into each glass coffee cup. "What do you want to know about? Her work?"

Fraser shook his head. "No. I've already looked into that. I was curious about what made her take in one foster child and nobody else. I've learned all I can about her work life, so this is my next line of inquiry."

She cringed to imagine what kind of investigation he could have done: interviewed the dean, her colleagues, even her students? He could research her online portfolio and see her entire academic history online. Suddenly, the free information Elise was so passionate about seemed like a violation of her privacy.

"You want to know what made her a victim. Why someone would target her and how."

Fraser sighed. "It would be easier if you'd let me be the cop. My questions don't work if you know my motivations."

Jil grinned. "Then you'll have to ask better questions. Try a little discretion, Nic."

He shook his head. "Are you always this difficult?"

"Sometimes more so."

"Has anyone ever tried to rein you in?" His eyes sparkled with mischief.

She reached for a tin of chocolate biscuits. "Yes. And you should stop flirting with me. I'm gay."

He laughed—a deep, reverberating sound that lit up his eyes and put a flash of pink in his cheeks. "I wasn't—I wasn't flirting."

"Don't feel bad about it. Happens all the time." She enjoyed watching him grapple to regain his upper hand.

"You're gay?" He squinted at her.

"What? You didn't do your research?"

He raised his hands. "I've barely opened this case! And I haven't been investigating *you.*"

"Well, get with it, Nic. The more you know, the more efficiently you'll work." She took a plate down from the cupboard and heaped the biscuits onto it before taking it to the table. The rich smell of coffee wafted through the kitchen, at once making the place seem alive again. Jil poured some of the strong hot brew into each glass mug and brought them, steaming, to the table.

She sat down opposite him and raised the cup to her nose, drinking in the vanilla scent of the Bailey's before taking a sip.

He lifted his cup. "Cheers."

She followed suit, touching her cup to his. "Cheers."

"To catching an art thief."

She grinned wryly. "And to finding you a straight woman."

Fraser chuckled and sipped. "Man, you have a talent for knocking people off guard."

"One of my *many* talents. That's why I'm good at my job."

With a serious look in his eye, Nic put down his mug. "Jil—"

She looked up.

"You have to let me work this, okay? Please. Let me do my job. I can find stolen Monets and emerald rings in my sleep."

Jil looked back, leveling her gaze at him. "She was my foster mother, Nic, and somebody robbed her. I'm going to find out why. I'm not going to stand in your way, because I know you have a job to do. But I'm not going to let you keep me from finding out."

CHAPTER TWELVE

In the middle of the night Jil woke with a start.

The emerald ring. She'd never mentioned anything about the emerald ring—to Fraser or anyone else.

How did he know about it?

She mentally retraced the path of their conversation, trying to remember if she might have slipped it in somewhere.

No. She didn't think so...

She got up and walked into her dark empty kitchen, flipping on a light to keep from being trapped in the regret that seemed to linger more prevalently in dark corners.

The room was missing a vital presence.

She felt it physically—a painful clenching of her stomach. Elise was really gone. No matter what Jil found out about the last few days of her life, that knowledge wouldn't bring Elise back home.

And when she went home to her own place, it would be empty as well.

Had she really messed up this time?

What if...

No, she couldn't call her. No, she couldn't text her and say sorry. If Jess wanted to talk to her, she'd call. But she didn't. Of course she didn't, because this could never work. Jess was a married woman. A straight, married, Catholic woman who worked as a principal at a Catholic school. It didn't get much more complicated than that.

They'd been fooling themselves to think that an affair—no matter how great it had been, or how much they'd fallen for each other—could ever work.

For God's sake, Jess was still married—to her husband as well as her job.

Nothing had brought that home more than Elise's funeral. The best thing they could do now was to say good-bye with some dignity and move on before anything irrevocable happened.

But that didn't stop her from wanting to talk. Jess's brain made up half her attraction value. She'd tell her if she'd gone crazy. If she'd crossed the line from skeptical to suspicious. Conceivably, she'd mentioned the ring to Fraser and not remembered.

How many other things had she forgotten since Elise passed away? Forgetfulness was a classic sign of grief.

How else would he know about the ring?

She gave her head a shake. She suspected a police officer now? And not only a police officer, but a detective?

Where would that get her?

Nowhere on this investigation.

❖

Elise knocked on her door on Saturday morning as Jil lay in bed listening to a mixed tape and reading a magazine from a stack Padraig had brought over.

"Don't mean to disturb you," she said and took a sip from a steaming cup of tea.

Jil sat up and removed her headphones. "No, that's okay."

"Just wanted to say that on Mondays I don't have to be at the university until ten, so I can go with you early in the morning to register for school."

Jil swallowed hard. School. She knew she'd have to go, but had been hoping, somehow, to be emancipated from that as well. Another group of kids. Another loud, clique-filled cafeteria. Another library to hide in over lunch. Another round of bullies to avoid. Another roof to find access to, and another principal to forge excuse notes to. She'd give anything not to have to start over—yet again.

She managed a tight smile. *"Any chance of homeschooling?"* she joked. With a flick of the duvet—the best thing she'd ever slept under—she swung her legs over the side of the bed and grabbed the papers Elise held out: St. Marguerite's Catholic School.

Surely not?

Elise sat on the side of the bed and glanced out the window thoughtfully. *"I don't know much about homeschooling. Do you think you have the discipline for that?"*

Jil stared back at her. *"Discipline? Well, yeah, I think I do."*

Elise sipped her tea and frowned. *"You mightn't have many friends, studying at home."*

"Right," Jil said. It was nice of Elise to consider it, even if she did eventually say no. She didn't seem like she would say no right away, so maybe she had time to make her case. So many things she could try, but the truth seemed the easiest.

"I've been in a lot of schools, Elise. Like ten, I think."

"Ten?"

"Yeah. I...um...I don't tend to make friends there either."

Elise cracked a smile and patted her hand. *"Well...I guess the other students just have poor taste then."*

Jil smiled. *"Thanks."*

"Are you in the eleventh grade now?"

"Almost finished, yeah."

Elise sighed. *"Maybe I can talk to Padraig and see if it would be possible to finish your year at home. Your teachers could send your work."*

Jil sat up straighter, hardly daring to believe it. *"What would we tell them?"*

Elise took another sip. *"We'll tell them you've contracted a tropical disease. That it might last for years."*

❖

"Five minutes." The head secretary poked her head into Jess's office and disappeared as quickly as she'd come.

Jess looked up at the clock on the wall. Five minutes to what?

She glanced down at her day planner. Tuesday afternoon. The first Tuesday of the month. Her heart skipped a painful beat. She'd completely forgotten about the staff meeting.

As she'd sat there for the past fifteen minutes, staring at a chart for renovations of the science lab, teachers had been filing into the gym, waiting for her to arrive. She had a list of items to discuss—probably an hour's worth of information—and hadn't written down a thing.

No notes, no minutes from last week. She was completely unprepared. How could she possibly face a room full of almost one hundred teachers?

Her heart began to beat faster until she felt dizzy.

Mary came to knock again, a little louder this time. "Two minutes, Jess." She stopped in the doorway. "You okay? You look pale."

Jess cleared her throat. "I think I must be getting the flu or something."

"Well, you sure don't look like yourself. Do you want me to cancel the meeting?"

"That might be wise. Can you get Cynthia in here for a minute?"

"Sure."

A moment later, Cynthia, the junior VP, knocked on the door and came in, her expression concerned. "Mary says you're not feeling well."

"Must be a bug." Jess tried to smile, but her racing heart made breathing difficult. "I'll hold the staff meeting another day, perhaps just for the department heads." Her voice sounded ragged and she struggled to maintain a normal volume.

"That'll work. I'm sure the teachers won't be too broken up about leaving an hour early. Should I make the announcement?"

"Thanks, yes."

When the door closed behind her, Jess exhaled slowly.

What was happening to her life?

CHAPTER THIRTEEN

Jil stuffed her gym bag with her workout clothes, an energy bar, and a stainless steel water bottle, rummaged around to make sure she had a pass, then set about searching for her keys.

Zeus followed her into the vestibule.

"Are you going to be the man of the house while I'm at the gym?" Jil asked him. He barely raised his head. "Lazy thing."

She grabbed her keys from the pocket of one of her coats, then headed back out, this time making a mental note to stay connected to her brain while driving. Her pack of cigarillos sat on the console, and she almost lit one up.

Stop smoking, for shit's sake. And on the way to the gym!

She hadn't eaten anything for dinner, but the knots in her stomach would have made that difficult anyway. The sign next to the door said the gym would be open for another forty minutes— time enough to work out whatever continued to fire angry signals across her brain. Not quite enough time to get in a run too, though.

Running shoes laced, she jumped on the spinner, not even stopping to stretch first. As her legs spun round and round in faster circles, she shook her head, trying to not think of paintings and money and Elise. Or Jess.

Did Jess really think they should see other people?

Of course they should see other people! Lots of other people. Because they shouldn't be together!

Hell, they'd only known each other a few months. Jess should see other people, especially—maybe divorce her husband first. They weren't ready for a serious commitment.

Quarter to nine—the gym had almost emptied. She had the weights to herself, just the way she liked it. She plunked herself on a large yoga ball and grabbed some barbells.

"Careful with your form," said Sian, the personal trainer behind the desk. Jil looked up and made a conscious effort not to smirk.

"Haven't seen you around much," Jil said.

"Probably for the best," Sian returned, grinning.

Jil laughed. *Yeah, probably.*

Sian looked about her age, but she had a lither body with better defined muscles. She also wore much shorter shorts and kept her straight hair cropped short and slick, while strands of Jil's came sticking out of her ponytail and fell in her eyes, courtesy of the large overhead vent blowing out cold air.

"Or maybe you want to try the punching bag instead."

Jil shook her head. "I think I'll try that." She headed for the large hanging bag. Sian came around the desk and handed her a set of gloves, then helped her strap up. "You're here late," she said.

"Out of my usual routine. Sorry, I guess you want to close up."

Sian shrugged. "It's okay. No rush. I usually work out after everyone's gone anyway."

Right. That much she remembered.

Sian stepped behind the bag to hold it as Jil began to punch. "Keep your wrist straight," she said.

Jil revised her form and continued with the series she'd memorized.

"Ever consider kickboxing?" Sian asked. She grunted as the bag caught her in the shoulder.

"Focus," Jil panted. "I don't wanna hurt you."

Sian grinned. "It'd take more than that. Besides, I wouldn't mind."

Jil punched square into the bag, focusing all her anger and praying this would help her bury it again. When she finished her set, she stretched her arms and neck and turned her elbows, trying to ease the ache that tensed her forearm.

"Again?" Sian asked.

Jil locked eyes with her. "I thought we agreed the last time was the last time."

Sian pushed her tongue into her cheek. "I was talking about your set."

"Sure you were." Jil breathed out. Her stomach was still in knots, and she felt the jazzy electricity up and down her limbs that told her she'd never be able to sleep. Sian took her stance against the bag and Jil started another set.

"I don't need a workout now," she joked when they'd finished.

"Sorry."

"Nah, don't be. I'm going to wipe everything down, then hit the showers." She winked and Jil shook her head, unable to suppress a smile. She remembered pretty clearly the last time she and Sian had been left alone in the showers. "Don't worry," Sian said as Jil headed for the locker room, "I'll let you have it to yourself this time."

For a second, Jil almost asked her to come along, but even though she knew exactly what could happen, she just couldn't bring herself to get naked with someone else. She shook her head and pushed through the door.

The bathrooms in this brand new athletic center gleamed and glinted with dark green mosaic tiles and chrome fixtures. The showers were open concept, though each had a partial wall to set down shampoo and soap, and the whole place smelled of raspberry body wash and the vanilla candles that burned next to the carved-out sinks.

Jil chose the second inlet and stripped down on the bedrock floor, heaping her clothes over the partial wall onto the bench. She turned on the overhead rain shower and let the hot water run over her head, caressing her hair and face.

The doorknob turned and Rob came in. She froze in the glass-stalled shower as he stared at her naked body and grinned.

Why did she keep thinking of that day at the Hendricksons'? She thought she'd put that behind her…

He sat on the edge of the claw foot tub, on the other side of the bathroom, and slid his hand into his jeans.

She wished these memories would just fuck off.

She'd much rather remember the last time she'd been in here with Sian. If she couldn't have Jess, at least she could have her fantasies. Thinking of Jess hurt too much, but thinking of Sian was a pleasant enough distraction.

She hit the button for the wall jets and stood there while steady, pulsing streams hit every knot in her tense body. So nice. Two jets pulsated against the muscles under her shoulder blades. She concentrated on the water, letting her mind go blank.

"I'm never gonna get out," she muttered.

"You might have to. I do eventually have to lock up."

Jil opened her eyes and saw Sian turning on the water in the inlet across from her.

Sian's tanned skin gleamed in the streaming water as the rain head soaked her dark hair and ran in rivulets down her round, smooth breasts.

She stared for a second, without meaning to, feeling her nipples harden, then ducked back under the water.

She finished rinsing out her hair and dared to look up.

Sian's arms were stretched up as she pulled conditioner through her own dark strands. Her skin stretched taut over her front ribs and her ab muscles rippled gently—tight, but feminine. She hadn't crossed the line into body builder. As Jil squeezed body wash into her puff, she watched out of the corner of her eye.

Sian lathered soap all over her body, then, slowly, like she knew she was being watched, put one leg up on the lower shelf of the shower and ran one hand down her abdomen, down between her legs.

Jil gasped.

Sian opened her eyes and their gazes locked. "Do you want me to join you, or are you joining me?"

Jil felt her lower abs flutter.

A small smile tugging at the side of her mouth, Sian left her own inlet and came into Jil's. With a light shove, she turned Jil around and pressed her breasts to the gleaming mosaic tile, then took the soap puff from her. Starting at Jil's neck, she lathered her up—her back, her butt, all the way down to her legs. Jil groaned under her breath as Sian's perfect nipples made contact with her back and Sian's fingers ran up the back of her thighs, across her waist, and around...

"Christ," she muttered as Sian's finger and thumb gently squeezed her nipples. She felt herself melting under Sian's hot touch. Heat flared between her legs, and she slowly turned around, wanting more.

"What do you want?" Sian asked, her dark eyes searching Jil's.

Jil closed her eyes.

"Tell me."

Jil breathed out. "I want to be fucked until I can't think."

Sian ran her teeth over Jil's breasts, teasing each nipple with the razor-edge of pain before sucking one, then the other, back into her mouth. Jil hissed, her back pressed against the wall as Sian's mouth explored her.

Tongue and teeth assaulted her skin while Sian's hands slid around her back, drawing her closer.

She let Sian slide one leg between hers, parting her knees, and turn her around so one of the jets streamed directly, though not hard, against her groin.

"Fuck," she moaned.

"Yeah, that's the plan."

Sian stepped behind her, holding her up and paying solicitous attention to Jil's breasts with both her hands. Then one hand traveled down, parting her legs farther, and one finger slipped between her folds to caress her throbbing clit, while the water stream surged around her fingers, widening her pleasure zone.

Jil gasped and opened herself more, letting Sian explore her hot slickness while the water pulsed her closer and closer to an orgasm.

Sian took her time, stroking gently, then, as Jil's clit throbbed harder, pressed harder, faster.

Jil opened her eyes to see Sian flicking the jet switch on the wall.

"I'm going to come," she groaned.

Sian tightened her grip and put her mouth to Jil's ear. "Come hard."

The pressure built between her legs, surging higher and stronger as Sian worked her nipples. She moaned louder, not caring if anyone might be listening outside the door, as the sensations overwhelmed her, pushing her closer and closer. The water pulsed and carried her right over the edge. "Oh!" she cried, arching into Sian's tight embrace. "God!"

She felt her limbs go slack, and Sian pulled her gently backward, until she was sitting on the stone bench carved into the shower. She exhaled in a half groan.

"How was that?" Sian grinned.

Jil looked up and matched her smirk. "As close to fucked dumb as I've been in a while."

"Thanks."

Jil reached up and grabbed Sian by the ass, pulling her closer, then pressed her face into her hard lower abs. She felt the heat emanating from Sian's skin as her fingers caught Jil's hair.

"You don't have to," Sian said gently, even as Jil moved her hands around her waist to hold her hips. "It was a one-way offer."

"I like two-ways," Jil replied. She kissed down the inches of space between Sian's bellybutton and the dividing line of her close-trimmed hair. Sian braced a hand against the mosaic wall and groaned quietly, leaning her head against her hand.

Jil kissed lower, slipping one thumb into the tight, hot space above Sian's clit and stroking gently. Sian's legs melted, both hands on the wall now, parting her thighs to let Jil in.

Jil slipped in her tongue, using the tip to stroke up the underside of Sian's clit, slowly, maddeningly, toward the head, as her hand braced the small of Sian's back, holding her in place.

"God yes, just like that." Sian tilted her hips upward, and Jil complied with her unspoken request, angling two fingers and pushing them gently inside, deeper, as Sian's muscles clenched around her and she groaned.

Jil set a slow rhythm in and out while using her tongue to drive Sian crazy. She felt her edging toward climax and kept it slow and steady until everything felt hot and tight and throbbing.

"Please," Sian whispered.

Jil looked up and met her gaze, making sure Sian was really close. Sian groaned again, and Jil sucked her whole clit into her mouth until Sian bucked against her, moaning swear words.

Jil pulled her mouth away and looked up as Sian pushed away from the wall, then leaned against the far partial wall and slid onto the opposite bench to turn off the body jets.

Water still streamed from the rain head, making the inlet steamy.

"Do that often?" Jil joked.

Sian shook her head. "If I did, I'd probably be fired."

❖

When she came out of the locker room, Sian was waiting by the front desk, freshly showered, pink cheeks glowing.

"The men's showers were empty," she said in answer to Jil's unasked question.

Jil laughed.

"Want to grab a drink?"

Jil shrugged. "Sure. That'd be nice."

"You look like you need to talk."

"Ha." Jil walked out with her, across the street to a small pub. "Talking's not something I do much of."

"I noticed that." Sian grinned. "I would have been okay with the alternative. But something tells me you're seeing someone."

"I was, yeah. You?"

"Sort of. Not serious."

The pub was quiet, with only a few patrons, most of them with gym bags on their chairs.

"It's kind of pointless to work out if you're just going to have a plate of apps at eleven p.m." Jil pulled apart a mozzarella stick and dipped half into the marinara sauce.

Sian took a sip of her margarita and shrugged. "I think you probably deserve it."

Jil smiled wanly through a mouthful of cheese. "I didn't come to the gym to pick up a confessor."

"Yeah, well, turns out you didn't come to pick up a casual fuck either."

"No. Believe it or not, I came to hit things so I could sleep tonight."

"I saw that. Anyway, I think you'll meet your goal."

Jil looked down. Normally, a workout like that would put her in a coma, but she couldn't shake this aching feeling that kept her awake at night. Losing Elise had been bad enough, but losing Jess too…

"So, who is she?" Sian took a sip of her drink and put one foot up on her chair so she could lean against her knee.

"She's…this woman I've been dating."

"Yeah, I gathered that much. Does she have a name?"

Jil smirked. "She's, um, private about her private life."

"Ah. A closet case." Sian grabbed a mozzarella stick. "And you're not."

Jil shook her head. "I said I thought we could work it out, but I'm finding that a lot more difficult than I planned…"

"Is it her family or her work?"

Jil considered. She didn't know much about Jess's family. "Mostly work."

Sian bit off a bite of cheese and nodded, shrugging. "Well, out of the two, I think work is the easier one to overcome."

Settling back into her chair, Jil tucked one foot up. Was this something they could overcome, or were they over for good?

CHAPTER FOURTEEN

The next morning, Jil's eyes snapped open just as dawn started to break, and she watched the peak of the church tower light up with the first morning rays.

She rolled out of her bed down the hall from Elise's bedroom and straight into the en suite.

She'd thought about moving into the master, but it still felt like Elise's private sanctuary, and when she was here, she still felt like the sixteen-year-old runaway sleeping in the single bed down the hall.

A sound like an eagle screaming issued from downstairs. Zeus yawning. She stretched, wondering why her limbs felt so relaxed, then remembered the gym the night before.

She flashed to the memory of Jess storming out of her flat. Maybe she should just let her go. Things were complicated enough already without adding a relationship to the mix. She and Jess had been one step behind the ball the entire time they'd known each other. Was it possible to build something lasting out of so much conflict?

Jess was not a one-night stand kind of woman any more than Jil was a monogamist. But since Jil had met Jess, she hadn't even thought about other women—definitely unlike her. Especially when Sian had been ready and willing.

She'd told Jess she wanted a relationship and she'd meant it.

So why did she have this thorny, prickly feeling in her gut when she imagined making a home with her?

Sian's hands on her breasts. She felt her abs clench again, just thinking about it. But it wouldn't fulfil her and she knew it.

Downstairs, she opted for coffee and turned the machine on while she fed Zeus. He approached his raised water bowl and slurped noisily. Water splashed on his face and over the side of the dish.

"Get a little in your mouth, why don't you?"

Zeus raised his great head, reminding Jil of a hippopotamus emerging from a swamp—water pouring from his loose jowls, pooling on the floor. Jil rolled her eyes and reached for a large tea towel while the Dane moved on to his breakfast.

She waited for the coffee machine to fill the carafe. Sleep still edged the corners of her consciousness, and she couldn't quite wake up. Zeus finished eating, then stretched his enormous paws in front of him, his ass in the air in the perfect downward-dog. And farted.

"Charming."

Zeus shook his ears, his tongue lolling, then stared at the door.

"Ready for a walk, are you? Let's go, then." If it weren't for Zeus, she probably would have stayed out all night, drinking more than she should have at that bar, and doing God knows what with Sian. A tingle ran from her bellybutton down between her legs, thinking about what they could have done last night.

Coming home had definitely been the best decision. Until she figured out what she and Jess wanted, she didn't have room for any more women on deck.

She shook that thought out of her head for the next four blocks.

Jil approached the counter at the bank.

"How can I help you?" The young man behind the counter looked over his large square glasses.

"I have a key to our family safety deposit box."

"Do you know the box number?"

Jil read the number from the back of her hand, where she'd scrawled it. Normally, she would have memorized that without problem, but since Elise had died, her memory seemed to have followed her into the mausoleum.

"I'll have to ask you for some identification, please." He stared at her oddly.

Not this again.

Jil produced her driver's license and waited while he scanned it through a machine, then looked at something on his computer. "Do you have another piece of ID?"

"What would you like?" Jil asked. "Credit card? Library card? Passport?"

"I'll take whatever you have."

She handed over several pieces of ID. "Do you need a urine sample as well?"

He startled, then cracked a smile. "Sorry. I'll be right back. He walked over to an older man in a tie—probably the bank manager—and said something to him.

In a moment, they both approached. "Would you please come with me into my office?" the bank manager said.

"May I have my driver's license back, please?"

"We need to take a copy of it first, and then Tyler will get it right back to you."

Tyler made his way to the copy machine behind the desk.

"What's this about?" Jil asked as the bank manager ushered her into an office and closed the glass door—though she could already guess.

"I'm very sorry for the secrecy, but there's been an issue recently with that box number."

"What sort of issue?"

"Well, yesterday, a Jillienne Kidd arrived at the bank and requested access to the box."

"I never requested access."

"No, clearly not. The other woman looked just like you, but she could not produce a driver's license, and her other documents did not pass our advanced forgery screenings." She detected a note of pride in the bank manager's voice.

"Someone has been impersonating me here at the bank?" Now why wasn't that a surprise?

"It seems so. We reported the incident to the police, and they came to investigate. Then, just yesterday, we had a visit from another detective, who wanted access to the box as part of an ongoing theft investigation. I had to inform him that he would have to obtain a warrant for the contents."

Jil's heart sped up, but she maintained a neutral expression.

"Detective Fraser, by any chance?"

"You're aware of this investigation?"

Best to keep her suspicions to herself for now. "Yes. Something was stolen from our house, and Detective Fraser is assigned to the case. Has he been back?"

"No. He said he'd return this afternoon with the warrant, but in the meantime, you've arrived, and…you see…it's rather complicated."

"Yes, I see that." Jil sighed. "Well, to be frank, I'd like to get into the box first. There are some materials in there I'm not sure I want made public."

"I understand."

"So, without a warrant in place, is access to the box frozen, or can I get in?"

The bank manager sighed. "Well, seeing as your name is on the lease as well as Mrs. Fitzgerald's, it seems as though it should be business as usual until the warrant arrives, doesn't it?"

Jil smiled. "That would be my way of looking at things."

"Just so you're aware of the situation."

Jil held out her antique key. "Also, I think I have a slight advantage. No warrant is going to open that antique box."

He smiled.

"This way, please." Tyler led her past the wickets and through a large steel door to a room filled floor-to-ceiling with small metal boxes.

"Over here." Tyler gestured to a column of boxes, and Jil found her number, second from the bottom. He pulled her box out for her and laid it on the table, then turned and left.

Jil stood and stared at it for a moment, running her hands over the cool, smooth surface. A part of her didn't want to know what it contained. So many things seemed to come at her from the depths of Elise's life—things she didn't feel she had the right to know.

She pulled a thin folder marked "Inventory" out of the box and opened it. The folder contained fifteen pages, single sided, with thumbnail pictures and a caption and description of each item. In total, twenty-two paintings, four Fabergé, ten Anglo-Saxon artifacts, fifteen pieces of jewelry, and ten miscellaneous pieces, including the cigarette lighter. She put the folder in her bag. No time to examine it now. She would have to read it later.

In a small velvet pouch, she found another key.

"Of course," she muttered. When had Elise found enough time to orchestrate this elaborate treasure hunt?

Tyler met her when she'd finished and moved inside to put the box away. He smiled at her on the way out and mouthed, "Good luck."

❖

In the middle of the night, Zeus let out a howl and jumped from his dog bed. He growled low in his throat as he paced wildly.

Jil swung her legs out of bed, grabbed a flashlight, and headed to the door. For the first time since she'd left St. Marguerite's, she wished she had her gun back.

Zeus banged against the bedroom door with his enormous paw and would barely step back to let Jil open it. Once in the hall, he barked again. In the dark, ricocheting off the walls and chandelier, the sound was terrifying.

Jil followed him down the stairs and he leapt against the front door, both paws up on the glass. "Down, Zeus!" What if his paws went right through the glass?

She wrestled him away from the door by jamming her body in front of him. But by the time she slid back the deadbolt, unhooked the chain, and opened the door, nobody was there.

Zeus barked again, but the hackles on the back of his neck had settled down a little.

Jil looked down on the porch. There had been no snow, and the ground was dry, so she didn't expect any footprints.

Something glinted on the concrete. An earring…She picked it up. A gold hoop.

She grabbed her coat and the flashlight Elise kept in the front closet, then made Zeus stand guard as she scanned the front garden.

Silence.

She ran to the end of the driveway and looked up and down the street.

There.

At the top of the road, under the streetlamp. Someone turned the corner.

She swore and ducked back inside. That somebody was definitely interested in getting inside this house.

CHAPTER FIFTEEN

A rap sounded on her car window just as she was buckling her seat belt. Jil looked up, startled to see Karrie standing in the driveway. She rolled down the window. "What are you doing here?"

"I'm coming with you." Karrie opened the passenger door and slid into the seat.

"How do you know where I'm going?"

"I called your office. They said you were out sick for a week. And if I were a PI, I'd be going to find the woman who's been impersonating me and everyone else I know."

Jil chuckled. "I guess I'm not as hard to read as I thought."

Karrie handed her a cup of coffee, steam rising from the vent in the plastic lid. "Black?"

She smiled. "Thanks. So...why are you here?"

The funeral director pursed her lips. "I'm in a little trouble with my boss," she admitted.

"Because you gave my ring away to the not-real me?"

"Yeah."

"They know it wasn't your fault, right?"

"Well, technically, yes. It's not like they ID every family member who walks through the door. Honestly, not many people crash funeral homes."

"Do you want me to say something to them for you?"

Karrie smiled wanly. "Thanks, that's nice of you. But I'd rather just find her and get your ring back."

Jil frowned as she backed out of the driveway. "You know, something bothers me about that."

"What?"

"The fact that Elise gave you the ring in the first place instead of leaving it for me at the house."

"She really wanted you to have it."

"Yes. But I had the only key to the house. Why not just leave it with the rest of the jewelry?"

Karrie pursed her ruby lips. "I've been wondering that too."

"You have?"

"Well…I've seen the ring," she said slowly.

"And?"

"And…it's nice and all—" She bit her lip, as if afraid of offending Jil with her next words.

"But?" Jil prompted.

"But it's not that valuable, honestly. I mean, I've seen loads of jewelry in my line of work, and some of the stuff Elise wore to our meetings was worth a lot more money. I don't understand why she gave me this ring in particular—"

"When I inherited half a dozen more expensive ones straight from her jewelry box?"

"I see you've already thought of this. I guess I shouldn't be surprised. You know, with your line of work."

Jil chuckled. "Never assume. You know how they say doctors make the worst patients?"

"Yeah."

"PIs make the worst family members."

Karrie cocked a grin. "I'm sure that wasn't totally true."

Jil sighed. "I'm sure it was. I just wish she'd told me if she was in trouble."

"Why do you think she was in trouble?"

"Because I know Elise and I know she would never get involved in something like this if something bigger weren't at stake.

And dealing with those sorts of things when you're terminally ill has got to suck big time. So now I have to find out why she left me this little bread crumb trail, and what that ring really means."

Karrie took a breath. "Is it possible it doesn't mean anything?"

Jil looked at her.

"I mean, she would have been on pretty heavy medication at the end, right? Maybe she just got confused."

"See, that's the thing," Jil said. "She smoked pot, I know that, but I actually don't think she was taking anything stronger. I saw her not long before she passed away and she was walking around and talking—talking about death, of course—but still, she didn't look like she planned to kick it anytime soon. She would have known what she was doing."

"Yeah, she was lucid the whole time I knew her," Karrie said.

Jil shook her head as she waited for the light to change. "Tell me exactly what happened when Anastasia came into your office."

Karrie unbuttoned her coat. "I met her for only a few minutes, because we were leaving for the day."

"Right. So what did she say to you when she came in?"

"She said, 'Sorry to come so late. I know we don't have much time tonight.'"

"So she knew your schedule? She knew you were about to leave for the day."

"Yes."

"Then what?"

"She said, 'My foster mother left something for me here, and I'd like to have it before the service.'"

"She didn't specify what?"

"No, come to think of it."

"She never specifically mentioned the ring?"

"No, I don't think so."

Jil pressed her tongue into her cheek. "What happened next?"

"I gave her the envelope and she said thank you and left."

"She didn't open it in front of you?"

"No. Why?"

Jil merged onto the highway and turned to look at Karrie. "I don't know yet. My brain hasn't caught up with my gut. I have a lot of questions."

Karrie grinned again. "Like what?"

"Like what did Anastasia think that envelope contained? Ask me again in a few hours when I've had time to filter."

"Okay. So where are we going, anyway?"

"I'm afraid it's nothing exciting. Just the only lead I have at the moment, so I'm following up."

"Let me guess, you found her home address?"

Jil laughed. "I wish. I have no idea who this woman is or where to find her. She's a chameleon, and she's obviously been doing this a while because she's been one step ahead of me and everyone else. She's also extremely brazen, which comes with confidence and practice, so I have her pegged as a professional."

"A professional what?"

"Thief."

"How is that different from a run-of-the-mill thief?"

Jil turned to look at her. "The professionals treat it like a business. And that means they hone their craft and pay certain dividends—to other thieves, for help or to trade merchandise or skills. Also, the pros aren't opportunistic. They plan their heists, sometimes for months or years. The payoff is always big, and the preparation is always thorough. Anastasia will move in the regular world. She'll have friends, alibis, possibly even a suburban home with a fence and a dog. She could be a university student or an accountant. She'll look to lead a perfectly normal life, and she'll have a lot of money stored in offshore accounts."

Karrie breathed out. "Whew. Talk about the criminal next door."

"You'd be surprised. It's never who you expect."

"So you're going to track her through her regular life?"

"Yep. Starting with her wig maker. She always looks completely authentic, which means her wigs and clothes are made to fit her perfectly."

"Preparation," Karrie said.

"And money. Real hair wigs can cost thousands of dollars and can take weeks to make. So we're looking for an expensive professional wigmaker."

"Someone who works for a theater company?"

Jil wrinkled her brow. "Probably not. Theater wigs are grandiose and don't necessarily have to be precise because you can't see the fine details from the audience. I was thinking more like this guy."

Jil pulled into the parking lot where a sign read The Art of Hair. "The proprietor's name is Jacob Baumer. He's a world-renowned wigmaker and used to work in Hollywood before his mother got sick and he came back to Rockford to take care of her."

"Wow. You do your homework."

"I have to. Professional thieves require professional investigators to track them down. Otherwise their lives get too easy." Jil winked.

"Good luck. I'll wait for you here."

Jil frowned. "Maybe not. I think you should come with me."

Karrie smiled. "Really? I get to actually help?"

"Well, provided you don't blow my cover."

"I won't." Karrie grinned and gestured for Jil to move in front of her. "After you, boss."

❖

"Good day." Jil opened the door and ushered Karrie inside.

An older willowy man with a gray goatee stepped away from the counter and looked at them over his horn-rimmed glasses. "Hello. How can I help you?"

Jil smiled as charmingly as she could. "You must be Jacob."

"I am." His eyebrows raised a few centimeters.

"You were recommended by a friend," Jil said.

"Really? Who?"

Jil flashed her phone at him, revealing a picture of Anastasia.

"Oh. Rebecca Nelson. Yes, she's been a client of mine for quite some time."

Rebecca?

"She said you'd take good care of us."

"Well, any friend of Rebecca's will receive nothing but the best treatment from me."

"She keeps the lights on in this place, right?" Jil winked and Jacob laughed.

"I do have to admit she brings me a lot of good business, in her line of work, and in cash too, which I appreciate. Please come sit down and tell me what brings you here."

"My sister Karrie has unfortunately just found out she has alopecia."

"Oh, dear," Jacob clucked. "I'm so sorry."

"It's barely started," Karrie said, drawing her eyebrows into a sorrowful frown, "but I want to be prepared, and I understand a wig can take several weeks to be made."

"Normally, yes," Jacob said. "Depending on the length and color you want. But in urgent situations, I can always move more efficiently."

Jil smiled. "We always wondered how Rebecca got hers done so quickly."

"Four days was my record."

"Recently?"

"No. About a year ago. When she was going to that photo shoot in Berlin and needed a blond bob."

"Oh." Jil nodded, as if remembering details. "She looked great in that outfit."

"Did you see it? I never did. The bum keeps promising to bring me copies, but never does. I think she's shy."

"Well, it was a lacy bodice job and she looked fantastic." Karrie grinned and Jil suppressed a laugh. The girl could act; she'd give her that.

"So, what are you looking for?" Jacob clapped his hands, back to business. Clearly in love with his craft…

"Well, I thought of going as close to my own hair as possible," Karrie said. She frowned at herself in the mirror, appraising her own hairline.

"Do you have a portfolio I could look at?" Jil asked. She meandered through the shop, discreetly checking the place out and looking for anywhere Jacob might keep client records.

"Yes, right there on my desk." He gestured to a little table at the back of the store with a laptop on it.

And a rolodex.

How quaint. And how much easier to riffle than a computer.

Karrie caught her eye in the mirror, then captured Jacob's attention as Jil picked up the portfolio and leaned against the desk. The guy did nice work.

A few moments later, she met Karrie back at the mirror. "You look like you're getting comfy, sis."

"It's a nice place," Karrie said noncommittally.

Jil fought a smile. "We're interviewing a few wigmakers before making our final choice," she said.

Jacob looked mildly affronted. "But why? I'm the best there is."

Karrie shrugged, like she just played along with whatever her big sister said. "We have a few more appointments this afternoon—"

"So we'd better be off," Jil finished. "But I'm sure we'll be back."

"But I haven't even taken your measurements."

Jil smiled disarmingly. "I'm sure you're the best. We'll call for a proper appointment next time."

They smiled, thanked him again, and headed straight to the parking lot.

In the car, Karrie turned to her with wide eyes. "So?"

Jil held up the rolodex card and grinned. "We have an address."

❖

They pulled off the highway and into an industrial area—old warehouses that were in the process of being repurposed into loft apartments. An area very similar to where Jil lived.

She drove up to the building on the card.

Unfinished. Apartments available in six months.

"I don't think anyone lives here," Karrie whispered.

Jil frowned at the warehouse. Hardly surprising that Anastasia would give a fake address, but still disappointing. She sighed. "Another dead end."

CHAPTER SIXTEEN

More mail in the foyer. Jil picked it up and stuffed it into the antique clay pot that had served as their mail receptacle since she could remember.

She was always surprised to see envelopes with Elise's name and address on them. Privacy had always been her most preciously guarded commodity, especially as a university professor. Very rarely did she allow anyone into her private life.

But utility companies and the bank demanded rights. They got her personal information within the first thirty seconds.

Funny how people wanted to keep the most secrets from those closest to them and would give so much away to near strangers.

Jil stopped going through the mail. So how had someone wormed their way into Elise's life to the extent that they would be allowed in her home?

She'd been assuming that Anastasia had come in contact with Elise through St. Augustine, but what if that wasn't true?

What if she'd targeted Elise beforehand?

She picked her phone up again and thumbed instinctively to Jess's number.

Shit.

Calling to hash out a theory wasn't exactly the best pillow talk she could imagine, and she couldn't exactly apologize right now. How would she even start? Especially since she wasn't sure she could handle slipping back into their establishing pattern.

Yes, Anastasia had impersonated a St. Augustine aide, but how long had she been coming? How had she known that Elise was sick in the first place?

She paced along the upstairs hallway, stopping at every vantage point to scrutinize the painting. She stared at the corners and the joints of the frame, examined each discrepancy in the tone and texture of the painting itself. And the longer she stared, the less sure she became that any difference she noticed was actually there.

When was the last time she'd really paid attention to it? When was the last time she'd even been upstairs before she'd had to pack the bag of clothes for Elise's funeral?

This painting could have been here for days, or weeks—or even months. Because, of course, she'd let herself get swept up in her own life, and her assignments and wouldn't have noticed. She'd shown up sometimes for Sunday dinner, but also let herself off the hook when it wasn't convenient. Or when she didn't feel like leaving the house. Or when it seemed easier to immerse herself in a bachelorette lifestyle and forget about having been part of a family.

Elise loved her; she knew that. But holding herself in the center of that love took energy. It took willpower. Easier to retreat to her own den and pretend that solitariness suited her. That she had grown beyond needing a mother—of any type.

So really, she had no idea when someone might have come in. If Anastasia or the mailman had been responsible. It could have been a neighbor, a handyperson, or any one of Elise's students…

Students.

What if Anastasia had been one of Elise's students?

That would explain how she knew her. If she'd been enrolled in her course the final year or so she was teaching, she would know when Elise had taken sick. She might even have visited her at home…she could have seen her artifact collection, taken interest in the painting. She could even have suggested Elise get a home aide.

And then impersonated the aide to come and go whenever she wanted.

Like when Elise had hospital appointments.

Or after she'd died—when the door was open and she could sneak items out in her box of supplies.

Jil raced downstairs to Elise's office. Where would she keep her student files? Probably on her computer.

Which wasn't in her office.

Because it was probably still at the university.

Damn.

How could she get in there?

She scrolled through contacts until she found her friend Morgan. His picture on her screen, smiling in his police uniform, made her grin. He answered on the first ring.

"Morgan, it's me."

"Let me guess. You have a technical question."

"Your powers of deduction are truly beginning to border on the psychic."

"Or it could be that every time you call me, it's to solve a theoretical crisis with your computer."

Jil swallowed hard. Was she a terrible friend as well as a shit girlfriend? "I guess I owe you dinner."

He chuckled. "Invitation accepted. I was hoping to see you anyway. Have a few theoretical questions for you too."

"Really? That's a first."

"It is not. Anyway, I'm curious about your new flame."

"Ugh. Don't ask!"

"No! Don't tell me you're not seeing her anymore. I liked that one. She was fantastic for you."

"No lectures, please. Just name your time and place and I'll show up with my credit card."

"Okay, but I think we'd better go Dutch. If I'm paying, I won't drink as much, and something tells me you're going to need a designated driver."

Jil laughed. "Okay. Friday night? The Market?"

"Sounds good. I'll see you then."

❖

"It could be stress," said Jess's doctor. She frowned over the top of her purple-rimmed glasses as she squinted at the thick beige chart. "Flare-ups happen for a number of reasons. Could be the weather."

"It's pretty bad." Jess crossed her ankles because she couldn't cross her legs. The usual throbbing ache in her hips had intensified to a crackling burn that kept her up all night, despite her usual regimen of pills and a few more new ones. "And it's not just pain. I'm having trouble breathing. My heart keeps racing."

"Anxiety?"

"I hope so, because I don't like the alternative."

The doctor frowned and unwound her stethoscope from her neck. "Can you get up on the platform?"

Jess climbed on the stool and maneuvered herself awkwardly onto the crackling sheet.

Dr. Rosenfeld snaked the cool disc down her top and stood listening. Then she strapped the blood pressure cuff around her upper arm and blew it up.

Jess winced as the material bit into her elbow, closing her eyes as the pressure valve released and the metal disc made contact with her inner arm.

After a few moments of silence, the doctor asked, "Has your new prescription been working?"

Jess breathed through the pain and shook her head. "Not at all. I went back to the old stuff."

Dr. Rosenfeld squeezed Jess's arm. "Hey."

Jess opened her eyes and tried to smile, but couldn't muster the energy.

"We're going to figure this out, okay?"

"Could you make it quick?" This time, she did manage to smile a little. "I have a life you know."

Dr. Rosenfeld narrowed her eyes. "About that. I'm prescribing time off work, first of all."

Jess absorbed her words. Time off work?

She started to protest but noticed that the knot that had been crushing her stomach had begun to unclench a little. As she considered not having to get in the car tomorrow, not having to cross the atrium, through the heavy doors to her office, not having to hold staff meetings and pretend like she gave a shit about renovations to the science wing, her hammering heart began to slow down.

"I know you're going to fight me tooth and nail, but I insist."

Jess met her gaze. "I'm not going to argue. It's probably a good idea."

The doctor leaned in. "Okay, that's it. Now I know there's something really wrong with you. Is work getting to you? Personal issues? Is it Mitch's situation?"

Jess breathed out through her teeth. "All of the above."

"And more, I'd imagine. Not that you'd tell me."

She got down from the platform and returned to her chair. "Don't take it personally, Doctor. I'm this difficult with everyone."

"You are not. But I will admit that for a patient I've had for twenty years, sometimes I feel like I'm barely scratching the surface with you."

Her words struck Jess far more harshly than the doctor had probably intended. "I don't mean to be so aloof," she whispered. "It's just…"

"Hey, that's not what I meant. Not at all. Your independence is what keeps you strong. Keep it. But"—she sat down—"you don't have to do *everything* by yourself. It helps to have someone to swap war stories with at night. Whatever your war happens to be. You might consider some company, considering…"

"Considering my husband's been in a persistent vegetative state for the past five years? It's okay to say it."

"Well, since you put it that way." Dr. Rosenfeld laughed. "There's nothing wrong with wanting to have a life, Jess."

For a second, she wanted to tell her everything. About Lily, Jil. Hitting the wall at work. Wondering what the hell she'd signed up for as a lesbian in a Catholic school.

But secrecy had become so ingrained to her, she couldn't do it. Besides, confessions were for priests, not doctors.

She left the office and limped the twenty yards out the door to the accessible parking, staring hard at the blue emblem flipped down on her visor. Disabled. Handicapped. Crippled. The words flipped through her mind until she got into the car and slammed the visor up.

Never had she used the accessible parking spot. Other people had always needed it far more than she had. She'd parked close, but never in that spot. Even when her knees and hips were screaming, she'd rested, taken a few moments, and walked on.

But today, she physically couldn't navigate the distance between the back of the lot and the office.

She'd had to search for the sticker, buried in the back of the glove box, and for a second, she panicked, sure she wouldn't be able to find it and would have to cross the lot—possibly get trapped halfway, not able to push on, or retreat. But she'd found it. She'd used it. She'd hated it, of course.

But the visit had been worth it.

She had a new treatment option and time off work—something she'd never wished for in her life.

Later that night, Jil got in the car and returned to the warehouse. She didn't know what to expect, but something about that place had bugged her. Did Anastasia have any connection to it at all—is that why she'd chosen it for her alias address—or was it just a random number and street she borrowed for the purpose?

She turned her headlights off and released the seat so she could lean back. The coffee in her mug still steamed through the hole in the lid, and she took a long sip. She'd stay as long as her bladder could hold out. Maybe she'd get a sense of the neighborhood and the inhabitants—find a reason why Anastasia might pick it. After all, everything looked different in the dark.

Zeus had whined to come with her tonight, but she'd left him at home. An alarm system was great, but a dog was even better. It seemed like a better idea to leave the dragon in the lair tonight.

Across the street from the warehouse-cum-loft, residents of a fully finished mid-rise had begun to come home. Lights gleamed from most of the windows. The silhouette of a Christmas tree filled one pane, balls of red and silver glinting off the glass.

The building next door had only a small light glowing from the basement window. Jil squinted at the grimy glass, wondering who would be working so late in the basement of an abandoned building.

That didn't smack of an above-board activity.

She decided to wait and watch—not that she could really see anything. Maybe if she got closer…

She left the door slightly ajar and crept toward the window. From a few feet away, she spotted the bars on the window and the crisscross mesh inside the glass itself. No wonder she couldn't see anything inside.

Even now, she'd have to press her face almost against the bars to get a good look. Was it worth it? What if the person inside saw her?

She crouched down to the side of the window and waited to see if a shadow would pass. Nothing. After a deep breath and counting to ten, she decided to risk it. Slowly, she moved her face in front of the bars and peeked in.

Through the dirt and scratches, she saw a long hallway, and at the end, a large vault.

What would you keep in a vault in the basement of an old warehouse?

A guy walked down the hall and she pulled back a little—not that he could see her, probably, unless he looked directly at her. She watched him carry a flat, rectangular object wrapped in brown paper. He stopped at the door of the vault and punched in a code.

Something of that size and weight could only be a painting.

When the door swung open, she looked inside. Dozens of brown paper packages lined the room.

Back in the car, she sat for a long moment before starting the engine. She should tell Fraser what she'd seen at the warehouse. Certainly, this was an underground operation of some sort. A counterfeiting ring, possibly, or a depot to house stolen items. But if she told him, and he raided it, that might be the last chance she'd have to stake out Anastasia. For the time being, she had no other way to find her.

For the thousandth time, she wished she could talk to Jess.

But that door had closed.

Chapter Seventeen

It feels like a long time since I didn't arrest you for carrying a loaded gun into a high school." Morgan wrapped his arms tightly around Jil and she squeezed him back, the light scent of his cologne transferring to the collar of her jean jacket.

Jil groaned. "Don't remind me of that day."

She thought of Jess's face—drawn and tight—when she'd realized Jil was an undercover PI sent to investigate her, and not a first-year teacher named Julia Kinness.

"I really thought you two were gonna make it." Morgan pulled Jil's seat out for her before sitting down across the table. In the middle of the room, two pianists began warming up their instruments.

"Dueling pianos tonight?" She loved the push/pull tension of the pianos and would try her best tonight not to compare that to her relationship with Jess: beautiful, intricate, the combined effort of two distinct opposites making gorgeous harmonies.

If they didn't clash horribly.

Jil ordered a plate of potato skins and a whiskey sour from the server, and Morgan asked for a Manhattan with three cherries.

She grinned at him. Those extra cherries were for her. She didn't like the drink, but the liquor-infused maraschinos were fantastic.

"Too bad you wouldn't marry me," Morgan said. "Could have had them a few times a week."

She sighed dramatically. "If only. You're a big man to still be my friend, despite your heartbreaking crush on me."

"All right, come on now. It was only for a semester."

She gave him a look.

"Okay, a year." He accepted his drink from the server and took a sip. "But it's better to be friends than nothing at all, right?"

"Of course."

"Not everyone can get to the friend stage." He looked into his glass and swirled the ice.

Jil's thoughts strayed to Jess. No surprise. She constantly hovered around the corners of her conscious thoughts—infused into every dream.

They could never be friends. It just wasn't possible. They were too charged, too in sync with each other's thoughts and movements. That kind of intensity couldn't settle into friendship, no matter how much time passed.

She took a sip of her drink. Time to change the subject. "Listen, what do you know about counterfeiting in Rockford?"

Morgan leaned in. At first, he didn't answer. "It's not really my department," he said slowly.

She appraised him. "You're keeping something from me. What is it?"

"It's not something I wanted to tell you. And now that she's dead, I didn't think it would make any difference anyway."

"Elise? You know something about Elise that's connected to counterfeiting?"

Morgan sighed. "She was on our watch list for a while."

"Why?"

Morgan leaned back and kept quiet as the server laid down their plate of potato skins. He smiled at her but waited until she moved away before answering.

"It doesn't matter now. We were wrong."

Jil stirred her drink. Her stomach felt queasy.

"So who's on your radar now?"

"Well, I know Fraser's unit has been keeping an eye on Duncan McLeod. He was the only reason they were looking into her in the first place."

"Duncan McLeod? Seriously? I think he's too smart to get caught."

"Everybody knows what he's doing and nobody can catch him. But he's Fraser's white whale."

Something in Jil's gut clenched. He'd never mentioned that. "How long has he been after him?"

"Ever since he made detective, I'm pretty sure. He's come close a few times, but never actually had enough on him to pin him."

Fraser had lied to her. He knew way more about Elise than he'd ever admitted. Why keep it to himself? What was he hiding?

"Does this…vendetta…have anything to do with his father? Joseph Fraser?"

Morgan frowned. "That name sounds familiar."

"Arrested in the nineties for a heist at the Toronto Art Gallery."

Morgan's eyes lit up. "Yes. And later died in prison. That's right. He was recently cleared of that, though, right?"

Cleared? Now why did that sound like something less than a coincidence?

"You think MacLeod is tied up in that somehow?" she asked.

"Wouldn't surprise me at all."

"So why not just tell me all this? Why keep me in the dark? Lie to me?"

"Maybe he was just trying to protect you." Morgan shrugged. "He didn't want to tarnish your memories of Elise."

"Morgan, he didn't just obfuscate—he's hiding something."

"Whoa, wait. What are you suggesting?"

"I don't know." Jil put her head in her hands and closed her eyes. "I feel like I'm going a little nuts, Morgan. But I can't trust anyone. Every time I turn around, something else is getting added to this pile of things that don't add up. Elise wasn't sick enough to die of natural causes. Period. The home health care aide was a fraud and had access to our home. She's been impersonating me at the funeral home and at the bank—both places Elise went before she died."

Morgan frowned. "Go on."

"The funeral director gave Elise's ring to the imposter. Fraser knew the ring had been stolen, but I never told him about it. How did he know?"

"Maybe the funeral home reported it to the police?"

Jil shook her head. "No. I told Karrie I would handle it."

Morgan finished his drink and steepled his fingers on the table. "Jil, have you thought…have you considered…taking a step back from this?"

She fixed him with a stare. "You think I'm crazy, don't you? You think I'm seeing motives that aren't there?"

"No. No, not entirely. Just…is it possible that you're just taking this too personally? That Fraser is just doing his job and keeping confidentiality like he should?"

Jil sighed and drained her glass. "I don't know anymore. I seriously don't know."

Morgan took a potato skin, which had cooled enough to eat. "Is this what you wanted to talk about?"

She put down the potato she'd just picked up. "No, actually."

He grinned. "How did I guess? Something to do with hacking, am I right?"

"You don't hack, do you, Morgan? You investigate." Forging, replicating, hacking, researching. So many gray lines.

He shrugged. "I like your version better. What do you need?" He looked relieved to be able to help her with something after all.

She looked behind her. It was ridiculous to think that someone was looking over her shoulder, listening to her, but being impersonated had her more rattled than she'd admit—even to Morgan. She dropped her voice. "It's Elise's student roster at the university. I want access to it."

"How far back?"

"I don't know—five years?"

Morgan whistled. "How many names are we looking at?"

Jil considered. "I don't think that many. In her later years, she only taught graduate seminars, and those have—what—fifteen students per class? So forty-five a semester if she taught three classes in both fall and winter term."

Morgan raised his eyebrows. "That's still almost five hundred names, Jil."

"Yeah. Well, I've got to start somewhere." She picked the cheese off the potato skin and put it in her mouth.

He drained his drink, then handed her the cherries. "I'll see what I can do."

Chapter Eighteen

S he would only do it once, Jil promised herself.
Just to quiet that little voice in her brain. If she saw no evidence, she would never do this again. She'd concede to Morgan that she was paranoid, confess to Fraser about the warehouse, and let him handle his investigation.

A full block down from the police station, she parked the car. She didn't have to wait long before she saw Fraser exit the building and get into his own vehicle.

Her heart sped up. What would he do if he caught her tailing him? It may not have been a crime, exactly, but it had to break some sort of code of honor.

Unless she found something.

She followed him ten kilometers, through traffic on the highway, and got off near downtown. Downtown? Not exactly in his neighborhood.

He merged left, and she followed three cars back.

They crawled down the inner city streets and he pulled into a tiny parking space.

Damn.

She had no choice but to pass him.

He was busy reversing and didn't see her. She watched him in the rearview mirror as he headed to John A. MacDonald park—a large open-spaced park in the middle of the downtown core.

Luck sat on her shoulder. She found a second parking spot and pulled in just in time to see Fraser head through the park's iron gates.

She followed at a distance, but he looked over his shoulder, as if he were nervous. Did he suspect he was being followed? She reached a group of trees and hid behind them, taking out her binoculars.

When she looked out again, he'd disappeared.

Damn.

She was about to duck out of her hiding spot when she saw something that made her stop. The fountain in the middle of the courtyard had been turned off for the winter but still seemed to be a popular gathering spot.

A woman walked by—blond with long wavy hair and a navy trench coat cinched at her waist. She wore large chic sunglasses, and flawless makeup, but Jil studied her walk. The gait, even in high heels, was familiar.

Her stomach lurched. Nic must be here because of her. Did he plan to arrest her? Who had tipped him off?

Jil wanted to rush the fountain and tackle the woman, but she had to let Nic handle his own business. She didn't have the power to arrest her or detain her. That was a police officer's job, and she had to let him do it.

The woman stopped at the fountain with her large handbag, sat down, and lit a cigarette.

Jil watched her, manipulating the binoculars to get a better look at her face. The red lipstick was distracting. As she watched, the woman fished something from her handbag and held it in her lap. She looked discreetly over her shoulder before brushing the object into the basin of the fountain. She waited a moment, then got up with her lit cigarette, and moved on through the park.

What had she dropped?

Just as Jil made up her mind to go over to the fountain, she spotted Fraser coming down the walk from the opposite side.

He sat in the same spot Anastasia had just abandoned, then reached down and scooped up what she'd dropped.

Jil flicked the binocular wheels. A black velvet bag. He pocketed it and sat back up, then lit a cigarette.

Jesus fucking Christ. He wasn't tracking her—he was meeting her.

To her astonishment, he texted her not a full minute later. *Meet me at Elise's place. I have something for you.*

He arrived less than five minutes after her, wearing his dark brown leather jacket and trademark nonchalant expression. He lingered on the porch, smoking another cigarette.

Rage heated her neck and made her hands shake, but she forced herself to stay cool. Confronting him now would be a mistake. She had to find out what his angle was, and blowing his cover might mean she never got to find out.

"Good day, Detective."

"Hello."

She stood back to let him in. This time, when Zeus got up to greet him, his hackles were raised slightly. Channeling her feelings?

Fraser reached out to pat him, but Zeus stiffened and he pulled away. He gave Zeus a weird look. "I'll keep it short. I've found something that might belong to you." He held out the velvet pouch. The same one she'd seen him collecting from Anastasia.

What the hell was he doing? She took it from him and opened it.

Elise's ring.

She cradled it in her palm for a moment, staring at the twisted white gold knots and dark green stone ringed with diamonds. She felt hot tears stinging the backs of her eyes, and she gritted her teeth. Like hell she'd cry in front of him. He'd been lying to her since the day they met.

"Don't you want to try it on?"

Elise's fingers had been so delicate, she was stunned the ring fit her.

Even so, she'd probably lose it somewhere if she kept wearing it, so she opened the chain she wore around her neck and slipped the ring on, then tucked it inside her blouse.

"Where did you get it?" She refused to look at him as she asked. She couldn't take him lying to her face.

"I found the thief. She gave it back."

She looked up, even though she couldn't entirely trust herself to keep a straight face. "Just like that?"

"Well." He raised his eyebrows. "There might have been a deal involved."

"A deal that involved her telling you about my painting?"

He shot her a look. "She says she didn't steal it."

"And that's it?" Jil raised her voice. "You said 'fine, thanks for the chat'?"

"Well, there was a little more to it than that."

She rolled her eyes. She'd have to find her again herself now.

"So, tell me something." She fixed him with a stare. "How did you know it was missing in the first place?"

He looked at her quizzically. "What?"

"The ring."

"You told me."

Jil fingered the ring around her neck. She hadn't. She shook her head. "I can't remember what I had for breakfast," she said. "But I'm sure I never told you about this ring."

Fraser brushed his stubble with the back of his hand, his brow furrowed. "I can't say for sure, either, now that you mention it. Maybe it was in a police report connected to you."

Jil said nothing but looked straight up at him. "You're keeping something from me."

Fraser sighed. "Fine. You caught me." He rolled his eyes. "I'm guilty of returning a ring that someone stole from you. And paying a hefty price of justice, I might add."

"I suppose you can't tell me what that price might be."

He shook his head. "Now, if you'd done the sensible thing and stayed a PO instead of going rogue as a PI, I might be able to share this with you."

"That really bothers you, doesn't it? That I would actually choose PI work—not because I flunked out of the academy or got some sort of reprimand, but because I actually think I can get more done."

"You don't have the same access to information that you would on this side."

"Yeah, but I can choose my cases."

Fraser conceded with a nod. "I can see that."

"And if someone rubs me the wrong way, or I think they're lying to me, I can drop them. Just like that." She stared at him and he stared back at her, the traces of an amused smile forming on his mouth.

Cocky, arrogant bastard.

She'd ferret out his game. Trickier now that he suspected she was on to him, but maybe the extra pressure would make him slip up. Reveal his true motivations.

If he even had any. The logical side of her brain nagged her to give this suspicion up, but her gut usually won.

Zeus came to her side and bunted her arm, and she leaned down to scratch his head. He growled very softly, looking at the detective.

He winced a fraction and took a step toward the door.

"Nice to see you again, Nic."

He turned the knob. "See you soon."

❖

Jil made sure all the doors and windows were locked, then grabbed a large flashlight from the top of the mantel in the living room. "On guard," she told Zeus.

He sat up and cocked his head.

"Stay."

She proceeded to the library and flicked on every light, then took her flashlight and ran it over the top of the desk. Nothing. She shone the beam inch-by-inch down the front with the missing panel and back inside, wondering if she'd missed something when she'd taken out the will. But the compartment lay empty.

The rest of the desk yielded no results, and she stood back, disappointed. She didn't know what she'd expected, but she felt like she was on a scavenger hunt without the list.

She sat down heavily on the stairs that ran up to the library's tiny loft. As a teenager, she'd longed to climb up there and curl up on the plush window seat, but this was Elise's room, the one area of the house she needed permission to enter. Since Elise had given her the rest of the house, Jil never asked to come in here, to her private space, and the window seat had remained a forbidden pleasure.

Now, she climbed the narrow spiral staircase to the top and sat down, her back against a wall, to look out the window. From this vantage point, she had almost the same view as from her bedroom, and the church tower was clearly visible.

Her phone bleeped and she pulled it from its holster. An e-mail from Morgan.

I've got the list of names. Now I just have to match them with the student ID profiles and pictures. Should have everything in a few days.

A thrill ran through her. This was important. She could feel it.

CHAPTER NINETEEN

Jess knocked twice on the sliding barn door that led to Lily's studio. Classical music surged over the sound system—a cellist—and Jess remembered what had drawn her to Lily in the first place. Her elegant taste in wine and music had been a good start. The way she walked around stark-naked half the time had taken her interest further.

Too bad she was as fickle as she was beautiful.

"Jessica?" Lily looked up from the long rustic table and raised her eyebrows. Her silk dressing gown had slipped down over one shoulder, and the wide sleeves billowed out as she got up from the table and walked down the short flight of stairs to where Jess waited in the entrance. "Was I expecting you? I don't remember."

"Sorry to disturb you. I suppose I could have called."

Lily laughed, her black hair bouncing off her shoulders. "You know better. I haven't answered that thing in years. Come in." She grasped Jess's hand in her cool, strong fingers, and Jess felt the dampness of the clay she'd been touching seep into her own palms.

She led her up the stairs and to the table.

"Hello." Down in the galley, a young woman knelt on a small table, her breasts displayed as she clasped her hands behind her head and arched upward.

Jess looked down to the sculpture Lily was creating. Her lines were perfect. The clay seemed to be moving, breathing, like the ribcage of a real person. She looked back at the model but felt Lily's eyes on her.

She turned. "What?"

Lily's mouth quirked. "You've changed."

"What do you mean?"

"You always blushed before, looking at my models. You could never meet their eyes, let alone appreciate their forms. What's happened? Have you found a lover?"

Jess turned away.

"Don't tell me you're a lesbian, finally!"

"Stop it."

"You're right. I shouldn't tease you. You have enough on your plate with all those naughty schoolchildren."

Jess didn't bother to correct her.

"Do you mind if I just finish this? Miriam has been stretched out waiting for hours. I have to release her soon."

Jess shook her head slightly, tongue pressed into her cheek.

"Up once more, darling," Lily called down, and Miriam stretched back into her pose. She turned to Jess. "Feel free to look around. I shouldn't be more than half an hour."

Jess slipped quietly down the stairs and over to the window where Lily kept shelves of art supplies and several kilns. Browsing through her collection was half the reason she'd come.

The other half of her reasoning was up for debate.

"I want to know about paintings."

"Paintings? That's not really my specialty."

"Please." Jess quirked her lips. "There's nothing about art you don't know. Even if it isn't your specialty."

"Well, I suppose it was a happy coincidence that my parents insisted I get a degree, even if it was art history. Who knew it would end up being useful?"

"I know of a retired art history professor who just recently passed away," she said.

"Elise Fitzgerald. Yes, I read it in the *Post*. Devastating." Lily tightened the lid on a pot of glaze. "She was something. I had her for three straight semesters. She even had me over to her house a few times—art appreciation."

Jess had to shake her head to clear her thoughts. The thought of Lily in Jil's house gave her goose bumps.

"Are you sure you're well, Jessica? You look pale and tired."

Jess shot her a look. "Don't hold back."

"I never do." Lily traced her finger up Jess's bare arm. "I wish the same could be said for you."

"You never know. Things could have changed."

"I doubt you'd change that much." With a flick of the silk tie, Lily let her robe fall to her feet.

Jess looked away. She could feel unwelcome heat coloring her face—and other places.

Lily smirked. "See?"

"You had your chance," Jess murmured, meeting her eyes without flinching. "You didn't want me."

"Don't take it personally, darling." Lily slid one finger under Jess's chin and tilted her face so their faces were inches apart. "It really wasn't about you."

"I know."

"You do have someone else. I can see it in your face. You love her, I think."

Jess took a deep breath and exhaled. She would not talk to Lily this way. She couldn't fall apart. Not after everything she'd been through, trying to rebuild her confidence, her identity.

Loving Lily had been intoxicating and wonderful, but it had made her lose herself on a profound level, and she couldn't slip back into that.

Not if she planned to survive losing Jil too.

"I need you to help me with something, but I can't answer a lot of questions because I don't know exactly what I'm looking for."

Lily reached up to replace a book on a higher shelf, and the red tip of her nipple grazed the case.

For a second, Jess imagined giving in to Lily—putting her hands on that creamy porcelain skin and falling into the soft-scented bed to kiss and caress all night like they had in the very beginning.

Before Jess had gotten sick.

Before Lily had started leaving her behind.

Before she'd decided that loving a cripple was too much work.

She blinked to stop herself. *Focus.*

But why was she looking for answers in this case? She was no detective, and what did she plan to do with the information? Call Jil and say, "Hi. I know I've been smothering you to death, but I thought I'd let you know that I've been stalking your life and have answers to a mystery you never asked for help with."

What the hell was she doing here?

"Tell me about the art appreciation," she said.

"At Elise's house?"

"Yeah."

"Why?"

"I'm interested in culture."

Lily narrowed her eyes. "Does this fall into the 'don't ask' category?"

"Sort of."

"You want to know about her painting specifically?"

Jess nodded.

"Well, she did have this giant painting on her second floor. A virtually unknown Monet. It was amazing."

"A replica?"

Lily shrugged. "Elise said it was a replica, but if it was, the replicator was a genius. I didn't know enough then to be able to tell for certain, but I'd love to be able to see it again."

Jess smiled. "Sometimes you only get one shot in life, Lily."

Lily appraised her. "You're over it. I'm glad. I was afraid I'd broken your heart."

"You did," Jess admitted. "But I understand that our lives moved at different paces."

"An artist can't be held in a closet, no matter how much she loves the warden."

Jess exhaled. "You know, I'm sorry too, for hurting you if I did. I wish it could have worked."

"But we are so different. And that wouldn't have changed. Better we part as friends, isn't it? And I can leave you to your new lover, whomever she may be."

"You think you know a lot, don't you?"

"I know some things. And I know the sight of a woman in love."

"I'm not in love."

"You don't want to admit to being in love. There's a difference."

Jess took her coat and headed for the door. "If the Monet was a replica, and you wanted to find the replicator, how would you?"

"I don't know," Lily mused. "I guess I'd have to find out where she studied. And with whom."

"You mean there are schools to teach artists how to counterfeit?"

Lily grinned. "Not exactly. But she would have had to study technique somewhere. And probably she would have apprenticed somewhere afterward, with someone who knew what they were doing. Privately, I'd always wondered..." she trailed off.

"Wondered what?"

"Never mind. It's not important."

Jess searched. Lily's secrets didn't bother her any more, but this seemed important.

"Tell me."

Lily sighed. "Privately, I wondered if Elise had more talent in that area than she ever let on."

"Why do you say that?"

A line formed between Lily's eyebrows—something that only happened when she was truly bothered by something. "She was a very talented restorative artist. One of the best I've seen. And restoration is so closely related to replication...I've seen some convincing pieces on art tours, and I thought I recognized her influence in some of them."

"Her influence?"

"It's just a feeling. A fleeting thought I had. That maybe she taught someone..."

"One of her students?"

"Possibly," Lily said. "I have no proof, of course. But there's someone in this area who's very good at this technique, and Elise Fitzgerald was one of the most knowledgeable art historians in the country. I don't think it's a coincidence."

"You think she has a protégé in Rockford."

"Nearby, anyway. Maybe Toronto? Maybe Montreal? I may meet her one day if I'm diligent about it. I don't know how I would track her down, though. It might help if I knew how to use the Internet." She laughed.

Jess considered that. How would she advertise herself? An art replicator? A forger? "What do you think she's like?"

Lily tilted her head. "Probably young. You need incredibly supple wrists to be able to take on the technique of another artist."

Jess smiled. "If I find her, I'll let you know. You can have the first crack at a date. Deal?"

Lily walked back up the stairs. "That would suit me well. I won't ask why you're looking, but I do wish you luck. Bye, Jessica."

CHAPTER TWENTY

*E*lise had actually complained when the bank started opening on Saturdays.

"The world is so bustling, so busy, so distracted with everything else that people don't have time to do their business in regular business hours, and spend the weekend with their families, like they ought."

"Don't be anachronistic," Jil said.

Elise laughed out loud.

Jil grinned back at her as they walked toward the bank.

"You've been studying, I see."

"Just wanted you to know."

"Well, the school year's almost finished. Your teachers report that your grades are quite good—better, even, than when you were attending school."

"That's no surprise," Jil muttered. Fewer distractions and a strong desire to prove she could do it so she wouldn't have to go back.

Elise stopped at the streetlight and turned to her. "What are your plans? When you've graduated?"

"Straight on to college and then finish at university," Jil said. She wanted to get the hell out of high school and onto a campus with more choices. "It's less expensive to take part of your degree at college first."

"What will you study?"

Jil looked down. She hadn't been on a tour yet and didn't have the program book.

Elise punched the button, and they waited for the little green man. "You know...college tuition can add up."

Jil met her gaze. "The province has stipends for foster kids who have good grades and want to go on to college. I was hoping to get one."

Elise nodded carefully, and Jil saw something in her face that gave her the impression Elise held something back. It scared her to think Elise might know something that could thwart her plans.

"Elise?" she said quietly. "Is there..."

"There's nothing," Elise said. "I will help you get that scholarship if that's what you want to do. You're a smart young lady, and I know any college is lucky to get you."

Jil grinned. "Thanks."

The light turned green, and they traveled across the street to the bank. "So, will you study at home again next year?"

Jil stopped, holding her breath. No new school, no new teachers, no cafeteria full of students looking at the freaky new girl. Days of studying at the park, in the library, walking around the zoo to look for interesting animals to draw...

"Yes! If that's okay with you, I would like to finish my year at home, on my own."

"Right." Elise walked toward the bank. "I'll send a request in. I'm sure they'll find me a suitable supervisor."

Jil smiled and backed away from the doors, off to search out the gelato shop. "Meet you back here in half an hour."

At the elephant enclosure, Jil sat on a park bench, her knees tucked up to her chest as she watched the mama elephant corral the youngster away from the rocks. She took out her sketch pad and attempted to capture the elephant's stance, the trunk, the soulful

eyes that looked up from under long, dark lashes. Drawing would never be her forte, but since she needed an arts elective to graduate, and it was difficult to complete a drama or music requirement on her own, she'd chosen Sketch.

She only needed a sixty-five percent.

She looked down at her pad—and that's all she would get... The idea of drawing elephants had seemed pretty romantic, but the result, unfortunately, was not.

Across the stone quad, she spotted another girl her age climbing a tree, a satchel slung over her shoulder. She watched as the girl settled into the crook between the trunk and a large, low branch. In a moment, she opened her satchel and took out a camera.

Jil watched her for a while longer, then went back to her drawing. She needed three different poses of the same subject, and guessed she had one reasonable attempt. The assignment was due next week. She could come back on Monday.

On the weekend, the place bustled with shrieking children and adults with large bags and hats. Impossible to get a clear view of the animals. She liked to come during the week.

"Aren't you lonely?" Padraig had asked her during one of their Wednesday night dinners.

"No." She didn't want him getting any ideas about putting her back in school.

"What about a class of some sort, Jil? Cake decorating or Kung Fu..."

Jil fixed him with a stare.

"I mean it."

She rolled her eyes. Privately, she suspected he was right, but she didn't really know what to do about it. What did he want her to do? Call up some of her old foster siblings and get together? She didn't exactly keep friends from one placement to another. Often, she had to move clear across town when she moved homes.

She just wanted a fresh start.

"Hey."

Jil looked up and saw the girl in the tree smiling at her. She waved back.

"Are you cutting school?" She took off her hat and ran a hand through her short, dark hair—a little damp from the heat of the day.

"No, I'm…" Jil almost said "homeschooled" but wondered if that made her sound weird. "I study independently."

The girl nodded and picked up her camera again, pointing it at the elephant enclosure. "I'd love to do that. The high school here is so big that the teachers never even notice I'm gone, so I do a lot of 'independent study,' and by that I mean cutting school every second day. I keep my grades up, though," she added, putting her camera down again. "I want to go to college and everything."

"For photography?"

The girl grinned again. "Yeah. How'd you guess?"

Jil laughed. "Are you taking it now? Photography, I mean?"

"No. I'm stuck in Sketch. But I take the pictures first, then develop them and draw from there. It's easier when the target isn't moving."

Jil nodded. Of course! She held up her notebook. "Wish I'd thought of that."

"You take Sketch 'independently'?"

"Yeah. Not very well, obviously."

She shrugged. "Who cares? 'Art is all in the interpretation.'" She sounded like she was imitating someone—probably her teacher. "Also, elephants are hard. Too many shadows and shading because of their skin texture. Try a leopard or something. I have pictures of those if you want to borrow them."

Jil nodded. "Thanks. That might help."

The girl climbed down. She wore a faded print T-shirt that fell off the shoulder, and even more faded jean shorts. "I'm Gigi, by the way."

"Seriously?" Jil bit her lip. She hadn't meant to say that out loud.

Luckily, Gigi seemed to have a good sense of humor. She rolled her eyes. "Well, Georgia. But, I mean, c'mon…" She adjusted the strap around her shoulder, and Jil caught sight of a rainbow badge on the top flap.

Jil winked. "Maybe that's a little formal, you know, for your style."

Gigi followed her gaze to the badge, then met her gaze. "I'm more of an alternative girl than mainstream."

Jil shrugged. "Sounds good to me."

CHAPTER TWENTY-ONE

Jessie! What are you doing here?" Henri opened the top of the desk at the animal rescue shelter and bolted through to wrap Jess in a bear hug.

She winced as his arms crushed her elbow joints, and he loosened his grip a little. "What's wrong? You sick again?"

Jess gasped. "Just a flare-up."

Henri let her go but still held her by the forearms.

"What's going on? Why are you here in the middle of the day? And how's that beast?"

"Zeus is fine. He eats a truckload, by the way. I'm off work for a bit."

His brow furrowed. "You're that sick?"

Jess blew her hair up on her forehead. Why was it so hot in here? "Just a setback."

Henri popped the counter open and led her into the back room. "You've never been off work as long as I've known you, Jessie. Not after Mitch's accident. Not even when what's-her-name left you."

She felt her throat tightening, and she turned away, concentrating on swallowing.

"Is it that girl? Julia?"

"Jil," Jess whispered.

"Jil? I thought her name was Julia."

Should she even bother trying to explain that one? What difference did it make now? "We're...we're over. I think."

Henri sank down into a broken chair. "Shit."

Jess snorted. "Sorry to disappoint you. You liked her?"

"Hell yes! Anyone who'd take a rescued Great Dane has my vote."

"Mine too." The words were out before she could stop them. She missed her. She loved her. Before her mind could get any further ahead of her emotions, she bit down on her lip. The clenching feeling had returned, and she felt like she was free falling through the air.

Something must have shown in her face because Henri jumped up from his seat.

"Let me get you something to drink." He opened the fridge and rooted around along the bottom shelf which looked like it hadn't seen a dishcloth in years. "Got a Coke."

She shook her head. With all the trouble she had sleeping, the caffeine would just make things worse. "Thanks anyway."

"Tea?"

"You have tea?" She managed a smile.

"Well, I have teabags and a kettle. Mary, the girl who comes in on the weekends, likes the stuff." He flicked the kettle on.

"Thanks."

"Are you going to tell me what happened to Julia—Jil?"

She leaned against the wooden break table, debating the merits of trying to get up and down from a chair, and deciding not to bother. "We had a fight. She said she wanted space. Then she left to go and stay at her foster mother's house."

"Why? Doesn't she have her own house?"

"Yes. But I was there." She laughed shortly.

"You sure that's the reason? She could have just asked you to leave. Wouldn't that have been easier?"

Of course that would have been easier.

She'd spent so much time taking Jil's reaction personally that she hadn't considered the reasons behind her decisions. Why was she staying at Elise's? She'd said something about her art collection… but that couldn't be the whole story.

Henri reached to the top of the cupboard for a clean mug, a triumphant look on his face. "High class." He winked.

"You surprise me, Henri."

"Well, you surprise me too, Jessica." He leveled his gaze at her, and his chocolate eyes seemed to hold a trace of something she'd never seen from him before—reproach.

She stared back at him. "What?"

"This wasn't a fling, Jessie. You're too smart for that. To get involved with her in the first place, she would have had to be something."

"I think you put too much faith in me. Look at Lily."

Henri's eyes narrowed. "Her, I didn't like. But she was still a quality lady. Beautiful, talented. Her problem was selfishness. But Jil doesn't seem selfish to me. And she's got all the pluses Lily had—looks, brains—and more. And she's trustworthy. That's the key, Jessie. She's someone you can count on."

"You can tell all that from meeting her once?"

"Yes, I can."

Jess smiled. "I believe you, actually."

"Of course you should believe me. I might not be the schoolbooks type, but I know people, and I know she was a good one. So it has to take more than just a little fight and some space to make a rift you can't repair."

A spasm seized her. Her knees began to shake, and Henri grabbed her arm and helped her into the one wooden chair that didn't have broken legs. She looked up at him. "Sorry. Thank you."

"No, I'm sorry. I think I was too hard on you. I just don't like to see you give up on something that might finally make you happy."

She looked down at the table. "Thank you." All her emotions fought for room at the surface, even as she tried to clamp them down. Talking wouldn't help. It hurt way too much. She breathed out through the threat of tears, fighting to keep her voice steady. "I don't know what to do."

He wrapped her small hand in his huge one. "Do the thing that makes you happiest. Even if it's hard."

The kettle roared as it came to a boil, then switched off. Henri looked at it for a moment like it was an alien creature, but he picked it up and poured the hot water into the mug.

"You'll need a teabag." Jess winked.

He shot her a look but grabbed a bag from the tin and pushed it under with a spoon.

"Milk?" He read her hesitation. "It's fresh."

She laughed. "I didn't say a thing."

"I know what you were thinking."

"Well, where the hell have you been then? I don't even know what I'm thinking!"

"Okay, well, let me tell you then. You're thinking that you've finally met someone—someone who likes dogs, by the way—and she's perfect for you in every way. And now you have to ask yourself how the hell you're supposed to keep a girl like that and keep your job at the same time."

Jess felt the color draining from her face.

Henri passed her the tea and sat beside her, then folded one of her hands into his rough fingers. "How'd I do?"

She couldn't even speak.

"You don't want to call her because you haven't made up your mind yet about the job."

The realization that she might not be able to return to school hit her like two paws to the gut. "I'm off work," she whispered. "Off work. I don't even know how this happened. I can't lose both her and my school, Henri. What the hell am I doing?"

"I think you're figuring things out."

"By visiting a dog kennel in the middle of the day?"

He smiled, showing a glimmer of gold tooth on the upper side. "Well, since you're playing hooky, you can always help me bathe the dogs. Maybe that's why you're really here. Some hard manual labor might be good for you."

She looked down at her legs. For a moment, she'd forgotten about the fire in her joints. "Why not? Seems like I could use the distraction. If you don't think I'd be more of a hindrance in this state."

He helped her to her feet. "Never a hindrance, Jessie. Never have been, never could be."

She signed on for two days a week at the SPCA. From principal to dog groomer—who would ever have guessed? Nobody even asked how long she would be off.

Cynthia called to ask if she could check in occasionally. Jess said yes. But she hoped she wouldn't call.

She hoped she wouldn't call? She didn't want to know the details about her own school?

What was *happening* to her life?

CHAPTER TWENTY-TWO

*S*he's not home," Jil said. Elise taught a class until four on Wednesdays, then had a staff meeting. They always ate out on Wednesday nights.

Gigi slipped her arms around Jil's waist and pulled her in for a kiss. "Benefit number one to skipping class," she murmured.

Jil pulled Gigi's shirt over her head. "You're still going to graduate, right, even with all your absences?"

"I have an A-average."

"In what?"

"Erogenous Discovery. Don't worry. Making out with you won't prevent me from moving on in life." Gigi stood in her pink bra and short stretch shorts, her hair tousled and a faint pink flush creeping from the base of her neck to her strap line.

Jil pulled her onto the bed and ran her hands over her soft skin, kissing her neck, her face. They both lay topless in the cool air of the room, hot fingers exploring.

Gigi leaned her head to the side as Jil kissed her from her earlobe to her collarbone. Her nipples stood stiff and ready for tweaking. And Jil obliged. But when she went to pull down Gigi's bike shorts, she giggled and moved away.

Jil stopped. "No?" She saw genuine shyness in Gigi's eyes— hesitation.

She bit her lip. "Sorry. I'm just...I'm not ready yet."

Surprised, Jil took her hand away from Gigi's waist and put it back on her shoulder. "Don't be sorry. I'm sorry. I thought..."

"I know." *Gigi looked away, pink tinging the tops of her cheeks.* "I guess I'm all talk."

Jil snorted. "Well, not all *talk.*"

"Can we just go back to..."

"This?" *Jil kissed her again, biting her lower lip.*

Gigi sighed. "I'm so lucky you're homeschooled—"

The door opened.

Jil sat bolt upright, pulling a pillow up to cover her chest, and met Elise's surprised stare.

"I'm sorry," *Elise stammered.* "I didn't realize you were home. I was in search of the letter opener." *Her glance fell on Jil's desk where the antique bronze letter opener glinted from the side of her homework. Jil had used it to make perfect paper cuts in an art project.*

"Hello, Gigi." *Elise nodded once and firmly closed the door.*

After the door closed, Gigi put her arm on Jil's shoulder and waited. "Does she know?" *she asked in a whisper.*

"If she didn't before, she does now," *Jil muttered.* "I've never told her, though..."

"You think she'll kick you out?"

Jil bit her lip and pulled her shirt on slowly. "I don't know. Would you mind going home now? I'll call you later?"

"Yeah. Okay." *Gigi grabbed her satchel and hat, pecked Jil on the cheek, and headed for the door.* "Good luck," *she whispered.*

Jil heard her light footsteps on the stairs.

"Bye, Elise," *Gigi said.*

"Bye, dear." *The front door opened and closed.*

Bye, dear?

"Jillienne?" *Elise's voice hailed her from below.*

She opened the door cautiously and peeked out, down over the banister to the lower level.

Elise stood brandishing the letter opener in one hand and an envelope from the bank in the other. Her multi-colored scarf highlighted her bright blue eyes and silver hair, making her look even more like a sophisticated art professor than usual.

"Reservations are for seven tonight."

Jil made her way slowly down the stairs.

Elise watched her descend, a tiny smile tugging at the corners of her mouth. "You can tell me all about your romantic interest."

Jil felt herself blushing and put her hands to her face.

"Oh, darling." Elise put her arm snugly around Jil's shoulder. "You must feel free to tell me these things. Let me relive my youth."

"Really?" Jil mumbled. "You want to know?"

"Of course I do. I was in love at your age. With a boy who wasn't at all good for me…"

❖

Dawn broke over the church steeple, and Jil squinted as the light hit her eyelids. She hadn't meant to fall asleep up here in the library loft, but after Fraser left last night, she couldn't bring herself to go to sleep upstairs. She needed to stand guard in a place nobody would look for her.

Unfortunately, it had been a long time since she'd been on a stakeout, and the stress of the past few weeks had taken its toll. She'd fallen asleep as the bell tower struck midnight.

She felt something digging in to her hip and shifted, groping beneath the throw blanket to retrieve the key ring that had fallen from her pocket. The teeth from Elise's mysterious key had bitten into her skin, and she rubbed the sore spot.

She sat up and swung her legs over the side of the bench. Her heel struck the side of the face with a hollow thud.

Hollow thud?

She threw the blanket off and knelt down. With her knuckles, she rapped along the side of the three panels of the face. The far left sounded dense, as did the middle, but the far right echoed when she knocked.

Why?

She felt along the corner, pressing and fingering the seam—looking for anything that might spring open or move back. There. At the bottom corner of the square facing, a thumbhole. She pulled gently and felt the entire square shift. With a tug, she popped it off.

She sat for a moment, holding the square face in her hand. *Seriously?*

Inside, she groped around.

A box.

Square.

Six by six inches.

With a lock.

She slipped her key into the lock and caught her breath as it turned easily, and the lock popped. For a moment, she didn't lift the lid. Every time she opened a box, she found something else she didn't want to know—and another clue she didn't want to follow.

But this box was small. She lifted the lid and saw three small items—a flash drive, a program for a studio tour, and, *for Christ's sake, Elise.* Another key.

❖

Zeus greeted her with a yawn, then stood by the door until she opened it.

As she waited for him to do his thing, she started the coffee and examined the program. It was dated for last year. Why on earth would she keep an old program in a box in the window seat and not with other keepsakes if it meant that much to her?

She squinted at it, looking for a clue, but nothing looked obvious. Just a brochure for a standard studio tour—the kind Elise loved to go to—churches, this time. It looked like five churches had participated, opening their doors for members of the public to tour their art and stained glass.

Elise had circled one church in particular—her own. Why would she go to a studio tour of her own church when she could see the artwork every Sunday?

At the bottom, in small font, she saw a possible answer. One of the older and more valuable paintings, usually protected behind glass, would be opened for the day. Spectators would have a rare chance to admire the painting up close, without barriers.

Jil sighed and pocketed the brochure. So many questions and nobody to ask.

Why did she have the feeling Elise had done this on purpose—one last treasure hunt from the grave? Except this time, the real treasure would be finding out about Elise's secret life.

She put the third key onto her keychain and grabbed her computer and headphones. Time to look at the last clue.

As the coffee dripped and hissed, she connected the flash drive to her laptop. It made a dinging noise, and she squinted at the screen and pressed some buttons—next, next, next.

This file requires the use of Audible-Me. Install new program?
She hit yes.
Next. Next. Next. Accept.
"Good Lord," Jil muttered as she waited for the circle on her desktop to stop spinning.
Finish.
"Yes, please!"
Suddenly, Elise's voice filled the room.
"Hello, Duncan. Just so you're informed, I'm wearing a wire."
Duncan?

Her stomach clenched. Not Duncan MacLeod, leader of organized crime? What was Elise doing talking to him—and recording him, for that matter? What was he going to do to her?

The sound of a door closing. Something dropped on the floor and the scuffling of boots obscured the first part of the man's sentence.

"...supposed to keep that a secret, generally?"
"No. This is a transparent part of my terms."
"Fine. You'll go down too if the recording is ever released. There's no statute of limitations on that you know."
"It's insurance for when I die."

He growled. "…should have you thrown in the drink for what you did."

Jil pressed pause on the screen, then turned up the volume and backed the cursor up a few centimeters.

"Then who would keep you on the straight and narrow?" Elise said.

"Maybe I'm tired of all your interference. Maybe I just want you to get the hell out of my way."

"You're a free man, Duncan. You'll do what you like when I'm gone. You think I don't know that?"

Jil frowned and paused the tape, then rewound it again to make sure she heard it correctly. Yes, that's what she'd said, and her tone had a familiar quality to it that could only mean Elise knew MacLeod. But how?

Jil strained to make out the sounds coming from the speaker.

"You're taking advantage of that girl." His tone sounded almost accusatory.

"I am not. She came to me willingly."

"I'm sure she did. She's talented. And she has a dark side as wide as yours."

Elise snorted. "We're not in that game anymore, Duncan."

"But part of you misses it, don't you? You must. Otherwise how could you have pulled off that switch?"

"You robbed a church!"

"Your morals are getting in the way of my profit. And I want to know who this bitch is who's working for you instead of me."

"You'll never find her. But even so, I'll tell you right now, Duncan, you lay a hand on her and I'll haunt you from the grave, no matter how many candles you light."

He cursed under his breath, and Jil felt her heart accelerate. What was Elise doing messed up with this guy? "You forget what I know about you."

"I don't care anymore. I'm going to be dead soon. Tell the world for all I care."

"You don't care about the world, but you do care about your daughter."

Elise's breath caught. She had to clear her throat before speaking. "We'll come back to that. But I have one question first—how did you get the Madonna across the border?"

"The fake one, you mean?" He laughed bitterly.

"Doesn't matter. You thought it was real."

"You need a lesson in smuggling, Elise?"

"Maybe."

"You do! What do you plan to pull off?"

"That's none of your business."

He snorted. "But you have the nerve to ask how I move my goods? Don't you know me better than that?"

Elise sighed. "It's been a long time. I'd hardly say I know you now."

A shuffling sound, like he was moving closer. "Once you know someone that well, you don't ever forget…"

"Years ago. We were practically children. And we both made bad decisions."

"Which you don't want to be reminded of. That's why you're really angry with me, isn't it? Because I made you do something that reminded you of how good you used to be? What a thrill it is to get away with it?"

"You're on shaky ground here, aren't you? Getting upset about a piece that didn't belong to you?"

"Do you know how many months of planning went into that heist? You stole more from me than just money."

"You got paid."

Duncan snorted. "Well, that's only because the replica was so good. The buyer didn't even realize it was a forgery. He left with your replica; I got paid. But I want to know how you switched them and when."

"And I'm going to take that with me to my final breath. Just know that I have beaten you for the last time."

"Yes, you have. And now, you're purposely keeping a valuable replicator in the wings when she rightfully belongs on my team. Tell me why I shouldn't kill you right now?"

Elise chuckled. "We both know why. But I need something else from you."

"What?"

"I want to make a deal."

"Why should I? You'll be dead and gone soon."

Elise sighed. "Because I plan to give you something you've always wanted. But you have to give me your word that you will not go looking for my replicator."

"I'll promise no such thing."

Her laugh was barely audible. "Yes, you will. And this is why."

A rustling of paper.

He inhaled sharply. "You wouldn't. You swore you'd never part with it."

"I earned it."

He chuckled. "You did. But I still want it."

"I know. I've come up with a solution. It will give me what I want—"

"You want something more than that? You've never wanted anything more than that. Not even—"

"Not even you?"

He didn't answer. But after a long pause, he cleared his throat.

"She deserves her life, Duncan."

He sighed. "I give you my word."

"I'm going to have to trust you to keep my secrets. My memory is all she's going to have when I'm dead."

"I know. Me too."

"You're never to make contact with her. And if she finds you—"

"How would she find me?"

"You might be surprised."

He sighed heavily. "If she finds me there's not much I can do about it."

This didn't make sense. Why would Anastasia go looking for Duncan MacLeod?

"I need more than that, Duncan."

He chuckled. Another rustle, like he was digging into a pocket or a small bag. "Here. Pin it on yourself. Take it as my promise."

Elise whistled slowly. "That's never the…"

What was she looking at?

"It is. And don't you go giving me any lectures. It never belonged to that museum in the first place. And if it doesn't convince you, then nothing will. Besides, with the amount of money that thing's worth, it's a fair trade."

Elise breathed a sigh. It sounded like relief. "I'll make sure she knows. And that she keeps this safe in case you ever need reminding."

He chuckled. "That might be difficult. But I imagine you'll find a way. You're nothing if not resourceful."

White noise faded in, obscuring the voices. She played with the settings on her laptop's sound, but the white noise persisted—almost like Elise was holding something to her chest, or putting on a sweater, muffling her response.

Jil tried once more, but couldn't clear the audio. This job belonged to someone else with far better technical skills than she possessed. Trouble was, though, she didn't know what Elise might have said on the tape, and what it might imply. But she wanted to know—she needed to know—what she'd given MacLeod to keep Anastasia safe.

And if she'd kept her relationship with Duncan MacLeod a secret, what else had she been hiding all this time?

She downloaded the file onto her iPod, backed it up to two separate e-mail accounts with the file name "Banana Bread Recipe," then took the flash drive out of her computer and popped it back into her pocket. She planned to put it back where she'd found it—in the crevice under the window seat. Elise had kept it hidden for a reason, and until she knew why, she would keep it out of sight.

At the door, Zeus stood waiting for her to let him back in. He nuzzled her hand on his way over the threshold, and she paused to scratch him behind the ears. So many questions raced through her thoughts that she couldn't catch a single one to process or analyze.

Instead, she poured a large cup of coffee and leaned against the counter, just trying to absorb all the implications.

Elise knew Duncan MacLeod.

Duncan MacLeod was a known leader of organized crime—specialty, counterfeiting.

Elise had double-crossed him in some way, created a forgery for a painting he had stolen, it sounded like.

What painting was it? How had Elise switched them? How had Elise even known about his activities?

Jil sighed. These actions and knowledge of the underworld belonged to other-Elise. Not the Elise who had raised Jil and held a prestigious professorship at a respected university. This other-Elise was a criminal.

CHAPTER TWENTY-THREE

Technically, their relationship was over. Fraser had taken her report. He'd delivered her ring and had let the thief go. She didn't owe him anything.

But if she wanted to talk to Duncan MacLeod, she'd have to know where he was. And after listening to him threatening Elise, she didn't mind at all if she had to speak to him in jail.

She texted Fraser. *What if I knew about a warehouse operation?*

He answered immediately. *Why would you tell me?*

She thought for a moment. *Because I'm pretty sure I can guess whose ring it is.*

As she was waiting for Fraser's reply, her phone rang and startled her. Jess's name lit up the screen.

Shit.

For a second, she considered not answering, but she didn't want to be that person. She'd worked hard to learn to confront her problems, and she wouldn't let one rocky relationship change her.

"Hi," she said.

"Hi." Jess's voice sounded soft—like she'd just woken up, or hadn't had enough caffeine to properly start her day. Usually she'd say, "I'm calling from work."

Code for *keep it straight.*

Jil waited for her to say something else—to direct their conversation—but she didn't. Why did it have to be so fucking complicated? This used to be a little game with them—how many different ways could they role-play having a professional conversation, laden with code only the two of them would understand?

"Your order is ready at the photo shop, Ms. Blake." *I can come pick you up after work. I'll meet you at the shopping mall down the road.*

"What time are you open til?" *I'll meet you in our usual spot. Tell me what time you'll be there.*

When it was clear Jess wasn't going to say anything but "hi" Jil jumped in with her most neutral response.

"How can I help you?" Her tone came out flat. She knew she was going overboard with the professionalism, but just couldn't muster the energy to play games today.

"Oh," Jess sounded disappointed—flustered, even. "I thought we should have coffee or something." Her sentence came out rushed.

"Sure," Jil answered. Better in person anyway. "Do you want me to bring anything?"

"Like what?" Jess asked.

Like your stuff?

Jess suddenly seemed to comprehend her meaning. "I just want to talk, Jil. Is that okay with you? Do you have other ideas? Unless you've decided you want to…make a more permanent decision?"

Jil felt a knot unclench somewhere in the region of her large intestine. She'd never had a fight like that before and continued a relationship.

What the hell was it with her and Jess?

"Listen, can you please text me the time and place? I'll be the one sporting a messy ponytail and bags under my eyes." Her lame joke contained more truth than she'd intended, but when Jess made a sympathetic noise, she cut her off. She didn't have time for sympathy right now, nor did she really deserve it. "I'll see you later, Jess, okay? Just text me."

And she hung up. Jess's voice had sent her reeling, both physically and emotionally. Did she want to see her? Of course she did. But how would they even begin to bridge the chasm that had slowly opened between them and now seemed like the wide maw of a huge beast, ready to swallow them both?

She couldn't explain her investigation, and she couldn't very well keep it a secret, while also blaming Jess for her own skeletons in the closet. Hypocrisy—one of the relationship kisses of death. The other might be *not seeing one another.*

Unless she wanted to break up.

No, she didn't want to break up. She just wanted to solve this case so she could make some sense of her life, and then maybe— possibly—consider putting her energy back into her future instead of her past.

Which meant she had yet another date with Nicolas Fraser to take care of.

❖

Jess grabbed her coat and sat gingerly on the bench beside the front door, confronted with three possible pairs of boots. One, she eliminated right away because it had a zipper that stuck and she couldn't pull it up. The second had laces, which might work, depending on the time of day she wanted to tie them, but as nervous as she felt, probably not right now.

The third pair wasn't nearly warm enough, but with a shoehorn, she could squeeze her foot in without any extra steps.

Option three. Old and a little scuffed, but they were boots, and to hell with fashion for the moment.

What if Jil wasn't happy to see her? How would they talk to each other? It felt like months had passed, though in reality it had only been a few weeks. What would they say?

She grabbed her purse and fumbled with the key, taking three tries to lock the door. The damn thing froze and stuck all frigid winter long. With more care than normal, she made her way to the car, ignoring the fluttering in her stomach and the tears that hovered just behind her eyes.

Part of her wanted to go back home and close the door on this relationship that had put her through every conceivable emotion—and then a few more she'd never experienced before. And part of her couldn't wait to sit across the table from Jil—to be able to read her face, hear her words and laughter. Maybe touch her hand.

At the coffee shop, she arrived first.

The clock on the wall showed 7:27 a.m., so she stood in line for her coffee, then snagged a table where she'd be easily seen. She took out her mobile and laid it on the table next to her: 7:28.

Someone bumped her chair, and her stomach lurched as she looked up.

"Jessica Blake, hello."

She looked up to see Phil Kelsey, a science teacher. "Phil, hello." She smiled, trying to look pleased to see him.

"We've all missed you. How are you doing?" He swung himself into the chair opposite her with a flexibility she hadn't expected from a man of his age, then leaned intently over his coffee.

"I'm okay," she replied, trying not to flinch at his closeness.

"That's good to hear. The school isn't the same without you. I mean, Cynthia's great and all, but it's not the same as having you in the driver's seat."

She glanced toward the door. "Thanks, Phil. I appreciate that." She tried to focus on his face. To give him the illusion of her full attention. "I hope to be back soon."

Really? Did she?

"Good. Good. No rush, of course. We hope you're taking all the time and help you need."

Time and help? She stared back at him—at his too-sympathetic expression, his open hands. He was looking at her as if she'd just come out of a psychiatric hospital.

But of course, even though they'd been told the truth—well, mostly the truth—about her illness, they probably all just assumed she was covering up a stress leave. In their position, that's what she'd assume too.

Maybe she should just play along with it. Tell him she was waiting for her psychiatrist or something. That might get rid of him faster. She dragged her attention back to his words. Something about provincial testing and his class's scores.

She glanced down at her mobile: 7:32.

"Sorry—are you meeting someone?" Phil asked, looking chagrined. "I should have asked instead of parking myself here like an idiot."

Jess smiled. The words "just a friend" formed in her mind, sliding down the space to her tongue, but she couldn't say them. She couldn't lie anymore. The weight of secrecy crushed her from the inside.

"You're not an idiot," she managed. "I was glad to see you." And she was, in a way—if only to force herself to confront the truth about what she cared about. Math scores weren't high on her list.

"I have to get going anyway. Don't want to be late for homeroom." He got up from the table, shooting her an apologetic smile.

She waved as he wound his way through the tables to the door.

Homeroom. She mulled the word over in her mind. Such an adolescent word. She wondered how many times in her career she'd said it, like it meant something, like it had weight and importance. Get to homeroom. Homeroom teachers, please send down attendance folders. Locker assignments will be given out in homeroom. She repeated it in her mind until it stopped meaning anything at all.

❖

Jil came out of the bathroom at the coffee shop and spotted Jess right away. She sat with her hand wrapped around a large cup of coffee, her short blond hair illuminated by the early morning sun, staring out the window, as if waiting to catch a glimpse of Jil.

Jil just stood watching her for a moment, hidden partially by the cream and sugar stand.

Jess took a sip of coffee and looked at her watch. A patron came in the door and nodded to Jess. She flashed him her professional smile. Jil had seen it so often when she was undercover at St. Marguerite's. So often.

Her principal's face. Her wall of secrecy.

Now she shifted in her seat, orienting herself toward the other man, closing herself off to anyone else.

If Jil had walked in the door right then, she would have kept walking—straight up to the counter, not pausing to say hello. She would have kept up their façade, not compromised Jess's job. She would have waited until the man left, then joined her.

Really, though, she could have sat down. Could have pretended to be Jess's neighbor or a friend catching her at 7:30 in the morning, before they both had to get to work. But Jil didn't lie well, and even acting out a lie, without having to say anything, made her belly twist.

Funny, for someone who had to go undercover so often to have such a problem with deception.

For a minute, she considered getting into the coffee line. She could do just what she'd thought of instinctively—order, wait out of sight. Neither of them had seen her. Then, as soon as the coast was clear—

She kicked herself mentally. *What the hell am I doing?*

With a shake of her head, Jil walked the three steps to the side door of the coffee shop and out to the parking lot.

In her car, she took out her mobile and texted. *I'm sorry to have to cancel.* For a moment, she hesitated. Should she add something else? Try to make an excuse? Her mind rejected creativity. She just couldn't come up with something else. Why bother? Jess could never truly be hers.

She hit send.

CHAPTER TWENTY-FOUR

How to catch a counterfeiter? Jess wondered. If she were even in the region.

Googling "art counterfeit" would hardly do.

Then she remembered something Lily had said about art tours. What exactly was an art tour?

She looked that up instead.

Hm. People opened their homes—well, estates, it seemed like—for the public to view their art and artifacts. She found a list of forthcoming tours on the site, along with the regions and prices.

Prices weren't bad.

She had to start somewhere—why not here? She might meet some interesting people.

Or open a can of worms she had no business even holding in the first place.

For a moment, she considered calling Jil, but what could she say? Besides, Jil should be the one to call her. She'd been the one who canceled, so she had to be the one to close the gap, if she wanted it closed.

In the meantime, the waiting would drive her crazy, and if she couldn't work, she needed to occupy herself. Otherwise she'd be a lonely, unemployed woman housebound with chronic pain.

To hell with that idea.

An art tour was scheduled for this weekend, Friday through Sunday.

With three clicks, she signed up and printed her itinerary.

❖

Jess boarded the bus to the tour and found her assigned seat. The bus ride would take two hours. That didn't seem too far if she could stand up and walk around.

"Excuse me, you're in my seat." A large man with a dripping nose loomed over her.

She glanced up at him. "I don't believe so. My ticket says B, and this is B."

He gripped his ticket in his hand and stared at it through thick lenses. "Damn. I specifically asked for an aisle seat. Windows make me nauseous. Would you mind trading with me?"

"I'm afraid I can't," she said. Being boxed in by this guy wouldn't help her cause at all.

He sighed loudly. "Great. Just great."

She moved back as much as she could to let him in, but even so he stepped on her foot—heavily.

"Sorry," he muttered as he stripped off his coat, jarring her again with his elbow. "This is why I like the aisle seat."

Jess rolled her eyes and settled back in her chair. Three days on a bus with this guy? Maybe she could trade seats at the first stop.

"So is this your first tour?" she asked, trying to change the subject.

"No." He turned to look out the window.

She rolled her eyes and settled into her seat, then put in earphones and turned on her music to block out the sound of him sighing in her ear.

When they arrived at the first house, he stood up abruptly, almost crashing into her.

She gave him a look. This would be a long day.

She barely made the bus on time the next morning, and when she slipped into the seat next to Bernard without saying good morning, he turned to her. "Rough night?"

"Didn't sleep well," she muttered.

He gave her a sly grin. "Oh. I see."

If only it had been sex that had kept her awake, and not her hips and back and every other fucking joint in her body that had flared up from a day of walking and sitting in a bus.

"Can we just ride in peace, please?" She closed her eyes and sighed. Her stomach churned acid from missing breakfast—that, and the handful of pills she'd taken last night.

"You want a muffin?" Bernard held out a dented chocolate muffin, still wrapped in plastic. Looked like he'd nicked it from the breakfast buffet and stuffed it in his jacket pocket. But it was in one piece, and she wouldn't have anything until lunch, so…

Gingerly, she took it from his fingers. "Thanks."

"Some mansion yesterday, right?" She opened the plastic wrap and took a small morsel from the muffin top.

"A whole lotta marble for no reason," Bernard grunted.

She smiled in spite of herself. The floors, the walls, the bathrooms…all a pristine alabaster marble that was supposed to be beautiful, but she could think only about how cold it would be on your feet every day.

"Did you see that Rembrandt above the fireplace in the library?"

"Yeah. It was well done—for a Rembrandt."

That seemed rather an odd assessment of a famous artist.

"Not a Rembrandt fan?" she guessed.

"Oh, I'm a Rembrandt fan. But that wasn't a Rembrandt."

The tour guide had said Rembrandt. And she recognized the style—Lily had taught her a thing or two during their time together. "I'm confused. What do you mean?"

He turned, giving her a quizzical look. "It wasn't real."

A faint feeling of déjà vu overtook her. "How do you know?"

He took another muffin out of his pocket and unwrapped it. "I can just tell."

He knew more than he'd said.

"Tell you what, you tell me what you know, and I'll give you the aisle seat on the way home."

She'd just have to take an extra long bath. Her body was already a mess. It would be hard to make it worse.

"Fine." Bernard wiped his nose on his handkerchief and leaned in. "I figure it's not really a secret anyway. But all the same I'd appreciate if you kept it to yourself."

Jess crossed her fingers under her purse. "Agreed."

"I can tell because I have studied a lot of replicas. I even have a few myself."

She nodded to encourage him. "Where did you...come across them?"

He squinted at her for a moment, as if deciding how much to trust her. "I wanted a Picasso. They're not the most expensive pieces in the world, but I couldn't afford the real thing, and a print just doesn't have the same quality. So I asked around at a studio tour a couple of years ago and I found this woman."

"Do you remember her name?"

"Mila. Never did give her last name. She was talented, but a little bit—I don't know—odd."

"Well, I guess you would have to be a bit odd to work as a forger."

"It's only forgery if you try to sell it as real. If you admit it's a replica, then it's called a replication." He looked intent about this point.

Jess nodded. "And replication is legal?"

"Well...I guess that depends." He eyed her suspiciously. "Are you a cop or something?"

Jess laughed. "Hardly. I'm a high school principal, if you really want to know."

"A principal? Well, good for you, I guess. How do you have time to be on an art tour?"

Jess shrugged. "Turns out I needed a break."

"You're kind of young to be burned out, aren't you?"

"Tell it to my arthritis." She tried to smile, but didn't quite manage.

"Arthritis?"

"Rheumatoid arthritis, yep. It's a bitch."

Bernard looked at her in surprise. "My mother had that. But she didn't get out much. She could barely walk. She had fingers that were all curled over. Seemed like it was pretty painful though she never said much about it."

Jess shrugged one shoulder. "Some days, it certainly is. Keeping active is the best way I know how to beat it. Hence the annoying aisle walking."

"Sorry," Bernard muttered. "I shouldn't have bugged you so much about the seat. I thought you were just being a pain, but I guess you really did need it. You can keep it. No charge for the chat."

Jess stood up. "No, a deal is a deal. You've told me what I wanted to know and I'm a woman of my word. You take the aisle."

Bernard stood up to let her move over. Then he leaned in. "That's nice of you. Thank you. I'll gladly let you out if you want to walk around."

"Agreed."

"Listen, I wasn't going to say anything, but I think I know where you might be able to find this girl. Mila."

"Where?"

"She hangs out at this club in the art district. The Cracked Palette?"

"I don't know it, but I can find it."

"They have a get-together once a month. Some sort of wine and cheese. I think that's where she gets most of her clientele."

"Thanks. I'll look into it."

"Good luck."

CHAPTER TWENTY-FIVE

Jil stuck a bag of popcorn in the microwave for dinner. At the sound of the kernels leaping against the paper bag, Zeus roused himself from his bed and loped into the kitchen. He looked at the bowl Jil had put on the counter, then tilted his head toward her.

She rolled her eyes and took down a glass pie tray from Elise's top cupboard. "Can't you catch kernels like every other service dog?"

He grumbled. Sometimes she swore he talked to her.

Bowl and plate in hand, Jil led Zeus to the living room, then settled down on the couch and flicked on the TV. Zeus sat at her feet, and she put down his pie plate of popcorn. He ate each piece delicately, and she gave up channel surfing to watch him devour his snack.

"And in a record-breaking sweep, detectives at the Rockford Police Department have reportedly arrested Duncan MacLeod, on charges of counterfeiting artwork, theft, and trafficking of stolen property. Police were tipped off to the location of a warehouse containing several million dollars' worth of forged and stolen materials. MacLeod was arrested earlier this evening in his home in South Rockford."

Jil almost knocked her popcorn over, she sat up so fast.

Zeus sat up, responding to her agitation. He whined.

"Shh, shh." Jil patted his head and he settled back down.

"An interview with lead detective, Nicolas Fraser, will air tonight at eleven."

She sat down slowly. That hadn't taken him long.

❖

Jil presented her identification to the corrections officer and waited.

Would they let her in? Would they ask her a hundred questions about her motives and intentions?

"You're here to see Mr. MacLeod?" The gatekeeper said. "What makes you think he'll agree to see you?"

Tell the truth as far as possible. Jil remembered her basic training. She didn't need to lie. "I need to ask him some questions about a private case I'm currently trying to solve. Theft."

"Was the theft reported to the police?"

Jil winked. "Not all reports are taken seriously."

The corrections officer rolled his eyes. "Ain't that the truth?" Then he snapped back into his serious face. "Let me see if MacLeod will agree to the visit, and we can take it from there."

They brought him in to the visitors' area in handcuffs, which the CO fastened to the table.

"Do you know how many visitor requests I've had?"

"Well, given that you're probably the most notorious boss of organized crime in the city, I'd guess—none."

A slow grin lit his face. "You're right. My no-visit list is three times the size of this table." He leaned forward. "So how did you get in?"

"Well, I'm a former police officer, so I think that probably helped."

"You think I don't have former POs on my payroll?" MacLeod's dark eyebrows drew together until they formed one giant caterpillar across his forehead. His large brown eyes, which seemed to have gone slightly rheumy with age, still held her full attention. He crossed beefy arms over his broad barrel chest, and his gray beard brushed the top arm at the elbow. "I've got everybody from priests and doctors, right down to the guard I just bribed so they wouldn't record this conversation."

She didn't know exactly what she wanted to ask, but for now, it seemed best to keep him talking.

He studied her for a moment. "Why don't you tell me why you're here, Jil?"

Why was she here exactly? To counter-spy on Nic?

"The detective who arrested you…?" She let the question hang. "Fraser?"

"Nicolas Fraser. Did you know him prior to this?"

MacLeod chuckled again, but didn't answer. She waited him out.

"I can't tell how much you know and how much you're bluffing, girl," he finally said, a grin on his face. "But you tell Fraser that I'll be sure to say hello to his dead daddy's ghost if I get shivved here in prison waiting for this bogus trial."

"Nobody's going to shiv you, Duncan. You're worth more alive than dead to most of the inmates here."

He guffawed. "You'd make a great squint for me some day."

"I learned from the best."

"Aye, I know that much. Your foster mother was one hell of a woman."

"Seems you liked her a lot." She paused. "From the tape I overheard."

His mouth drew shut, and, like a string pulled him from the ceiling, he sat up in his chair. As she waited, he licked his lips. "What tape?"

"The one Elise left me."

He kept his face straight, impassive, but a muscle in his jaw twitched, and she knew she'd surprised him.

"Why?"

He just stared at her.

She stared back. He couldn't admit to anything without incriminating himself more, so she didn't expect him to volunteer the information. But she was also coming at this from a personal angle, not from the side of the law.

She'd given up that right when she'd given up the badge.

She laid her hands on the table. "Here are my terms. I get to interview you. In exchange, I agree not to share the tape with anyone else."

"That would assume I trust you to keep your word. I don't even know you."

Jil shot him a look. "Really?"

MacLeod shrugged a little, conceding. "Fine. You know, I always wondered why she'd bother to take on a foster child. Especially a fucked-up teenage brat. But then I realized—who would ever suspect a university professor with a kid?"

Jil felt the air being pushed out of her lungs, like someone was squeezing her.

The perfect cover.

MacLeod smirked. "But you are just like her. I can see it now. You could have been hers. And Elise's daughter would keep her word." He looked as though he was puzzling something out. For a moment, she thought he might actually ask her a question back, but then he settled back down in his chair and waited.

Suddenly, all the questions she thought she had for him fizzled in her brain. She'd been so sure that meeting him would open doors for her—doors to understanding Elise's life, her choices—but now it seemed like she was intruding on something she had no business knowing. Something Elise purposely hid from her.

Who would ever suspect a university professor with a kid? Is that the only reason Elise had taken her in? To doctor her image?

MacLeod leaned back in his chair, a smug look crossing his face. "You had no idea about her underground life, did you?"

She met his gaze but didn't say anything. She could ask, but she really didn't want to know.

"She was good, you know."

Jil's head seemed to be nodding without her volition. "I know."

MacLeod tugged on his beard. "But everybody has a dark side. You know that."

Jil swallowed. She stared straight back at him. "You were her dark side."

He licked his broad lips and chuckled. "Yes, I was. But she was a match, even for me, back in those days."

"That's not what I want to know." *No*? Wasn't that exactly why she'd come?

"I think you do. Otherwise you wouldn't be here. But have it your way. Ask me whatever other question you think you need to ask. But make it count."

Jil took a deep breath. She wasn't wasting her time on Fraser's vendetta or anything else. There was only one thing she really wanted to hear from him. "About the Monet."

He frowned, and this time, his surprise showed.

"The one she hung upstairs. It's gone."

He stared at her. "The one that's hanging there now is not the one that I grew up with. It doesn't make sense that someone would switch a replica for a replica. So I need to know—the painting that hung on our wall...was it real? How did she get it?"

MacLeod chuckled. "That's it? You can't figure that out for yourself? Or you just don't want to believe Elise Fitzgerald could have talents that weren't exactly above board? Well, believe me: Elise was no innocent. She had a game to play and she played it well. You want to know where she got that gorgeous painting? She stole it. Forty years ago. With me."

Jil felt the color drain from her face.

MacLeod shook his head, looking like he felt genuinely sorry for her. Then he rapped on the top of the table with his knuckles. "Time's up. I enjoyed our chat."

❖

Jil drove home slowly, not caring that she hit every red light. A few times, she failed to accelerate fast enough for the driver behind her and heard honking. The second time, she felt her chest constrict. Hot pins pricked her nape and hairline, and she pulled off into a Tim Horton's parking lot to get a grip. Believing in *innocent until proven guilty* was getting harder by the hour.

MacLeod's words kept pounding against her ears. "She had a game to play and she played it well."

What role had Jil played in Elise's game, exactly?

And could this money have been a payoff for the truth she was only now discovering—that Elise had only ever used her to create the image of a family? That she'd never loved her at all?

CHAPTER TWENTY-SIX

The Cracked Palette smelled of incense and melting scented wax which dripped from broad sconces in the gathering space. The lights had been dimmed, but the spotlights shone warmly on the walls lined with exhibited art. Jess took a glass of wine from a proffered tray, then joined the people who stood milling around holding crystal tumblers of spirits and glasses of the same ruby Bordeaux she sipped. She considered perching on one of the high metal barstools, but if she sat down now, she'd have a hard time getting up later.

In all likelihood, she probably shouldn't drink with the medication, but arthritis could fuck itself tonight.

She browsed the art, working her way slowly from one side of the room to the other, scanning each piece carefully. Many pieces she recognized. Perhaps she'd absorbed more artists' culture during her time with Lily than she'd realized.

She'd looked through the book of famous stolen artwork—Mila's specialty—but she couldn't be entirely sure which of the pieces in front of her might be from that list. There were several she knew for sure were not included, and she could skip over those.

Any piece belonging to Mila would have a tiny signature mark etched into the frame at the lower right hand side—a symbol few would ever notice unless they were looking for it explicitly. Bernard had tried to describe what it looked like, but his art skills were definitely lacking. She had a vague idea but wondered if she'd be able to see it, even if it stared her in the face.

On the last picture in the first row, she spotted something that looked like a pencil lined scrawl. It might have easily been part of the texture of the wood, but she couldn't be sure from this distance. As she stood squinting at the piece, a hand brushed her fingers. "You like it?"

She turned to the speaker. A slight woman with chestnut hair stood inches from her. The faint scent of turpentine and coffee wafted from her paint-stained pants. Her jewelry and top were pristine, so clearly the pants were a statement—a way to stand out from the buyers? Make it easier to be found?

Jess noticed an angel wing earring dangling from one ear. "I do," she answered. "Any idea who the artist is?" She smiled slightly.

"I might. My name is Mila." She held out her hand and Jess shook it. It was dry, almost chalky. She wasn't nervous, then. This must have been routine for her.

Jil would be proud of her sleuthing skills.

"I hoped I might find you here." Stick as closely to the truth as possible. Trying to feign surprise would only make her stand out.

"You're looking for me?"

"Well, I'm looking for an artist. My friend Bernard has the most amazing painting…"

"Bernard? There's a name I haven't heard in a while." Mila winked. "He was fun."

"He's something. You come highly recommended."

"I hope so, after everything he put me through. But I'm surprised he sent you to me. We had a confidentiality agreement." Her eyes scanned Jess's, searching for something—deceit, maybe?

"Which I think he's maintained," Jess put in quickly. "He wouldn't tell me much, only that I should show up here during the wine and cheese and I might get lucky."

Mila looked her up and down in a slow, appraising way, a teasing smile lighting her lips. Her eyes traveled back to Jess's face, and Jess felt a hot prickle travel up her neck. Mila was flirting with her. Which meant that she was either bisexual or that she had sussed Jess out in the three minutes they'd been standing there and was now using her knowledge to charm her.

Either way, Mila outmatched her. This woman was a professional forger and possibly a thief. Jess had to play her hand and get out of there before she ruined her own plans.

What could she say?

As close to the truth as possible.

She gestured to Mila to follow her and snagged a barstool. Normally, she would be embarrassed to have someone see the robotic way she maneuvered into the chair, but tonight, it might actually help her cover. "I'm glad I found you now because I'm afraid I'm running out of steam and I have to go."

"Are you tired?" Mila frowned, and Jess realized she'd failed to conform to the script that Mila must have been expecting. She was like a newly minted drug user negotiating her first heroin deal—badly.

"That's my normal state of affairs, I'm afraid. A slight mobility problem."

"I see." A brief flicker of confusion crossed Mila's face.

Could it be that she'd gained the upper hand, if only for a second? Thrown her off enough that she might be able to do this?

She let Mila fill the silence. "Well, why don't you tell me what you had in mind?" Mila said.

Jess leaned back in her chair. "Something small for my home office. I have a few art pieces left to me by my…aunt…and I'd like something to complement them."

Mila leaned in, cocking her head to the side. "Why not go to an art gallery? Pick up something that matches the decor?"

Jess sipped her wine. "Well, Mila. My decor leans more toward the classics. It's hard to find those for sale at the gallery."

Mila pursed her lips, seeming to think for a moment. "Why don't you give me your number? I can meet you again this week and show you some photos. You can pick the style you like and we can go from there. Agreed?"

"Yes, that would be great."

❖

Jess closed the front door behind her and laid Mila's card in the tray on the table. What exactly could she do with this contact information? Take it to Jil? Only to find out the whole thing was a giant misunderstanding and Mila was not involved at all? Worse, that Jil had moved on—in more than one way?

She felt like crying. This evening had been a waste of time. In fact, the whole studio tour and amateur sleuthing were just an embarrassment. She and Jil weren't speaking, and that wasn't likely to change.

She needed to forget her. Stop involving herself in her life. Move on.

She ran the bathtub, turned on the jets, and lowered herself into the hot, soapy water. She couldn't shake Jil from her head—no matter how hard she tried to concentrate on something else.

A vision of Jil, naked, sitting across from her in the tub, flashed through her mind. She'd love to swing her around, wrap arms and legs around her, and kiss all the way from her hairline to her shoulder...

A tear fell from the corner of her eye. She missed her so much.

Just the thought of Jil's naked body sliding against her own had been enough to stir heat in the pit of her stomach. She imagined Jil's hand sliding up her thigh, higher, and her fingers making deft, gentle strokes...

The hot water made her tense muscles relax. She leaned back in the tub and closed her eyes, let her thighs fall apart, and slipped two fingers between her legs.

The contact made her moan immediately.

Just fantasizing about Jil was still enough to get her to come almost effortlessly—the way Jil made her come.

She'd never experienced that before. And maybe she never would again.

She pushed that thought out of her mind and imagined Jil's mouth on her breasts, teasing her sensitive nipples with her hot tongue. Jil's hands on the small of her back, pulling her closer, pushing her down on a bed, on the floor of the closet, on the couch at her place, where they'd been the first time...

Heat melted her from her core and spread through her thighs and legs. Her breasts popped out of the water as she stroked herself. Nothing felt as good as Jil touching her, and the memory of it made her dizzy.

A jolt of pain shot down her legs as her hip locked, and she gasped in pain. She dug her fingers into her thigh to loosen the spasming muscle that twisted her ankle out and splayed her toes.

She breathed out, willing the pain to pass. Then, clenching her teeth, she eased her legs closed.

CHAPTER TWENTY-SEVEN

The knock on the door came just after dark—loudly enough that it made Jil jump. She pushed herself out of the chair at the kitchen table and followed Zeus to the door. A quick peek outside revealed uniformed police.

She slid back the dead bolt and let them in.

"Are you Jillienne Kidd?"

"Yes."

"I'm going to have to ask you to come with me to the station, please."

Jil looked at the officer's weathered face, his furrowed brow, and the tight set to his jaw. "What's this about?"

"We'll discuss it at the police station."

Jil stood firm. "According to the law, I have the right to know why I am being questioned, particularly if I am to be detained."

The officer nodded once. "You're a person of interest in the death of your foster mother, Elise Fitzgerald."

Jil felt her heart squeeze—too tight—and all the air rushed out of her lungs. "I didn't kill Elise!"

"You'll have to come with us, please."

Zeus whined.

"I need to make a phone call, please. Someone will have to come look after the dog."

The officer handed her his own phone. "On speaker only."

If Padraig had been here, of course she would have called him. And in the midst of the chaos, something clicked in her brain. Why the hell wasn't Padraig here? This timing wasn't just shite; it was convenient.

He was keeping something from her. Seemed to be a theme lately.

She took a deep breath and dialed the only other person she could imagine might come for her.

The line clicked. "Hello?" The sound of her crisp, clear voice sent a shiver from Jil's ear to her arm.

"Jess, it's me," she said. Before Jess could say another word, she rushed on. "I don't have time to talk, because the police are in the foyer."

"The police?" Jess's voice rose in concern.

Jil felt a rush of gratitude that she hadn't hung up as soon as she'd heard her voice. "They're taking me in to the station."

"Why? And which one?"

"Oxford Street..?" Jil looked at the officer for confirmation. He nodded. "Did you catch that?"

"Yes, I did." She was using her principal's voice, and Jil felt a surge of hope.

"Can you please come to Elise's and let Zeus out if I'm not back? I'll leave the door open. You're the only one he'll let in the house."

"Yes. I will be there."

Jil handed the phone back to the officer and followed him out to the car, remembering at the last minute to leave the key inside where Jess would find it.

"On guard," she told Zeus.

❖

"Laine St.Clair, homicide." The slender detective with the crisp white blouse and large belt buckle set her files on the table between them and hovered over the table. Jil sat with her hands folded on the tabletop and met her gaze.

Her dark red hair spilled to her shoulders in loose ringlets, and light hazel eyes followed Jil's every move.

"We have reason to believe your foster mother, Elise Fitzgerald, may not have died of natural causes."

"Could you be more specific, please? And how did you come to suspect this?" Karrie wouldn't have said anything. Which only left Nic.

Laine raised her eyebrows. "I'll ask the questions."

"Fine. Ask away."

"You don't seem surprised to hear this. Did you know?"

Jil thought about lying, but what would that accomplish? "I was told the results were inconclusive."

"No evidence, in other words."

"That's what I assumed."

"So you inquired about the tox screen results? To make sure you had covered your tracks? To be certain the ME didn't find anything?"

"What do you mean? If I'd killed her, why would I inquire about her tox screen? Don't you think that's a little stupid on the part of a murderer?"

"Well, I don't know. It seems pretty suspicious to me already. You're the primary beneficiary of millions—*millions*—of dollars, you're not actually a blood relation, and you were the last person to see Mrs. Fitzgerald alive. Now, you're admitting that you knew she was murdered. Why wouldn't you report it?"

"To whom?"

"To the police—who do you think?"

"And how would you suggest I do that? Elise's body had already been taken to the funeral home, prepared for burial by the time I got to see her. The ME had examined her and found that she'd died of natural causes."

"And?"

"And I'm not a doctor," Jil said. "I had no proof. When I brought the robbery of our house to the attention of the police, I practically had to pin Detective Fraser to the floor to get him to take my report. How do you think they would have reacted if I'd said I had a hunch Elise had been poisoned? The ME admitted he'd found some irregularities but nothing conclusive. Did you want me to ask them to run more tests? They would have said 'thank you very much—we'll get back to you' and never called me."

"Maybe they would have suspected you of murdering her. Maybe you did murder her. Maybe that's why you didn't say anything—"

"Or maybe I'm a PI who's doing a better job of investigating a theft, and some detective's got his nose out of joint. Who reopened Elise's file, anyway? What reason was given?"

"I'm not at liberty to discuss that, Ms. Kidd."

"See, this is why I flipped the bird at becoming a police officer. I can get things done without yards of red tape and city politics always in my way."

Detective St. Clair leaned over farther. "I'd be very careful about my next move," she said in a low voice.

Jil knew she was treading through dangerous territory here, provoking the officer who could detain her, but the whole situation made her so angry she could barely speak. No help from the police from Day One, and now they were actively getting in her way—accusing *her* of murdering Elise?

"Are you going to arrest me?" Jil leaned in, until she could smell the detective's light vanilla perfume and the faint after-scent of her cucumber deodorant. "Because if not, I have things to do."

"Such as?"

"Such as live my private life as a private citizen."

Detective St. Clair stood up straight, then fixed Jil with a careful stare. "We're getting an exhumation order for Mrs. Fitzgerald's body."

"Exhumation?" Jil echoed. "She's not buried yet. She's at the mausoleum at Beechgrove cemetery."

"We need an order to unseal the casket," she said. Almost immediately, she straightened up again and regained her detachment.

But for a moment, she'd dropped her guard. For a moment, she'd treated Jil like an equal. And from that, Jil knew—as much as she might have wanted to pin this on her and solve her case—she didn't really suspect Jil had killed Elise.

"Can you provide an alibi?" Her tone was frank, almost gentle.

Of course she could. She'd been in bed with Jess when she got the call about Elise. But she could hardly say that out loud. Jess couldn't even have dinner with her in public, let alone make a public statement about sleeping with her.

"No."

St. Clair sighed. "Now's not the time to hold back, Ms. Kidd."

"Thanks. I'll take my chances. Get some evidence and I'll come with you willingly. But it seems like all you have at the moment is suspicion, otherwise I'd be arrested. Am I right?"

She took St. Clair's icy silence as a reply.

Jil stood up and dropped her card on the table as she left. "When you open that casket, I plan to be there. And if you have any questions in the future, call me and ask me to come in. I don't need any more officers at my door, treating me like a criminal."

As soon as she got to the car, she called Nic Fraser. Bastard owed her an explanation. But of course he didn't answer.

Chapter Twenty-eight

Jil got home a little after midnight.

Zeus trotted to greet her, bunting her arm with his giant head.

"Hi, buddy. How's it going?"

A light switched on in the living room, and Jil followed the light to find Jess curled up on the couch.

"Hi." Jil blinked as her eyes adjusted from the darkness of the hallway.

"Hey." Jess sat up and ran a hand through her hair. "I tried to wait up for you, but I guess I fell asleep."

Zeus settled back down at the foot of the couch, by Jess's feet, where, judging by the size of the dent in the cushion, he'd obviously been lying for several hours.

"Thank you for coming. I didn't know who else to call, with Padraig being away and everything." Jil bent to undo her boots and slipped them off. Her feet protested the long day.

"He's still gone?" Jess sounded surprised.

"Yeah."

"When's he coming home?"

"I don't know. Hopefully, this week."

A silence fell between them that lasted a few beats too long. How quickly people fell out of that intimate space. Not long ago, they'd had their own shorthand, their own codes and language of touch and movement. Now, they had awkward silence—worse than a first date, because they'd already reached that first kiss and had drawn back, afraid.

"Did he eat?" Jil asked, for something to say. Of course she knew Jess had taken excellent care of him.

"Yes. Sorry I couldn't take him for a walk." Jess sighed and sat up awkwardly.

Instinctively, Jil reached out and helped her, noticing the awkward way she propped her feet up on the coffee table. Stiff.

She sat on the couch beside her and looked at her—really looked. "What's happening?"

"We'll talk another time," Jess said quietly. "You don't need the details right now."

Jil touched Jess's cheek softly. She didn't pull away, so Jil trailed her fingers along Jess's jawline and cupped her chin gently in her hand. "Whatever it is, I want to know."

Jess closed her eyes, pressing her cheek lightly into Jil's palm. A tear hovered on the end of her eyelash.

"So I take it you're not going to be arrested?" she said, her eyes still closed.

"No." Jil looked down.

"What is it?" Jess's tone turned concerned. "They can't seriously think you did it?"

She attempted a smile. "I doubt it'll stick. Seeing as I obviously didn't kill her."

"Well, of course you didn't. You were with me…" Jess's voice trailed off. She exhaled slowly. "Which you didn't tell them."

Jil shook her head. "I'm handling it."

They fell into silence again.

"I was waiting for you at the coffee shop when I got your text," Jess said.

"I know."

"You do?"

"I saw you."

Jess stared at her incredulously. "You were there? And then—you left?"

Jil looked down at her hands. "Yeah."

"Why?"

It seemed silly now, with Jess just inches away from her, to think of telling her how distant she'd felt. How far removed she felt now that she wasn't part of Jess's day-to-day life. Jess had been so omnipresent, so powerful in her own domain. Outside, things had changed.

"When that other man came in and started talking to you…"

Jess frowned. "Mr. Kelsey?"

"Sure. Whoever…"

"That's when you left? I don't understand."

Jil sighed. "Neither do I, really, Jess. I'm just worried…" She exhaled deeply and tried to think of a way to express her doubts, which now seemed so petulant. "Sometimes…I just worry that we're never going to be able to have a relationship that doesn't involve looking over our shoulders to make sure nobody's watching. And then, when we are together, I forget about how terrible it makes me feel when we're apart. Until we're apart too long."

Jess drew her knees up to her chest and met Jil's eyes. "When we're apart, you think about how easy it would be to move on to another woman who wasn't so complicated? Someone who'd go to the Pride parade with you and give out candy from a float?" Her voice held an edge that Jil couldn't quite place.

Jil sighed. "I don't expect you to change who you are, Jess."

"No? I get the impression that you'd like to."

Jil felt her insides heat up again, and she took a deep breath to remind herself to take things slowly. One step at a time. Rome wasn't built in a day, and all that. "I just can't see our way clearly to the future, when I can't count on you to be there for me."

"Like today?" Jess returned. She sounded a little incredulous; annoyed, maybe.

Jil looked up. "No. Like at Elise's funeral." Her voice cracked. She hadn't meant for that to happen. She thought she had tighter control over her emotions.

Jess's face softened. "I wanted to go with you," she whispered. "I told you I wanted to go."

Jil swallowed hard. She would not cry. "And that's exactly what I mean. You wanted to be there. I wanted you to be there. But you were at school and I was there alone."

"I thought about you all day. I wondered if I could pretend to be sick so I could be there, but being a Catholic funeral, someone was bound to see me, and I'd be caught in a lie. I thought of claiming to know Elise, but then if someone saw you there and me there…well, people already talk, you know. I think the stress of this double life is really the reason I'm off work right now."

"Wait, what do you mean? You're on leave?"

"Disability." Jess almost choked getting the word out.

Jil took both her hands. "Why didn't you call me?"

Jess looked away. "I didn't know what to say. Nothing had changed. And I knew this situation was impossible for you. At first, I tried to get back to being a leader, and…" She took a shaky breath. "But going down that road meant I couldn't have any more indiscretions."

"I don't want to be an indiscretion, Jess. I want—"

"I know," Jess said softly. "I want that too. It's just—it's not easy saying good-bye to my whole life."

"Of course it isn't. And that's not what I'd expect."

Jess bit her lip. "Being apart from you was hard, but also, eye-opening. I saw clearly what I really wanted from my life. And I know being a lesbian isn't something that's going to change for me. It's part of who I am. And I like it…"

"Were you seeing someone else?" Jil knew she didn't have the right to ask, but the thought of Jess sleeping with another woman made her a little sick, and she had to know.

Jess folded her hand over Jil's and squeezed softly. "No. It's better with someone you love."

The warmth from her fingers and the light, gentle pressure sent a tingle of energy through Jil's hands and left her body buzzing lightly. "Do you?" she wondered aloud.

"What?"

The words stuck on their way out of her mouth. She couldn't say them without tears welling in her eyes. "Still love me?"

Jess stared at her. "Of course I still love you," she said quietly. "Why do you think I tried so hard to get over you?"

Her words echoed off the walls in tiny waves that penetrated Jil's ears over and over in a sweet buzz.

Jess took her face in both hands and kissed her, long and slow.

She reached back, circling Jess's waist with her hands and pulling her in closer, tighter.

"I just want to know one thing," Jess said.

"Okay."

"You've slept with other women, so...I'm just wondering...do you sometimes wish it was easier?"

"Easier?" Jil thought of Sian's lithe dexterity. Her stamina. The way her athletic body held her upward and the strength in her grasp. It had certainly been more acrobatic. But easier? She hesitated.

Jess circled Jil's nipple with one finger. "What?"

"I kind of like taking it slow."

"Do you?" Jess's voice trembled a little. "You don't find it...I don't know...tedious or something?"

Jil thought about it. She'd had a lot of sex in her life, but nothing as intense as with Jess. Nothing that pulled everything out of her like this and still, somehow, left her wanting more. "No." She kissed the top of Jess's head. "I like it."

"Even if we don't do it as often?" Jess whispered onto her neck.

Jil grinned, and Jess tweaked her nipple. "Yeah. I'd much rather make love to you than anyone else."

Jess's hand slid down Jil's body, over her hip, then turned so their mouths could meet. They kissed, searching each other out, reconnecting. Jess's arms encircled her, and she kissed her back more deeply, cupping the back of her head.

A jolt shot through her body—the same electric heat that had jolted her the first time their skin had accidentally met. She felt it buzzing through her fingers and toes, behind her ears and deep between her legs.

Jess pushed her onto her back and leaned over her, kissing her mouth hard and working her nipples until Jil gasped. Jess's mouth moved down to her already aching nipples, sucking one, then the other into her hot mouth while her hand traveled down, pushing Jil's thighs apart.

When Jess's finger made contact with her clit, Jil arched up.

Jess kissed her mouth again, stroking her gently while waves of heat and dizziness washed over Jil like the ocean pounding the unsuspecting sand.

Jess pulled away, kissing down Jil's neck, across her collarbone and breasts, then down the faint line between her abs to the crest of her pubic bone.

"No," Jil whispered. "I will seriously die."

Jess kissed her mouth. "I'll be gentle. Promise."

She kissed a line down again, and her hot tongue grazed Jil's most sensitive spots, igniting them like fire rings that heated her core.

She couldn't stop the moan that welled up from her stomach and through her mouth. It felt so good to be fucked like this. Jess's fingers probed and sought her permission, and Jil relaxed, loving the feeling of Jess bending her fingers up and inside her, finding and stroking her G-spot as her tongue glided over her clit—gently, like she promised.

Her pace was slow—maddeningly slow—but exactly what Jil needed. Her orgasm built like red-hot coals, drawing energy from every cell in her body. An earthquake that started deep inside and cracked her body in every direction.

Her hips rocked on their own and she moaned louder. Like magic, Jess's tongue pressed harder. Pleasure surged through her, tightening her muscles and making them grip Jess's fingers in their own sweet rhythm. "God, yes."

She looked down and saw the flush of Jess's face, the curl of hair that had dampened on her forehead. Jess let out a soft moan— pleasure at seeing her orgasm—and Jil surged to the top. The waves crested between her legs.

Jess stopped licking her, but kept her fingers inside for a few more moments before drawing them out slowly. Jil shuddered.

Sex with Jess felt so amazing. She'd almost forgotten. Almost.

She pulled Jess up to lie beside her and cradled her in the crook of her arm. Jess's eyes were dark with desire, and Jil took her time touching every inch of her body with featherlight strokes of her fingertips.

Jess began to shiver, and Jil pulled the white fleece blanket from the bottom of the bed to lay over her. "I love you," Jess whispered.

"I do too." She did. She always had.

She ran her hands up and down Jess's thighs, warming her and relaxing her muscles at the same time.

"It's..."

"What?" Jil kept her hand on Jess's hip, gently working her fingers into her tense butt muscles. "You don't want to...?"

"Oh, I want to." Jess took Jil's hand and moved it so she could feel the slickness between her thighs.

Jil chuckled. "Yep, I can see that."

"But..."

"Don't worry," Jil whispered into her ear, echoing Jess's own promise. "I'll be gentle."

She turned Jess away from her so they were spooning, then pulled Jess's top leg over her own, exposing her flesh.

"I'm afraid," Jess said. "I don't want to stop, but I've been so sore for the past few weeks, and the last time I tried..." she trailed off, seeming embarrassed.

"The last time?" Jil prompted her.

"My hips locked open and—it just really hurt."

"Okay." Jil stroked her face, and hair. Her heart clenched when she saw Jess's tears on her fingertips. "Baby, it's going to be okay."

"Yeah." Jess sniffed. "I know." Her voice wavered. "I'm just afraid of where it's heading. What's happening to me."

Jil kissed the top of her head. "It's a setback, I know, but maybe that's all it is. You've had flare-ups before, right?"

Jess pulled Jil's arms tighter around her waist, and Jil enfolded her gently.

"Tighter," Jess whispered.

Jil squeezed tighter, locking Jess in her grip until her biceps ached.

"Thank you."

They lay like that for a while, Jess's heart beating quickly under Jil's forearm. It slowed little by little, and as Jess shifted in her arms, Jil eased her grip, aware of Jess's breasts under her hands.

"It's okay," Jess said. "I like it."

Jil pressed her palms into Jess's nipples, and Jess exhaled deeply, arching back.

Jil felt a fresh surge of heat radiating from Jess's body. "Just tell me what you want, and I'll do it."

Jess leaned into her arms, guiding Jil's lower hand back between her legs. "Just make me come. Please."

"I can do that."

Jil took her time, caressing Jess's skin across her neck and stomach, kissing her earlobe and the edge of her hairline. She took the weight of Jess's body, draped across her own, careful not to let Jess's hips open too wide.

Listening carefully to the sounds of her breaths and moans, she found a gentle, steady rhythm. Jess's clit expanded under her fingers and she stroked along the shaft, drawing louder sounds from Jess's mouth. Her hand got slicker as Jess got wetter, and within seconds, Jess's clit pulsed pink and ripe.

Suddenly, Jess's thighs shuddered and Jil stopped.

"Take a break?" she asked.

"Just for a sec."

Jil made lazy circles on Jess's inner thighs, squeezing her breast with her free hand. Jess turned to kiss her, and Jil bit her lower lip gently as she rolled Jess's nipple between her fingers.

"You okay?" Jil whispered when she pulled away.

"So good," Jess whispered back.

Jil massaged her thighs, her hips, until Jess's pelvis rested, relaxed, against her again. "Let me know."

Jess kissed her again, her eyes rolling back as Jil squeezed her nipple.

"It could take a while."

"Luckily, I have nowhere else to be." Jil brushed Jess's lip with her thumb and kissed her softly.

"Thank God for that." She sighed and guided Jil's hand back between her legs.

Jil started again, this time taking in wider circles. Jess's weight on her pushed her down into the bed, but she'd never felt so solid— so secure. She held her, stroking her like a delicate instrument.

Jess's breathing changed again, a shallow, edgy panting, and Jil eased up.

"Still okay?" she said.

"God, yes."

But as Jess started to climb, a muscle in her butt clenched. Jil felt the movement on her thigh before Jess gasped in pain. She wrapped her legs around Jess's thighs, holding her until the spasm passed, then let Jess resume the way she wanted to.

Jess rested her hand lightly over Jil's and guided her hand, pulling up and pressing down, playing herself to the crest.

CHAPTER TWENTY-NINE

Jess turned on the kettle as Jil put the bread in the toaster.

"It's weird to have you waking up with me in this house."

Jess shrugged. "Two people, three houses to watch. I guess equal time in each is logical, right?"

Jil laughed. "Yours is getting the short end of the stick then."

Jess reached to take down the teapot and loose-leaf tea.

"See? Making yourself at home already."

"I feel sympatico with Elise," Jess said. "I would have liked to meet her."

"Me too." Jil tried to smile but found tears clouding her eyes.

Jess put her arms around Jil's neck, kissing the top of her head lightly.

"It's okay to miss her. You don't have to pretend it's easy being orphaned."

Jil snorted. "Twice!"

"That's right," Jess said, as if the thought had just occurred to her. "You're far too young for that."

Jil hugged her back, expecting to hate feeling like she needed Jess to hold her, but finding she didn't mind. It didn't make her feel weaker.

"I don't know why it bothers me so much. It's not like she owed me anything. It's not like she was my real mother. If she didn't love me, if I was a convenience to her—a front—what difference does it make? She clothed me, fed me, made sure I got my education..." She broke off. This road was rough with emotional potholes.

"Of course it matters," Jess said softly.

Jil looked up at her.

"And of course she loved you. How could she not?"

Jil breathed out through rounded lips.

"Sometimes, a person's past life is complicated. Sometimes, people make a real mess of things, Jil, and wiping the slate clean and starting over again is difficult, if not impossible. But that doesn't mean they can't love someone in their future. It just means they have to make compromises. Sometimes very difficult compromises."

"Are you talking about Elise or you?" She gave her a small smile.

Jess ran her fingers through Jil's hair and kissed her cheek. "Both."

"I missed you so much," Jil whispered. She linked her fingers through Jess's.

"I did too."

"Promise me we're not going to do that again. No matter what happens between us—what problems come up—we're going to have to find a way to talk them out. Because losing you a second time isn't possible for me. I wouldn't survive without you again. Hell, I don't even want you to go home at night."

Jess went to grab the boiling kettle and poured the water into the teapot. "My house is dragging me down anyway. I've been considering making a switch."

Jil wiped her eyes on the sleeve of her flannel pajamas. "Really?"

As she brought the teapot to the table, Jess smiled. "Yeah. I think it's time for a few changes."

Jil's phone pinged and she picked it up. A text from Morgan—the results of the student roster at the university had finally come in. A thrill of anticipation surged through her body. She sprang up to grab her laptop and opened the list Morgan had sent to her.

"What's up?"

"Morgan's sent me Elise's student list. I'm about to track an art thief."

Over five hundred names and faces, but she'd know her when she saw her. There. Four up from the bottom on the fifth page.

"There she is," Jil whispered.

Jess looked over her shoulder. She took in a sharp breath. "That's the artist I met at the Cracked Palette. Her name is Mila."

❖

"So you're going to go in first, talk with her for a minute, then I'm going to join you, okay?"

Jess pursed her lips. "Do you think she'll run?"

"She might. But I can see the street from the bathroom window. I might even have time to get a license plate or something."

"I'm not that keen on her knowing where I live."

"Of course not." Jil grinned. "I've booked a hotel room for the occasion."

At eight on the dot, a knock sounded on the hotel room door. Jil tiptoed into the bathroom and closed the door, holding her breath as Jess went to answer.

"Thanks for coming," Jess said.

"Interesting home you have." Flirtation mixed with irony in Mila's voice.

What is her game, exactly?

"I'm not sure I'm ready for that step yet." Was Jess flirting back? Maybe Jil should have given her more credit.

"But you're ready to meet me alone in a hotel room?"

Jil opened the door. "Not exactly alone," she said quietly. She took in Mila's long bouncy curls, her delicate nose. Without her strawberry blond wig, Jil probably wouldn't have recognized her. She was a talented chameleon.

Mila's eyes flashed. "I see." She turned toward the door and reached it in two steps.

"I will find you again," Jil called. "And I only want to talk. I'm not interested in having you arrested. Yet."

Mila let her hands fall to her sides, the fight seeming to have gone out of her. "I guess I knew you'd find me eventually. Maybe

I'm even a little glad about it. I didn't like this whole business. Elise was a good person, and I cared about her."

"You cared about her? Are you kidding me? You robbed her. Stole my heirlooms. Pulled a Catwoman in our home." Jil's voice rose and she struggled to keep her anger in check.

Mila snorted, and Jil glared at her. "I didn't steal from her, Jil."

"Well, you stole from me. My ring?"

"I gave it back, didn't I?"

"You impersonated me."

"Sorry. But when I couldn't find the key to the safety deposit box, I had to try something else. I took it as a sign from the universe, being there when you found it. I should have known you'd keep it with you and it was useless to try to find it."

"So that's why you came back to the house after you came as Anastasia?"

"Yeah. I climbed in the window, but obviously I couldn't arm the security code and close the window, so…"

"So you left it open and hoped I'd think I'd done it myself."

"Exactly."

"And you still didn't find it."

Mila sat down on a wing chair. "No. But you did."

Jil shrugged. "I had home field advantage."

"I thought it would be easy to get into the bank. Who would have thought Elise would have an antique box inside a safety deposit box?"

Jil smirked. "It doesn't surprise me at all."

"It shouldn't surprise me either, really. Elise was savvy."

Jil shot her a look. "So you admit to breaking into my house to find the key, but still insist you didn't steal from her?"

"Yes."

"You were all alone in my house in the middle of the night and didn't think about taking *anything* else?"

Mila looked at her seriously. "I didn't steal from her, Jil. She let me in. If I'd wanted something, I could have taken it any time."

"So then why did you need to impersonate a St. Augustine aide?"

Mila exhaled. "Because I couldn't come and go from her house as myself."

Jil paused. Something about that made sense. "In case anyone was watching."

"Yes."

"Why bother to go to all that trouble?"

Mila tilted her head. "Because Elise was double-crossing a very dangerous man."

"Who?"

"Someone she knew from when she was younger. Someone who makes his living as an art thief and would love to get his hands on someone who could replicate paintings the way I can."

Jil exhaled. "I knew it."

"Who?" Jess asked.

Mila and Jil answered at the same time: "Duncan McLeod."

Mila sighed. "She found out about my ability to replicate during my first year of university. I was already a mature student by then, but I'd never been able to afford a proper art education—a theoretical one, anyway. But after I'd sold a few replicas, I decided to go—to see if I could make a living at selling my own work."

"But you went back to forging—um, replicating?" Jess asked.

"It pays so much better than trying to eke out a living as an artist. Elise never approved of what I did with my skills, but she understood my talent. She helped keep me safe. Specifically, she told me to stay away from Duncan MacLeod. To never let him find out my name."

"Because once he knew about your talents, he would exploit you," Jil guessed.

"Exactly."

"And that's why she went to the trouble of having you impersonate an aide."

"That's right. But I also needed practice if we were going to pull off this heist. Impersonating Anastasia was our final test before—"

Jil held up her hands. "Hang on. A heist? Elise wasn't a thief."
Anymore.

"No, but Duncan McLeod was. And to get back this painting he'd stolen, we had to beat him at his own game."

Jil frowned. Of course. Who better to double-cross a pro than the woman who used to be his partner in crime?

Mila smiled. "I think Duncan would have been a hell of a lot worse if Elise hadn't thwarted some of his more ambitious plans."

"But why did he stay here where he knew she was watching? Why not move to New York—or hell, to Paris?"

"I think…well, from what little she's said…"

Jil tipped her head back. "Of course," she whispered. "He was still in love with her."

Mila nodded.

"I'm sorry. Are you saying that Elise and Duncan MacLeod were lovers?" Jess's voice rose incredulously.

"They were young," Jil said softly. "He was probably a very charismatic young man, and she was talented and ambitious…"

"How long have you known about this?" Jess turned to her.

"Not too long. Elise never talked about her past life much. And she never mentioned him by name at all. She just said she'd been in love once with a boy who wasn't good for her. I didn't know what she meant by that. But it makes sense when I think back. I always thought she'd inherited her love of art because of her father's amazing collection, but of course romance had to have something to do with it."

"You'd have to have a pretty compelling reason to steal a Monet you could never sell," Mila said. "Although I have to say, it was pretty impressive."

"You saw it?" Jil asked.

Mila smirked. "Who do you think replicated it for you?"

"For me?"

"Of course. You inherited it, didn't you? Elise could hardly pass on the original, could she? And she knew you'd wonder where it went."

Jil shook her head. "I wish she'd just told me the truth ages ago."

"You weren't supposed to know. You were supposed to inherit the house, the legitimate artifacts, my replica to keep as a memory, and go on with your life. But apparently, you're too damn nosy for your own good."

"I'm sorry. You're angry with me? You don't think that's a little ironic?"

"You're making things very difficult, that's what I think. I was trying to do you a favor. A favor Elise asked me to do. And you just keep stepping on my toes."

Jess stepped between them. "Why don't we all take a breath? I think this is a lot for everyone to take in right now." Her cool hand on Jil's arm felt reassuring, comforting, but she couldn't let her guard down yet.

"Why did you need to get into the safety deposit box anyway?"

"Because I was looking for a recording Elise made of a conversation she had with Duncan. I knew that if the police found it they would put Duncan away, yes, but I was afraid they would also make the connection to me. I couldn't take the risk that she'd said something on that recording that could bring me down. I could be arrested for counterfeiting."

"I thought you replicated," Jil said sarcastically.

Mila shot her a look. "I have many talents, okay? I went to find it so I could destroy it."

"I don't understand why Elise would make that recording after everything she'd done to try to protect you."

Mila gave her a quizzical look. "She was protecting me from MacLeod, yes, but she was also protecting you. My guess is that she made that recording as a fallback in case he didn't keep his word."

"His word about what?"

"The deal they made. I don't know exactly what the deal was, but I do know she gave MacLeod that painting. That's why I had to make the replica—to replace it."

Jil took a deep breath. Her head hurt. She felt like she'd sidestepped into an alternate universe.

With a sigh, Mila crossed her legs. "Can I have a drink please, if we're going to continue this?"

Jess moved to the side bar. "Any requests?" she asked wryly.

"I'm not particular."

Jess grabbed a handful of minibar vodkas and a shaker.

"I'm sorry she never told you," Mila said over the sound of clacking ice.

"Told me what? That she educated young counterfeiters?"

"Not on purpose. I was an exception. I came with a dark side. She didn't create that."

"But she took advantage of it, right? She knew what you could do."

"She let me help her right a wrong. And that's what I'm doing."

"By robbing me of an original Monet?"

"For the last time, I didn't steal it. The painting was switched before Elise died. And I made you a perfectly acceptable replica. I still don't know how you figured out it wasn't hers."

"Wait a minute, you're insulted? Isn't that a little ironic?"

"I'm very good," Mila said defensively.

Jil squinted. "You are. And honestly, if it had been any other painting in the house, I wouldn't have noticed. But we have a history."

"Yeah, you knocked it over. An original Monet!"

Jil's stomach flipped. That painting was priceless. And yet, Elise had never even batted an eye about the damaged frame. Never told her to be more careful, or forbidden her to go near it. "Obviously, I didn't mean to. And there's one thing I still don't understand. Elise was married—for a long time—to another man. She should have been rid of MacLeod years ago."

"Sure. Except that he knew things about her past life that she didn't want anyone to know—including you. It seems to me that she felt it was better to know what he was up to than to let him disappear."

"And he blackmailed her right back, I think."

"More like they had a mutual understanding."

"So what changed?"

Jess cut in. "It seems to me that Duncan MacLeod is an impatient man. Maybe he got tired of having his wings clipped by Elise. She'd gone on and become a successful professor and artist. She inherited her father's collection. She had talent."

"And he was jealous?" Jil finished.

Mila shrugged. "Possibly. Or maybe he was too invested in his own line of work. Replicating really is an art, you know."

"So she got on with her life, and he didn't. And he resented her?"

"Maybe he did. Elise did say that as soon as she got sick, all bets were off."

"How?"

"That's when he planned the church heist."

Jess murmured something, and Jil turned to look at her. "What?"

"That was how he dealt with his grief over losing her," Jess said softly.

Mila looked at her. "I think so too."

Jess smoothed her pants across her thighs, pushing the palms of her hands into the muscles at her knees. Jil closed her hand over Jess's and squeezed. "You can go lie down if you want to."

"I'm okay." She smiled.

Mila sighed. "The sicker she got, the more brazen he got. Almost like he kept daring her to get better and stop him."

Jil sat on the chaise at the end of the bed, her stomach clenching. "The church studio tour. That's what this is about, isn't it?"

"Yes. The Madonna. It had started to show signs of disintegration, so this tour would be the last time they'd agree to open the glass to display it for art viewers. Elise knew it would be a temptation for him, and sure enough, she found out he had a plan. That's when she decided she had to take action. She had to beat him at his own game."

"So she came to you for help making a replica of the Madonna?" Jil said. "That's what you were doing at her house?"

"She couldn't do it herself in the time she had left. She could help me, observe and critique, but she couldn't do the work. So I did it. I studied the painting behind the glass. For hours, I'd sit there in the church, pretending to pray. I'm sure the priest thought I was considering taking vows or something."

Jess frowned. "The Madonna at St. Patrick's? I never heard about that theft."

"Nope. It's because nobody ever reported it. The church doesn't even know it was stolen."

"How is that possible?"

"I'm telling you, MacLeod was organized. He committed the theft in broad daylight. It took one minute and ten seconds. The last day of the tour, after everything fell quiet."

"You timed it?"

Mila grinned. "It was pretty amazing to watch. Especially knowing he had no idea."

"No idea about what?" Jess asked.

"That we'd already stolen it."

Jil sat on the bed. "Of course. You switched it on the first night."

"We did. There are two perfect times to steal a painting: one, when the place is packed. The second, when the place is deserted. We knew he'd go for the deserted option, so we had to beat him. On the last night of the tour, MacLeod pulled his heist. He stole what they thought was the original Madonna—"

"But was actually your replica," Jess finished.

"Exactly." Mila grinned. "We watched them load the van and take off, then we bustled in with the original."

"I don't understand why she'd go to all this trouble," Jess said. "Why not just go to the police if she knew he'd planned this robbery?"

Mila just looked at Jil.

"She couldn't," Jil said. "This was her final good-bye to him. One last dance."

She remembered something she'd heard on the recording Elise had made of her conversation with MacLeod. "He thought she'd switched the paintings after he'd stolen it."

Mila's eyes crinkled. "But he stole the fake in the first place. I don't think he's ever figured it out."

"No. But if he does…"

Mila's face sobered. "I know. If he does, I'm in trouble. Right now he thinks Elise hired some team of thieves to switch the paintings at the dock. If he finds out we carried it off between us right under his nose…"

"You'd be invaluable to him with your dual skill set," Jil said sardonically.

"Hey, I might have a few skills in that area, but I don't use them often. Occasionally, I liberate paintings from their unrightful owners to their rightful ones. But I don't want that to be my life. Especially after Elise has gone to the trouble of trying to keep me away from the guy."

"He can't force you," Jil said.

Jess snorted. "I'm sure he has many persuasive techniques. Better to keep her safe."

"Don't worry," Mila said. "Nic's taking care of that."

"Nic Fraser? Now why doesn't that surprise me?"

CHAPTER THIRTY

Jil arrived at Beechgrove cemetery and followed the winding narrow path, originally built for horse and buggy, through the old part of the graveyard where headstones had been washed out and tilted by years of harsh weather and erosion.

She wondered, for a moment, what the cemetery would look like one hundred years from now—if cemeteries would still be used at all.

Two police cruisers, lights off, stood by the wide doors to the mausoleum. She noticed the coroner's vehicle and two black town cars belonging to the funeral home. She parked at the end and got out.

Karrie greeted her at the door. "Thank God you're early. They wanted to open it already without you, but I've been stalling," she murmured.

"Why are they all here already?"

"Detective St. Clair called, asking if we could meet half an hour earlier, and I agreed. I didn't realize she wasn't going to call you."

Jil followed her down the dark corridor and joined the company gathered around the casket. She noticed Detective St. Clair standing next to Detective Fraser and three uniformed officers. The ME, his face hidden behind a mask, stood waiting in his isolation robe and gloves. Jil recognized Karrie's eyes behind the mask.

"Your dad?" she asked.

Karrie nodded.

She pointedly ignored Fraser and stood next to Karrie, glowering at him when he attempted eye contact.

When St. Clair gave the signal, two workers bearing tools began the process of unsealing the casket. "I'd like to warn you all that this might not be pretty," Karrie's father said through his mask. He laid out a metal tray on which he placed several syringes, containers, and swabs.

"Why doesn't he take the body back to the lab?" Jil whispered.

"He's looking for something specific," Karrie said. "He only needs a few samples. That's all they have a warrant for."

Several minutes passed before one of the workers announced, "Ready."

They lifted the lid, which creaked indignantly, as if protesting this interruption to Elise's final rest.

A dank smell filled the room as the mouth of the lid yawned open to reveal Elise's body. If she'd thought burying Elise the first time had been hard, it was nothing compared to this. Her breath caught in her throat and her knees buckled.

Karrie caught her arm. "You don't have to be here," she whispered.

Jil breathed out deliberately. She wouldn't leave Elise alone for people to prod at her.

"Excuse me, please," Detective Fraser muttered, weaving his way through the people assembled. Jil noticed his face had gone a peculiar shade of white, and he staggered a bit on his way to the door.

Apparently, this exhumation wasn't any easier on Nic.

Outside, a car started, and Detective Fraser drove off. She hoped he hadn't puked in the bushes on his way out. Her own stomach felt queasy enough already.

Jil studiously avoided looking at Elise's face—afraid it might show signs of decay, or worse, be exactly the same. She looked instead at her scarf, her jacket, remembering the day she'd brought all this to Karrie.

Her gaze fell on her lapel, to where the butterfly brooch should have been.

It was missing.

A wrenching feeling in her gut threw her off balance. Why would it be missing, when Elise had been so specific about having it buried with her? Who could have taken it, and when?

Something felt wrong here. This brooch was the key to something. She could feel it. Where the hell had it gone?

Her brain caught up to her gut. She recalled Nic's face—the haunted look in his eye, the fear in the lines that pulled down his mouth. He wasn't affected by the dead body. He had another reason for rushing out.

He knows something.

But by the time she got to the parking lot, his car had disappeared.

She drove straight to the precinct, imagining seventeen different ways to have this conversation with him.

The first scenario involved running him over with her car...

The second involved beating down his office door and strangling him with her bare hands.

But she didn't have time to consider any more because when she got there, his spot was empty.

Where the hell have you gone now?

Had he fled? Did he have a plan? If so, what was it?

With no other choice for now, she turned around and headed home.

❖

"Good news," Elise said. "Your funding's approved for September."

"What? Really? That's great!"

"It is."

"Enough for tuition and books?"

"And a little stipend for meals." Elise smiled and passed the roast chicken to Jil.

"Well, clearly, that's important." Jil helped herself to the chicken and potatoes, then reached for the carrots. She looked down at her plate.

By the time she started college, she'd be eighteen, and would age out of the system. She would need to find an apartment to live in and a job to pay her bills while she attended school. It would have been impossible to pay the tuition on top of all that, so having the funding was great, but she still worried about how she'd manage it all.

"Penny for them?" Elise said gently.

Jil looked up and attempted a smile. "Nothing. Just thinking about how much things are going to change."

"Really?"

"I'm going to be eighteen soon."

"I know. I've already ordered the cake."

Jil felt tears welling up in her eyes, and she swallowed hard. This was the deal. It had always been the deal. Elise had been great to her, but in a foster situation, kids didn't get to stay.

"Have you heard who you're getting when I age out?" she asked, trying to look up, but failing.

Elise dropped her fork. "What?"

"Well, you know—who's going to replace me?" She hated the idea of someone else sleeping in her bed, drinking out of her mug.

"Ah." Elise reached over and folded her hand over Jil's. "That's what you're thinking about."

Jil took a shaky breath. Good-byes had never been this hard for her. She looked up, forcing herself to smile.

"I'm not taking anyone else."

She blinked a few times. "No?"

"No. You're it for me. I don't want anyone else sleeping in your bed. It would be too awful. Besides, I hoped that you would be sleeping in your bed while you were in college."

"But I'm out of the system, Elise. They won't pay you anymore."

Elise shrugged. "Well. I guess I'll have to take the loss. They were lousy paychecks anyway. Never did cover the amount of dessert you eat."

Jil laughed, but then stopped short. "I can't ask you to keep me for free."

Elise met her eyes and smiled. Sadness hovered behind her eyes. "It's not a favor, Jil. It's a blessing for me. You've spared this old widow from loneliness and grief, and I don't know what I'd do without you now."

❖

"He's fucking with me, I swear to God."

Jess raised her eyebrows. "I don't disagree with you."

Jil exhaled a long breath.

"But..."

Jil turned to look at her. "What?"

"I think you've had a very long day. And I don't think there's anything else you're going to accomplish tonight. You're out of steam. So I'm running you a bath." Jess didn't wait for an answer. She just moved past Jil into the en suite of Elise's bedroom and turned on the faucet.

As the smell of strawberry wafted into the bedroom, Jil sighed and relented. She stripped off her clothes, leaving them in a pile on the floor. They probably needed a wash as badly as she did.

Jess met her in the doorway and glanced up and down, biting her lip.

Jil smiled, despite herself. "You don't want to get too close, believe me."

Jess winked. "Get in before I do something to delay you."

She got into the hot bath and sank below the surface, blocking out all sounds. The water hovered over her, a protective shield—a layer of calm.

When she broke the surface, Jess sat there with a bottle of wine and two glasses.

"Thanks." Jil accepted hers and took a long sip. The buzz ran through her whole body instantly and she could breathe. With the hot water, the safety of Jess's presence beside her, the heat of the wine—everything fell away.

When she finally got out, Jess handed her a towel and took away her glass. "C'mon. I want to take you to bed."

Jil nodded. "Let's go."

"We're going to consecrate your childhood bedroom?"

She snorted. "Believe me, it's been consecrated a few hundred times already."

"Seriously?"

"Oh, yeah. I was an early bloomer. But I'm not taking you there. It's not big enough for all the things I want to do to you."

"Agreed." Jess's touch lit her skin on fire. She let her towel fall and pulled Jess in again, backing her against the wall so she could kiss her mouth, her cheek, her neck—then ran her fingers along Jess's waist, pulling up her sweater so she could caress her bare back.

Her nipples were so hard they ached, and being pressed so close to Jess's sweet heat made her melt harder.

"Let's go." Jess's voice came out a little breathlessly. "Or we might not get there at all."

Jil pulled herself away, and her skin protested the sudden cold. She linked hands with Jess again and led her to the bed. At the edge of the bed, they stopped so she could pull Jess's sweater over her head, leaving her in her jeans and navy lace bra.

"You're gorgeous," Jil murmured, then kissed her again.

Jess clasped the back of her head and bit her lip as she kissed her.

"Wow, you're fast. Learn something in our time apart?" She searched her face. Had she slept with someone else?

"No, as a matter of fact, I learned it from you."

Jess pulled her down on the plush down duvet. For a moment, she got lost in the sweetness of the moment—of being close and safe, skin on skin, and faces so near, there was only a whisper between them.

"Don't ever leave me again," Jess said. "Or, if you're going to, do it permanently. Either way, I can't take the push and pull. It's too hard."

Jil kissed her cheek, a whisper on Jess's soft skin. "Agreed." She moved to her mouth, breaking away only to say, "You taste the same."

Jess's eyes met hers. "So do you."

Jess snaked her arms around Jil's torso, and caressed her bare breasts with open palms.

Jil sucked her breath in through her teeth as her nipples turned to stone.

Jess kissed her neck again, her breath hot and steamy on Jil's skin. "Do you want me to continue?" She pinched one nipple lightly and Jil arched into her hand.

"Yes," she managed through the surge. "Please."

Jil relaxed and Jess tweaked her nipple again, then ran her hands down her flat abs to the soft part of her stomach, right below her belly button.

Jess's hot hands massaging her bare breasts made it hard to breathe, let alone think. Jess's lips touched every part of her—neck, shoulders, arms—as she spoke, and her warm breath whispering over Jil's skin made her dizzy.

She leaned back into Jess's arms, and the phrase *sweet surrender* crossed her mind, before it was obliterated by a moan that escaped her.

"Next?" she said through the waves of pleasure that rushed from her nipples to her toes.

Jess used her superior positioning to explore Jil's body from her shoulders to her knees.

She traced a line around Jil's navel, making wider and wider circles...

"Christ." Jil turned her face into Jess's breast and captured a nipple through the dark lace bra.

Jess gasped in surprise. "Excuse me. This is about you."

Jil moaned as Jess's fingers traveled down farther still, parting her thighs...

She arched back into Jess's chest, watched Jess's fingers slipping in and out of her. Then she closed her eyes and let the orgasm take over.

CHAPTER THIRTY-ONE

The phone rang at seven thirty in the morning. Jil groped along the nightstand in her bedroom at Elise's until her fingers found the flat face of her phone.

She sat up as Karrie's voice reached her ear. "Jil, I'm sorry to call you so early."

"It's okay. What's wrong?"

"It seems like there's a never-ending parade of problems with this burial." She sounded scared, maybe like she'd been crying.

"What now?"

"I don't know whether I should call the police, but…"

"But what?"

"I don't think they'd believe me. They'd just think I made a mistake. But I thought you would. Believe me, I mean."

Jil raked the hair back from her face and blinked hard to clear the sleep from her eyes. She flung off the covers and reached for a robe. "Why don't you start at the beginning?" For a moment, she wondered if she should grab a notepad and pen—her current mental computing skills left a lot to be desired—but then decided that a strong cup of something would sharpen her wits and help her start her day at the same time.

"Okay." Karrie's voice dropped to a hushed whisper. "Every morning, I come in around seven o'clock. I have a lot to do lately because we've lost a few funeral directors, and they're a bit difficult to replace."

"So you're working long hours?"

"Yeah?"

"You're tired."

"Yeah. Wait. But that doesn't mean I'm not sure about what happened."

Jil took down the coffee canister and started filling the machine. Why didn't she do this at night so in the morning, she only had to hit the start button? She knew why—every morning, she told herself that tonight, she was going back home to her own place.

Only she didn't. She kept staying here.

"I'm here until seven thirty at night."

"So you work a twelve-and-a-half-hour day."

"Well, I break half an hour for lunch."

"That's still some workday, five days a week."

"Six, actually," Karrie said ruefully. "My husband and I are saving for a house."

Jil smiled.

"So every night before I leave, I lock my top drawer and put the key in the glass dish behind the pot by the door.

"Why?"

"Well, I'm not supposed to take it home with me."

Jil shook her head. Workplace politics had always baffled her. "Okay. So you have a top drawer in your office with a lock on it, but you're not supposed to take the key home. So you lock the drawer and leave the key inside your office, which you then also lock?"

"Yes."

"Do you take that key home?"

"Well, I'm not supposed to, but last night, for some reason, I did. I forgot to put it into the main box in the staff room. We keep them all together, you see, so that if one of us is away and another person has to take over, they have a key."

"There's no master key?"

"No. The building is a historic site. They've retained all the old character of the home, including the original handles and locks from the nineteen hundreds."

"Charming, but a bit impractical," Jil said.

Karrie sighed. "It is. Especially when a key goes missing."

Jil got tired of waiting for the coffee to fill the carafe, so she pulled the glass pot out and stuck her mug directly under the stream. "And has it? Gone missing?"

"No," Karrie said, "but someone was in my office last night."

"Who?"

"I have no idea. But they didn't use my key, because it was in my purse this morning when I came in."

"And how do you know?"

Karrie sighed. "This is why I haven't called the police."

"Why?"

"Because I have no proof. It's just that I always leave things in my drawers organized in a certain way—client envelopes alphabetized and filed by year in the bottom drawer, which is not locked, by the way, and the more valuable items in the top drawer. You know, like rings for burial and reminder notes from clients. Anything that could be confidential."

"And...?"

"So this morning, I went to retrieve a file from the bottom drawer, and I found Elise's misfiled—two spaces over from where it should have been."

"And it's not possible that you misfiled it yourself?"

Karrie sighed. "No. But even if it were, that doesn't explain why the top drawer was ransacked."

"Ransacked?"

"Yes. Everything had fallen out of order."

"Where was the key?"

"That's the strange part. I found it back in the glass dish behind the pot!"

"So, someone broke into your office, rearranged a file in your drawer, and ransacked your box of client items." She took a sip of coffee and felt it warm her from her stomach all the way to her toes. She took another sip and sighed. Bliss.

"I know it sounds ridiculous," Karrie said. "But someone was here."

"It doesn't sound ridiculous to me," Jil said. "Is it at all possible someone knew what he or she was looking for?"

"I do think I know, which is the other reason I called you."

"Okay."

"Remember yesterday, when you asked about the brooch?"

Jil set her mug down. "Yes."

"I lied to you."

"Why?"

"Because I had an obligation to Elise, who was my client. She made me promise not to reveal what I had done, especially to you, and I did. I promised. But now this is all a bit much for me, and I don't know what to do."

"What do you mean, Karrie? What did you do? Where is the brooch?"

"She made me swear to take it off her before the final burial. She said I had to make sure it was on her for the wake—that nobody removed it—and that as soon as the wake ended, I should take it off her and pop it into an envelope that she'd pre-addressed and stamped."

"And did you?"

"I did."

"Do you remember where you sent it?"

Karrie sighed. "That's the trouble. I wrote down the address, just in case I ever encountered a problem with her envelope and I had to try again. This morning, when I came in, that's what I found missing—my pink sticky note with the address on it."

"Do you remember the address?"

Karrie sighed. "No. It was a PO box."

"Do you remember for where?"

"I don't remember the number. But it was somewhere here in Rockford."

CHAPTER THIRTY-TWO

"Padraig's not back yet?" Jess sat on the side of the couch, squinting.

"No, and I can't reach him. It's making me paranoid."

Jess raised her eyebrows. "Not without reason."

"I feel like I'm suspecting everyone in my life, Jess. Everyone."

"Well, not everyone," she said softly.

Jess slipped off her lap and onto the couch. "And what do you think he's doing exactly?"

"I don't know. But on the recording, Elise asked Duncan how he managed to get the artifacts across the border. Why would she need to know that, unless she planned to do it?"

"But that doesn't mean Padraig is involved, does it?"

"Those two have been friends for their entire lives," Jil said. "For him to miss her funeral, then basically go off the grid, there has to be a damn good reason. What if he's involved in something he shouldn't be? What if he's in some sort of trouble? What if he's—I don't know—trafficking stolen goods or something?"

"It's almost impossible to sneak anything onto a plane these days, Jil. He'd have to have documents for all his checked luggage. Everything would be looked at upon arrival."

"Yes. I know. And I think that's what Duncan was trying to tell Elise. The day Padraig left for Ireland, I could barely have a conversation. But I do remember his car being full of stuff. I even joked with him about his insane amount of luggage."

"You said he was on the way to the airport?"

"Yes, but here's the weird thing. I've checked the flight records, and there was no flight at that time."

Jess frowned. "Maybe you got the time wrong."

"It's possible. That's been my problem this entire investigation. I haven't trusted myself to remember the key details."

"But you did some more digging."

"Of course. He left me a credit card to use for expenses during his trip, so I checked the records on it."

"What did you find?"

"The day he left, he drove to Nova Scotia. Then he got on a boat."

Jess breathed the bangs off her forehead and met Jil's eyes. Jil could tell by her expression that she wasn't wrong about this.

Jess pursed her lips. "Okay. Well…let's find out why."

"There's one more thing."

"What?"

Jil let Jess take her hands.

"He's the one who found her, Jess. He called me from her house. How did he know she was dead?"

When Jil got home, Fraser's car blocked the driveway. He paced along the front step, smoking a cigarette almost down to the filter.

He had come right to her front door.

Could that mean he was ripe for a confession? Why else would he seek her out?

He wanted to tell her everything—she knew it. And after the way he'd fucked with her life, she had no problems giving it right back. She knew exactly how to play him—gay PI attracted to a scruffy corrupt detective. She just had to give him an opportunity. He wanted to take it.

"Can I help you?" She slammed the door and headed toward him.

"Yeah." He dropped the cigarette and snubbed it out. "I think it's time we were honest with each other."

She stared at him. "You have to be fucking kidding me. Since when have you been honest with me? You've been playing a game with me since we met, Fraser, so if anyone's going to be called out on the carpet, it's you."

"Fine. I'll go first. Why didn't you tell me you'd found Mila?"

She fished her keys out of her pocket and opened the front door as he unwrapped a piece of spearmint gum and popped it in his mouth.

"Well, Nic, I didn't see the need to rub your nose in it. You doubting my PI skills and all."

"Or you purposely kept it from me because you knew what I would think."

She let him in and kicked off her shoes. "Or because you lied to me, kept me out of the loop, and chased your own agenda instead of figuring out the truth."

Zeus greeted them at the front door. He growled once at Nic, a little warning purr at the back of his throat, then shuffled off toward the kitchen.

"Do you know you could be charged with obstructing my investigation?" He spun her around and locked his eyes with hers. She felt a surprising jolt of heat and wrenched her arm away from him.

What the hell? She'd never been interested in a man—any man, but especially one as infuriating as Nic Fraser. This was supposed to be playacting.

"Tell me what she said to you."

Jil stared at him. "Why don't you ask her yourself?"

Fraser took a step toward her and pulled her close. She stared at him, inches from her face, his hot breath smelling of mint and cigarette smoke. "She won't return my calls."

She drew back an inch. "So how did you know I found her?"

He looked at her and refused to answer.

When their stare went on a beat too long, he cupped the back of her head in his hand and crushed his lips to hers. She let him kiss her for a minute, wrapped up tighter than she could have imagined in his strong arms. His full lips were surprisingly soft, and the stubble against her face felt foreign, but sure and solid and…masculine.

She pulled away. "What the hell are you doing?"

"I'm sorry." He took a step back. "You're with someone, right?"

"Hello!" She stared at him incredulously. "I'm gay, remember?"

"Really? You could have fooled me."

She glared. "You kissed *me*. I was just being polite."

He rubbed his hand over his lips and grinned wickedly. "If that was polite, I'd like to see you turned on."

She shoved him. "You're not the least bit worried about seducing someone involved in your investigation?" Her words doubled back at her, extra loud. "Take it from me, because I know from personal experience that it's a bad idea."

"Why do you say that?"

She skirted around him and headed into the kitchen. "Just trust me."

He made her angry enough to tackle him to the ground, but she made herself take a deep breath and go with the plan.

He followed her, and as they passed through the threshold to the kitchen, Zeus raised his head, then slumped back down.

"So are you going to tell me what you two talked about?"

"No." Jil left him at the table and stood at the counter, pouring a glass of wine. She gestured with the bottle, but Nic shook his head.

She smiled as she opened the cupboard and took down a small bottle of cognac some considerate neighbor had dropped off in lieu of Bundt cake.

Nic chuckled as she poured him a measure in a square glass and set it in front of him. "You know how I take my coffee and my booze. You're the perfect woman."

She raised her glass and made eye contact. "Except for one minor detail."

He cricked his mouth. "Well, I could get over that, if you could. Have you really...never..."

Jil surveyed him over the rim of her glass. "How personal do you want to get here, Nic?"

"I'm just curious." A faint pink tinge crept up his cheeks.

"Never met a lesbian?"

"Never one as attractive as you."

Jil tensed. "I'm sure you've crossed paths with many a young hot lezzie and have never even realized."

He stared at her again. "I guess nobody ever interested me before."

"I can't be switched, you know."

"Aw. Too bad. I was hoping to make you a vampire. What century do you think I'm from? I didn't mean I wanted to *convert* you..."

"Just bed me."

He took the final swallow of his drink. "The thought has crossed my mind."

The perfect opening. She downed her wine. "Fine. Let's do it."

His jaw dropped. "You're kidding me."

"Not at all. I've always wanted to get a little experimental."

He stared at her for a full ten seconds without saying anything.

How the hell did this work? *The same way it does with women, idiot.* Start with body contact. She slid her hand up his arm and rested it against his collarbone. "Well?"

He rubbed his fingers over his stubble. "Well, I'm game if you are. But don't you want to make up with your girlfriend?"

She ran her fingers through the lock of coarse brown hair that fell over his forehead. "How did you know I had a girlfriend?"

A shrug. "I knew there had to be someone you were trying to get away from. Nobody leaves their loft for their foster mother's house if they're not running away from a fight."

Okay, so maybe he wasn't that bad a detective. He'd figured out she was running away from Jess. But he obviously didn't know all the developments since then.

She topped up his glass. Seriously, she'd have to get him to talk fast before he got too drunk to speak, and she got too drunk to remember that this was just a ruse.

She led him through the living room to the couch. This felt safer. A bedroom would have been really dangerous.

He caught her arm and spun her into him, crushing her against his chest. "How much do you know?"

"Enough."

"How much?"

She reached up to loosen his tie, and he relaxed his grip enough to let her fingers work. "I have an idea. Why don't you answer my questions, and I'll give you a reward?" She undid his top five buttons and stepped back, pushing him onto the couch.

He made himself comfortable on the leather couch, bare chest showing through the gap in his shirt. "Do I get to choose what it is?"

She put a hand on her hip. "Within reason."

His lips twitched. "Fine. But I have some questions of my own."

"Fine," Jil said. "We're playing twenty questions striptease, and we both answer questions. Deal?"

"I've never played."

"Don't worry. You'll get the hang of it. I ask you presumptive questions, you answer and take your clothes off."

Nic rubbed his chin. "Fine. I'll play. But I get the first round of questions."

Jil rolled her eyes. "Fine." She'd get her turn soon enough.

"Where did you find Mila?" he asked.

She undid the zipper on her black sweater and took it off. "In a hotel room."

He paused for a moment. Not the answer he'd expected? "How did you lure her there?"

She took off one sock and threw it at him. "By pretending to be a client."

"Socks are one item."

"Of course they are." She peeled off the other one and dangled it in front of his face before chucking it next to the first one.

"What did she tell you?"

"I don't see the presumption in that question, Detective."

He sighed. "How much did she tell you about our relationship?"

"So you admit to having a relationship with her?"

"Sorry. You're in the hot seat right now. Which means you don't get to ask questions back."

"Quick learner." Jil stripped off her long-sleeved shirt, leaving only her camisole and jeans before she'd be in her underthings and nothing else.

He paused and she caught him staring at her breasts which popped out of her skintight cami. "Is that a red silk bra strap?"

"I'm sorry, is that a question?"

"No. I want to know how long you've suspected me." He paused for a moment, seeming to consider the lack of assumption. "I don't know how else to ask this," he finally admitted. "Why did you call the police when you suspected the painting was stolen? Why not just investigate it yourself?"

She fixed him with a stare that would break ice. Why had she called the police?

Because she didn't think surgeons should operate on their own kids? Because she didn't have the energy to look into a case involving her own life when she could barely keep that life together? Because she had been taught since kindergarten that in an emergency she should call 911 and wait for help?

Or did the reason run deeper than that? Did she want to be told she didn't have a case? That the house was safe and so was she?

She stripped off her jeans. "I don't know how to answer that."

His glance dropped to her red silk panties, and the tips of his cheeks turned pink.

Guessing his next objection, she took off her camisole. "That's for not answering your question. I just don't know the truthful answer, Nic."

"I understand."

"Thank you. Okay, next. And make it count." She hoped that by provoking him, he'd show his hand—and maybe, just maybe, save her from having to get naked by getting it wrong.

He sighed so deeply it bordered on a growl. "I've only got one more anyway, but it's the most important one."

"Shoot."

He looked her straight in the face. "When did you have time to take Elise's brooch off her jacket?"

CHAPTER THIRTY-THREE

Thank God. He got it wrong. So many thoughts flashed through her brain as she stood staring at him. How much would he be willing to admit, exactly?

"Sorry. You're off base there. I didn't do it."

"Then who the hell did?" His brow furrowed.

"I have no idea. But now I have some questions for you." She pulled him off the couch.

Jil sat in his spot on the couch in her matching red bra and panties, taking a small measure of satisfaction in the bulge she saw pressing through Nic's dark wash jeans. She'd never much cared if men found her attractive, but this man got under her skin. She was curious in a way she never expected: what would his body feel like on hers—his hands on her thighs.

The fact that he had been investigating Elise and colluding with Mila didn't seem to dim that strange attraction at all.

But maybe anger made her hot for all the wrong reasons.

He loosened his tie even more and cleared his throat.

"A little uncomfortable being on the stripping end, Nic?" She couldn't help the sharp edge to her tone.

He looked her up and down. "Not sure I would be throwing stones, sitting there in your scant underwear."

"Panties. Underwear are for adolescent boys."

"Oh, pardon me."

"Call them what you want. I intend to see you in yours as well." What was wrong with her? Hadn't she had enough opportunities as a teenager and college student? She'd known what she liked since she hit puberty—tits and ass. Not once had a penis and facial hair ever factored into her list of fantasy items.

His eyes flashed. "Fine. Go ahead with your first question."

She planned to hit him fast and hard. "When did you begin investigating Elise?"

He startled. "That's what you want to know? Wait—how did you know I was investigating her? She couldn't have told you."

"Because?"

He cleared his throat and grinned slyly. "Well, if you want to know that, you'll have to use a question."

"I have no objection to that. But you have to answer this one. And take off your shirt too."

"What? I'm taking off my tie."

"Shirt and tie are one item."

He chuckled and slipped his tie off his neck, then peeled off his shirt. "There. Feel better?"

"A little. Now you can answer my question too. And add in the part about why you lied to me and pretended never to have met her."

He sighed. "Elise came up on my radar a few years ago because of a complaint from a student at the university about one of her art restoration courses. I didn't tell you about it because believe it or not, police investigations are confidential, and the fact that we let her go without incident means that my talking about it is actually libelous."

She was surprised he knew the meaning of the word. "Okay." She frowned. "I don't see what's objectionable about restoring art."

Nic shrugged. "It's a bit of a gray area. Restoration can lead to falsely representing a piece as original—or even to outright forgery, depending on the artist, and his or her particular skill set."

"Right. So someone thought Elise was too good at restoration?"

"More that she taught techniques that could be used in more questionable circumstances."

Jil grinned. "That'll be one more item, please."

He glared at her. "That was hardly a question."

"Of course it was. You answered it, didn't you?"

He shot her a death stare, but removed his socks.

Jil thought for a moment. This next question had to count. Who would have reported Elise to the police? It didn't make sense that the informant had actually been a student. Only one person logically would want Elise out of the way—metaphorically, or literally. It was the perfect move in a lifelong game of chess.

"How long before you realized your informant was really Duncan MacLeod?"

Fraser's eyes narrowed. "That's a reach."

"Is it? Am I wrong?"

"No," he said through gritted teeth. "But the fact that you figured that out so fast just makes me feel like more of a moron."

"You didn't realize at the time?"

"No. And I just wish I'd known what sort of Pandora's box I had in front of me."

"Belt, please."

Fraser wrenched open the buckle and yanked his belt through the loops. "You're a—"

"Careful," she interrupted him. "Swearing can become a bad habit. And you wouldn't want to let a PI get you all riled up, would you?"

He shifted to his other foot, and Jil noted that the denim at his crotch was straining. He caught her looking. "Shut up."

"Oh, whatever. I'm flattered."

"You're having a great time, aren't you? Men are at a distinct disadvantage, seeing as our attraction is—obvious."

Jil smirked. "Back to my question. What did Duncan ask for in exchange for his information?"

Fraser exhaled and shook his head. For a long moment, Jil was afraid he wouldn't answer. "I'd hoped I wouldn't have to tell you this story."

"Is that why you lied to me about knowing Elise in the first place? I mean, that and your strict moral code when it comes to criminal confidentiality."

His jaw twitched.

"Don't worry. I won't ask you for any more clothes."

He sighed. "Yes. She had asked me to keep you out of the investigation in exchange for her full cooperation. And even if she hadn't, having met you, I didn't think the story of how I screwed up my investigation with your foster mother would've made me a good candidate in your mind to investigate your own theft."

She took a deep breath, trying to recount all the ways in which she'd suspected him. His own professional pride had never factored into her theories about why he'd lied to her. "I see. So you screwed up with Elise. How?"

"By believing MacLeod in the first place. He had compelling evidence—"

"Fabricated?" Jil guessed.

"Of course. But he had me believing he could blow the whistle on some big heist that had been planned at the museum with a collection borrowed from Germany. Turns out he was just keeping me busy while the work got done, and giving himself an airtight alibi. He'd been with me at the time." Fraser shook his head, a red tinge creeping up his neck. "By the time I figured out Elise was innocent and MacLeod had orchestrated the whole thing, a bunch of valuable items had been marched right out of the exhibit."

"In broad daylight?"

"Of course."

She frowned. "Why you? Why did he target you? Because you were new, or was there more to it?"

Fraser's eye twitched. "We have a...history."

"Because of your father?"

He blew air out through his nostrils. "You've been investigating me, I take it."

"Only a little." She smiled sweetly at him.

"Yes. Because of my father. Because MacLeod framed him for a heist during my time in the academy and I was stupid enough—or ballsy enough—to make a threat to him, telling him I'd fry his ass one day."

Jil shrugged. "Well, you sort of have."

"It took too long," Fraser spat. "And it wasn't a clean victory either."

"Did you recover the goods?"

"A few, when we got lucky and closed in on a handoff taking place at the docks, but the most valuable piece was never recovered."

"The Fabergé brooch. That's what you've been looking for this whole time? That's why you've been at the safety deposit box, trying to find Mila—you thought she might have stolen it?"

Fraser nodded. "It's the clincher. The piece I need to put MacLeod behind bars for the rest of his life. It's the piece that proves his involvement in the Toronto heist of 1990."

"And clears your father," Jil finished.

Fraser ducked his head. "I'm sorry. I just needed to see it for myself. I needed the proof that my father was the man I thought he was. That trying to clear his name has been worth all the sacrifices I've made—for my integrity and my job."

"And you couldn't just come out and ask me?"

"Ask you what? Could I have back the piece of stolen property Elise took to her grave?"

Jil shot him a look. "Well, apparently, she didn't take it to her grave."

"I didn't know that. I assumed that it had been sealed in the casket with her." He ran his hand through his hair.

"How did you know Elise had it?"

"When I arrested McLeod and found his coded records with no indication of that brooch going anywhere. He confessed it was the one thing he'd held on to. He wanted it as a gift."

Jil frowned. A gift?

Something on the recording nagged at her. *Pin it on yourself. Take it as my promise.* Of course, he'd given it to Elise. As proof of the pledge he'd made. And she'd worn it to her grave to remind him to keep his word.

"And you couldn't just say that? You had to get me charged on suspicion of *murder*?"

He exhaled loudly. "Murder is the only evidence compelling enough to get a body exhumed. I had to see for myself. I had to try to put him away and make the charges stick to him. I needed to hold him accountable for his actions. His crimes."

Jil stared at him in disbelief. "Do you have any idea—"

Fraser held out his hands. "Yes. Yes, I know. But listen. Please."

"To what? You're going to try to talk your way out of this? Do you have any idea what you've done?"

"I know," he shouted. "But you don't understand. Do you know how much of an advantage he has now that she's dead? He can rewrite all sorts of history. Elise could make all the deals with him that she wanted, but he has the upper hand because he's alive. He is a powerful and well connected man. He can make people say and do whatever he wants. Do you think he'd care about her memory if pinning his crimes on her could save himself? I know how it would have played out: Elise's name would have been splashed over the front of every newspaper in the city. They would have dug into her whole life, then yours by extension."

Jil sat down, her knees shaking. "You don't know it would have happened. You just cared about having your father's name cleared."

"Yes, that too. I admit it." Fraser took a seat beside her. "I'm sorry. I know how it looks."

"It looks like you're an asshole," she muttered. But the venom had gone out of her words.

"I knew the charge would never stick." Fraser touched her arm. "I risked something big, and I told myself I was doing it for you as well as me. I still believe that, but…I'm sorry."

She turned away from him. The memory of the coffin being cracked made bile rise up from her throat.

All for the sake of a fucking brooch.

A brooch that was now missing.

She stood up and walked to the door. "Go to hell."

CHAPTER THIRTY-FOUR

I can't." Jil tugged Gigi's hand and led her away from the door to Elise's forbidden library.

"Oh, c'mon, aren't you curious?" Gigi turned back toward the door. She never could resist temptation—one thing Jil normally loved about being with her, but which today she found mildly infuriating.

"Just one peek. Then we can go upstairs and listen to sappy music and make out." Gigi pulled Jil close and kissed her, slipping her tongue in to her mouth. "I was thinking today...you know..."

Jil's jaw dropped. "Today? Well, hello, let's skip the breaking-and-entering and go straight for the 'today.'"

"I just want to see what secrets she's got in there..."

"Gigi, they're secrets. That's why the door's closed." Jil thought of the glimpses she'd got into Elise's private world—the marble elephant in the corner of the room, beside the lush indoor trees...

"Just one look, then we'll go."

Elise had left an hour ago for the market and would be home any time now.

Jil felt her nipples harden as Gigi brushed one breast with the back of her hand. God, that girl knew how to persuade anyone.

"Just one peek. That's it." Jil reached into the mouth of the jade fish with gold leaf gills and picked out an ornate silver key.

"Seriously?" Gigi stared at her. "Why bother to lock it if you know where the key is?"

"It's for other people. She's supposed to be able to trust me."

"Okay. I swear to forget."

"And don't tell!" Jil fit the key into the lock and felt the bolt shift back. Her heart beat faster as she pushed the door open, Gigi right behind her.

"Wow." Gigi took in the spiral staircase to the loft, and the two-story shelves of books. "What does someone do with all these? She can't have read them all!"

"Maybe eighty percent." Jil twirled around slowly and brushed her hand over Elise's giant mahogany desk. She reached out to touch a globe, the countries on which were made of semi-precious stones. When she pushed it, it twirled on its delicate silver axes. Mesmerizing.

"Look at this painting." Gigi had stopped in front of the fireplace and stood gaping. "What is it? Paris?"

"I think so."

"Wow. She sure likes her art."

Jil fixed her with a withering look. "You know what she does for a living, right?"

"Yeah, but still."

Jil smiled. "Elise thinks that the main purpose of life is happiness. She likes these things, so she surrounds herself with them."

"What about you?"

"Yeah, she likes me too. Probably would like me less if she found me snooping in her library."

"We're not snooping. We're art appreciating."

A blown glass ring holder glinted from the side of the mahogany desk, and Jil reached out to pluck off Elise's emerald ring. She slipped it onto her finger and admired the glimmering stone in the soft light from the stained glass lamps.

"Getting married?" Gigi said.

Jil stuck out her tongue. "Not unless they change the law."

She glanced in the mirror. In the distorted reflection, it looked like the side of the staircase had tilted. Or was it a crack in the paneling...?

She was about to turn around and examine it when the front door opened.

They both froze.

"Quick!" Jil shoved Gigi toward the library door.

"C'mon!" Gigi pulled her.

Jil scampered out after her, and with trembling hands, managed to lock the door.

Gigi ducked into the main hall bathroom as Jil slipped the key back into the fish mouth just before Elise passed by, carrying canvas bags of groceries.

"Let me help you." Jil rushed forward to grab a bag.

"Thank you." Sweat dotted Elise's brow, and she loosened her sweater with the hand Jil had freed from a grocery bag. "It's warm out today. Have you girls been outside?"

"No, not yet." Gigi emerged from the bathroom. "We're thinking of heading to the zoo."

Elise smiled. "Have they still got the elephants?"

Jil nodded. "Five of them. They're building a bigger enclosure."

"That's what we've been watching."

Elise's glance dropped to Jil's hand. Jil looked down and swallowed hard.

She didn't say a word, but the look that crossed her face seared Jil more than anything she might have said.

"I'll meet you outside," she said to Gigi.

Gigi nodded and dashed out the door.

Slowly, Jil removed the ring and handed it to Elise.

Later, when Jil went back to the fish, the key had been moved.

CHAPTER THIRTY-FIVE

Jil woke up, remembering that day like it had just happened. The cold fish mouth against her hand. The missing key.

The ring on her finger—solid and heavy.

It had only been a dream. So why did it feel so important?

Jess lay sleeping, the early morning sun lighting the blond hair that fell across her forehead. Jil turned over and stared at the ceiling.

This wasn't solved.

She wasn't satisfied.

If that brooch had been meant to keep Duncan away from Mila, then where was it? She closed her eyes, trying to get back inside her dream.

The staircase. The crack in the side.

She opened her eyes.

Was she imagining it, or remembering?

Elise's face when she saw Jil with the ring on her finger—surprise, disappointment, but also...fear? Was she afraid of what Jil had seen?

She sat up. That crack in the staircase had been there—in reality, not just in her dream. And she suddenly knew why Elise had left her that ring specifically—yes, in part to say she forgave her for trespassing, but also to remind her of what Elise knew she must have seen that day.

She crept out of the room and tiptoed downstairs. Zeus bounced up from his spot in the living room and stared at her, his head cocked to one side.

"In a minute, buddy."

She reached into the fish head.

The key was back.

She drew it out and stared at it for a long moment. The door to Elise's library hadn't been locked in years, but it had to—it must—open something else.

In the library, she studied the staircase from every angle. The wrought iron railing, the polished wooden steps—and the intricate paneling making one impressive column up to the loft. Jil approached the left side first, her face inches from the wood panels. Something here had to give.

But what?

She squinted into each corner, pressed her fingers along each seam. Then she knocked along the bottom.

There. A hollow thud. Just like in the window seat above. Only this thud sounded much deeper. The space under the stairs would be big. She slid her curved fingers down the hollow panel. There. A thumbhole. She lifted it and a small two-by-two inch piece of paneling came away, revealing a key hole.

"Of course." She couldn't help smiling. Elise's memories were fading already, but her love of treasure and treasure hunting would stay with her forever.

She fit the key into the tiny keyhole.

It turned.

As she stood, stunned, the entire panel opened outward—a small door. This is what she had seen reflected in the mirror that day—almost shut, but not quite back in place. She examined the hinges on the inside

Who had built this? And when?

Holding her breath, she stepped inside. She could stand upright with both arms extended. The space was approximately the size of Elise's walk-in closet.

"Are there any more rabbit holes in this house you'd like to tell me about?" she muttered to the air.

She searched for a light and found a switch by the small doorway. When she flicked it on, she sighed, partly in disappointment and partly in relief. The room was empty.

But what had Elise kept in here? Maybe nothing. Could it have been a panic room? A storage area?

She reached out to touch the walls. A quilted material lined the space from floor to low ceiling. She'd only seen padding like this used for one reason: to protect paintings.

Along the farthest side of the room sat a drafting table. Smudges of paint covered the surface and the walls nearby.

Her heart sped up. Could this be where Elise had worked?

She edged over to the table and picked up a thick red folder. When she opened it, a sheet of paper fell onto the floor. She bent to pick it up, recognizing it as a list of reference material—newspaper articles, it looked like, complete with volume numbers. She'd lived with Elise long enough to know that these volume numbers must refer to the ledgers she'd had made of her newspaper collections.

Jil put down the list on the table and flipped through the folder. Clippings. A few photographs. And another key.

Her eyes widened as she realized what she was holding. A stack of articles about art crimes, beginning with the 1975 theft of *Evening River Seine*. Elise had left her a reference list of confessions. A history of her other life.

She breathed out slowly, her hand shaking. Now that she had it, she wasn't sure she wanted to look.

The doorbell rang and she jumped. Before hurrying out, she slammed the door to the secret room shut. She'd have to look through the rest of this later. In secret. And then burn it.

She saw Nic Fraser's outline through the glass and wrenched open the door.

"What the hell are you doing here?" Jil glared at him.

"Are you always this hostile after people see you in your underwear?"

"Stay out of my way today, Nic."

He laid a gentle hand on her shoulder. "It would be easier if you'd let me help you."

"I think you've helped enough, thanks. Hard to see what more you could do after having me arrested for murder. A charge I *still* haven't been cleared of, by the way."

He spun her around. "Listen, I need to tell you something."

"I don't want to hear it. I can't take anymore bullshit, Nic."

He shook his head. "Just do me a favor, okay?" He didn't wait for her to answer. "No matter what you hear today, no matter what happens—don't do anything stupid."

"Thanks for stopping by."

He made an exasperated noise and left. She slammed the door behind him.

Half an hour later, a message from Morgan lit up her screen. *St. Clair got the arrest warrant for Fraser. Call me as soon as you can.*

Her heart stopped.

Is that why he'd come over? To tell her St. Clair had actually gotten him a warrant to arrest her? What evidence could they possibly have?

No way she planned to be detained today. Not when she felt so close to finding out the truth.

Don't leave town, St. Clair had said. Well, she was about to engage in some civil disobedience.

Padraig had a hell of a lot of explaining to do.

CHAPTER THIRTY-SIX

Jil pulled on a pair of jeans and a sweater, yanked on mismatched socks, and grabbed two spare outfits out of the closet. She looked at Elise's travel bag and decided to borrow it. Then again, what if it was lined with rubies or something?

"Do you have your passport?" Jess swiped hair out of her face.

"Yes, right here." She couldn't even remember the last time she'd used it.

To her credit, Jess didn't ask how long she was going, or why.

"I'll stay here with Zeus," she said before Jil could even ask.

She stopped long enough to kiss Jess good-bye. Properly. Then she grabbed her gear and got in the taxi.

How far had they gone? Had they suspended her passport? Would they be waiting for her at the airport?

At the check-in counter, she presented her passport and itinerary and waited, her heart beating so fast she felt the air in her lungs constrict.

"Hmm," said the flight attendant. He frowned and looked at her.

She met his eye. "Problem?"

"You're not in the system yet. Did you just buy the ticket, by any chance?"

"Yes, today," Jil said. *An hour ago.*

He clicked through to something else and smiled. "Ah. Here we go."

She waited, consciously not tapping her fingers on the desk as the printer chugged and spat out her boarding pass. "Here you go."

"Thank you."

As she moved away, he called out, "Hey!"

She turned back.

"Your passport."

Jil took it out of his hand and rolled her eyes. "Thank you. Can you tell I haven't had my coffee yet?"

He grinned.

Practical intelligence—that's what she'd scored highest on in all those stupid school tests they'd made her take. Her IQ was above average, but that didn't matter. Practical intelligence got people further along. Their ability to smile and say the right thing to the right person. Grease the wheels. Get to the next step.

How far would her practical intelligence get her today?

Down the elevator, past the smoothie kiosk on the mezzanine, and down another elevator to the security line. Fixing her gaze on the bookshop down the hall, she advanced with the line, one person at a time, until her turn came.

Jil dumped her carry-on bag onto the roller belt and threw in her phone, money clip, and boarding pass. She'd timed it on purpose so she didn't have a lot of time to loiter at the gate. Just in case. She avoided looking over her shoulder, or down at her watch. These people were trained to look for anxiety in travelers.

The security guard beckoned with one hand and threw his arms up, gesturing that she should come through the metal detector. It beeped. Her damn steel-toed boots. She'd forgotten about those. She gave him a small smile and rolled her eyes. "Sorry. Footwear."

He waved her toward him and scanned her up and down, from side to side. "Boots off, please."

She complied, handing over her footwear to another guard who sent them through the small-items scanner as she waited barefoot on the thin airport carpet.

The other guard nodded and handed her back her boots. "Go ahead."

She grabbed her stuff and headed toward her gate. Ten minutes until boarding.

They ticked by slowly. She never imagined she could cram so many activities into one ten-minute period, trying not to watch the clock. Behind the bookshelves in the bookstore seemed like a good place to keep out of sight, so she browsed the literature section.

Every title reminded her of Elise.

She looked at the magazines for a while instead, but the glossy centerfolds of glamorous women irritated her even more than usual. What the hell did the photographers think they were capturing?

She looked for Ellen on a cover somewhere—found her—and felt marginally better.

Six minutes.

Exiting the bookstore, she looked up for a sign to the ladies' room and found one. Right next door. For once, she'd actually hoped for a longer walk. She ducked in anyway. Used the toilet and washed her hands.

Outside, she heard raised voices, and the door to the washroom burst open. She froze.

A kid ran in. Four years old at most. "Gotta go, gotta go," she squealed.

Jil stepped back quickly as the girl's mother hurried in after her. "Sorry." She flashed Jil an apologetic smile.

Five minutes.

In the hallway, flight crews marched by, rolling their carry-on bags behind them. Jil took note of the different uniforms. The scarves, short and pointed like bowties. The professional high heels. The silk stockings. She scoped out a coffee kiosk and made her way over.

Four minutes.

A female captain walked by in her wide-brimmed hat as Jil shuffled forward in line. She felt like saluting.

"What will you have?"

"Vanilla latte, please." Why not? If St. Clair planned to throw her in jail, she might as well enjoy her time on the outside. As she waited, she kept sight lines on the elevator, the gate, and the opposite hallway. This was the perfect vantage point.

"Vanilla latte?"

She took her drink and moved to the side. Two minutes.

"Calling all passengers for Flight 598 to Shannon, Ireland. Passengers traveling with small children, and those who need extra time to come on board are now boarding. Flight 598 to Shannon, Ireland, now boarding."

Purposely slowing her walk, Jil walked to the gate and stood at the back of the advanced boarding line.

Inside, sitting next to the window, she waited.

The plane taxied down the runway.

They were airborne.

CHAPTER THIRTY-SEVEN

J il didn't realize she'd dozed off until the announcement
came to buckle up for landing. She couldn't believe she'd
made it.

For a wild moment, she wondered if the police had called
ahead.

If they'd found out she'd boarded the plane.

If they'd be waiting to arrest her as she cleared customs.

But she got through without difficulty and breathed a sigh of
relief mixed with suspicion as she passed the luggage carousels and
searched out a sign for the taxi stand.

She stopped for a minute to think. Something didn't add up.
Why hadn't she been detained? Why hadn't someone come after
her? How had she made it to Ireland without any problems at all, if
she was the main suspect in a murder? It didn't make sense.

She pulled out her phone. *St. Clair got the arrest warrant for
Fraser.*

Stupid! St. Clair wasn't getting a warrant on Fraser's behalf;
she was getting one to *arrest* him!

She thought of turning around to help him.

*Hello? He's screwed up. He can't be trusted. Leave him alone
and look after yourself.*

Padraig. He held the key.

As she ducked through the revolving door, she almost missed
him standing on the sidewalk, smoking a honey vanilla cigar.

She stared at him for a second. How the hell did he know she'd arrived? And what cheek to meet her here, just like old times, when she'd come to give him a piece of her fist.

"What the fuck?" she spat as soon as she got within earshot.

He steered her through the crowd by the top of her arm. "You can yell at me in the car," he muttered into her ear. "Make a scene and we'll both be arrested. Airports are no joke around here."

She shook him off—subtly—but allowed him to lead her to the parking bay, where an old black two-seater sat waiting in the five-minute parking. She headed around to the passenger side.

"You don't know how to drive in this country, Kidd." Padraig chuckled, and she realized that she'd come around the driver's side.

She shot him a death glare but circled the back of the car and opened the passenger's side door.

"I knew you'd come," Padraig said when they were shut inside the car.

"You think this is funny!" Jil shot back. "Do you know they think I killed her?"

"Who?"

"Elise! Who do you think?"

"No, I mean who thinks you killed her?"

Jil slammed back in her seat. She felt like a petulant teenager all over again. She fixed him with raised eyebrows. "Detective St. Clair."

Padraig stroked his beard. For a while, he wouldn't meet her gaze, but then he looked over and sighed. "We'll take care of that when we get back."

Jil stared at him incredulously. "What the hell are you people, spies?"

He guffawed. "Spies. Oh, how I wish. Come on, I'll buy you a drink."

"I'm not sure I feel like spending time with you." Jil glared at him. She felt cheated. Abandoned. Downright pissed off.

"Aye, well, you've only got a few hours and then we're going back home. Too bad you couldn't have come earlier and helped me sort out this mess here."

"You might have clued me in."

He sighed. "I should have. I knew you'd figure it out eventually. But she hoped you wouldn't so I played along even though I knew better. So let me take you for supper and a pint, okay?"

They drove in silence. She turned on her phone and scrolled through the messages. Morgan.

Where the hell are you? Jessica was at the station this morning giving a statement. You've got an alibi. Should be cleared up soon.

Jil shook her head. She should have known she'd do that. She knew as well as Jil did that suspected murderers weren't allowed on planes so she'd tried to clear her name before she'd even taken off. Why hadn't she seen that one coming? And what was this going to mean for her job?

"We're going to have to sort out Jess too when we get back," Jil muttered.

Padraig frowned. "Right. You'll feel better with some fish and chips in your stomach." Padraig let Jil lead the way to their table, following the server. He ordered a pint of ale for himself and a glass of cider for Jil.

"Full or half pint for you?" the server asked.

"Half, please," Jil replied. "Apparently, I'm flying again."

Padraig nudged her under the table. "And two specials."

Amazing how easily she let herself collapse back into her role she'd tried to outgrow. When would she ever truly emerge from his shadow?

"You owe me a lot more than a pint," Jil growled. "Now start talking."

Padraig fixed her with a tired look. "I'm sorry to have left you alone with all this."

She looked away. His insight cut through her—every time. "I'm over it. But I came all the way here to find you because you wouldn't answer your fucking phone, and now you owe me an explanation."

Padraig stroked his beard roughly. "Aye. I suppose I do. But just because you ask some questions doesn't mean you get all the answers. Agreed?"

"Fine. Start at the beginning."

"The beginning? Well. That's going back a fair bit."

Jil waited while the server put down their drinks. "Go back to the orphanage. And the expatriation."

Padraig sighed and took a sip of ale. "You know we all grew up together, yes?"

"Yes. But it seems like that's a pretty loose term for kids who got sent over on a boat together, then grew up on a working farm."

"We were released when we were eighteen. We found our own lives. In different ways, obviously."

"Elise always talked about her parents like she'd grown up with them."

"Well, she did, to a point. They died when she was about fourteen. After that, the three of us were the only family we had."

"You looked after one another, you mean."

Padraig drummed his finger against the side of his sweating glass. "She was the only one among us who came over with anything. No money, mind you. None of us had any money. But she did have some very valuable jewelry. When we left the farm, she sold it all to help us get a fresh start. A real chance at careers."

"You took that chance, obviously, and so did she."

"We did. And then there was Duncan."

"So…how did Elise get the jewelry in the first place?" Jil asked.

"From her father, Mr. Fitzgerald. She brought it over on the boat, sewn into the hems of her coats and skirts. How she managed to keep them close to her for all those years afterward is a mystery to me."

Jil frowned. Elise had many talents, and secret keeping seemed to be one of her finest.

"She kept one piece though. Her mother's ring."

Jil looked up quickly. "The emerald ring you mean?"

"Her mother's engagement ring."

She bit her lip. Of course.

"Her father was a lawyer, wasn't he? What was he doing with jewelry like that?"

Padraig took a long sip, and Jil felt his resistance loosening. "You'll have to understand the times he was working in. Mr. Fitzgerald started his practice in the early nineteen thirties. He dealt with some rough folks back then. The Great War had just ended, and the Depression had just started. Times were pretty desperate. Lawyers were working for pittance—I mean, twenty-five dollars a deal, which could take them all week. Factory workers made almost as much as they did—even on reduced earnings."

Jil waited. She felt threads of a connection start to form in her mind. The 1920s cigarette lighter took on a whole new meaning.

"People had no money. Even their valuables weren't valuable anymore, because nobody could afford to buy them if they had to liquidate. Mr. Fitzgerald, though, he knew how to make a penny stretch. He'd been a poor kid too. He wasn't afraid to eat cabbage soup and neither was his wife. He said, fine, if the rich people wanted to pay him in art and artifacts instead of cash—because nobody had cash—then he would accept it. And wait for better times. Then sell the art and jewelry and everything else for their real value when the economy had turned around."

"But that took years. Didn't it?"

"Aye. Nobody knew when it started what the Depression would be like. They didn't know how long it would last. And certainly no idea it'd last for years. Mr. Fitzgerald developed quite a collection. By the time Elise was born in the late forties, the Depression had long since ended, and Mr. Fitzgerald was back from the war and back in business. He had cash flow again, as a lawyer, and a collection worth hundreds of thousands of dollars. But the situation in Ireland was getting a bit dangerous for him. He'd developed quite a reputation. He'd planned to move his family over to Canada, and had made all the arrangements. Boxed the items and had them shipped to a storage facility in Montreal."

The server returned with two platters of fish and chips. The smell of the salted fries made Jil's mouth water. Days of stress had taken a toll on her appetite.

She grabbed a steaming chip from the plate and blew on it while Padraig took a long draught from his glass. "Go on."

"Well, just as they were getting ready to go, Mrs. Fitzgerald took ill. She died of tuberculosis three months later, as did Elise's youngest sister."

"And both your parents," Jil finished.

"Aye, and both my parents."

My mother smelled of rosewater and told me stories as she washed the dishes. I miss her most while I'm rinsing teapots.

Not everything Elise told her could have been a lie.

"And what happened to Mr. Fitzgerald?"

Padraig squinted, as if trying to recall an elusive memory. "I'm not sure they ever did find out." His voice dropped even lower. "One night, shortly before he was supposed to leave for Canada, he disappeared coming home from the office. They thought he might have had a car accident or been run off the road. In any case, the police came to the door. Elise was only fourteen at the time—and she and her two younger sisters ended up on the boat with Duncan and me and all our lot. The youngest ones were sent to foster homes, but we went to the farm."

Jil shook her head, imagining the frightened cluster of kids separated and sent to live with strangers. A thought clicked. "Wait. What happened to the stuff Mr. Fitzgerald sent over to Montreal?"

Padraig smiled sadly. "Well, since he never came to claim it, a lot of it was stolen. Elise spent the next twenty years trying to recover it all."

Jil sat back. Now she understood what had attracted Elise to the underground world in the first place. She had to move like she belonged there to track down everything that had been stolen.

"Her father meant everything to her, and his collection was all she had left of him. She got herself an education, of course. A real career. But she kept one foot in the shadows, one ear to the ground."

"So that's why she and Duncan paired up."

"Aye. He was helping pay her back I suppose, for what she tried to give him by way of a start in life. He helped her track down some of the bigger items. But he was a bad seed. Once he made contacts in the underground, he never turned back. Made himself an entire career out of it, and dragged Elise right along with him."

"But she ended up on the right side of the law and Duncan didn't."

Padraig sniffed. "He was too greedy to be patient. For Elise, it was never about the money; it was always about the art."

"And for Duncan it was the other way around."

Jil ate in silence for a few minutes, digesting this part of Elise's history. Finally, the lump in her throat made it impossible to take another bite. She had to know.

"Why did she take me, Padraig? I want the truth."

Padraig put down his fork. "Elise had never been a foster parent before," Padraig said. "And I suppose you know that now."

"Yeah. So how did she get clearance?"

Padraig looked away. "She didn't. I did."

"What?"

"You were sixteen. Old enough to be emancipated. I knew they'd never find you another long-term placement at your age, and it would have been group homes for you. But I also knew my house—my long hours, with no set schedule—was not a good fit for a young girl like you, so I applied to be your legal guardian, and they approved me, based on our history."

"Well, since I was already sleeping on your office couch."

Padraig cracked a wry smile. "I didn't mention that. But I did call in a few favors to have things moved along. That situation at the Hendricksons'…" he trailed off and Jil suppressed a shudder. He shook his head, exhaling loudly.

"So then what?"

"Then you were off their docket and mine to worry about. So I asked Elise to look after you."

Jil felt the heat rising in her neck.

"But why did she agree?"

Padraig looked away but didn't answer.

Jil waited, and finally he said, "I owed it to your mother, and Elise knew that. I didn't even have to ask her, really. She volunteered."

So many conflicting emotions. "So I was out of the system at sixteen? She never told me. She never said the agency wasn't paying her to take me. All the clothes she bought me, the school supplies, the food I ate. God, Padraig, we ate like queens."

He chuckled. "I know. Elise cooked marvelously. I rather figured that's why you liked Jess."

Jil shot him a withering look.

"I just meant you liked to eat and having cooks around is handy."

"I can cook."

He laughed out loud. "Sure you can. And eat too. Good thing Elise was wealthy."

She shook her head. "She was paying my way, all this time."

"She didn't need the money, believe me."

Jil stopped, and grabbed his arm. "My scholarship."

He nodded, his eyes on the ground. "Aye. We put that together for you."

"You lied to me!"

"You never would have accepted it otherwise!"

"Of course I wouldn't!"

"Well, you needed an education. What good would it have done any of us to have you working in a pizza parlor with brains like yours?"

Jil exhaled loudly and took a swig of her coffee. "You put in your money, then?"

"Both of us, together."

"Well, I'll be paying you back now."

Padraig's beard twitched, like he was trying not to laugh. "I'll take your last case at St. Marguerite's as payment."

Jil stared at him. "Why do I feel like a puppet in some show?"

Padraig looked back. "Aye. I'm sorry about that. You know I only ever tried to protect you. As did Elise. She didn't want you to know about her past because she hoped she'd raised you properly. With a good moral code."

"Her life was complicated, Padraig. She dealt with so much alone. I wish…I wish somehow she could have told me."

"You know that sometimes you carry around the weight of your parents' lives?"

"Yeah," Jil said softly.

"Well, she had a lot of it from her father, and Duncan, of course."

"I just wish she'd shared that part of her life with me. I feel like there are a whole lifetime of conversations we're never going to get to have. She can't tell me her side. I can only guess."

He smiled sadly. "She never wanted you to know. At least until she was dead."

"But she left me clues. Why?"

He chuckled. "I think she knew you'd go looking. She wanted you to have the truth—as much as she could leave you—if ever you started trying to find it."

She fixed him with a stare. "What are you doing here really? What family business do you have to do? Or were you just running away?"

Padraig finished his ale. "Sorry. That's all under the category of mind your own business."

She waited him out. "I know you lied about your flight and that you took the boat over."

He narrowed his eyes. "Best be careful, Kidd."

She sat back. "You're seriously not going to tell me?"

"Not today."

"How am I supposed to trust you when you keep lying to me, Padraig?"

He locked eyes with her and she was forced to look into his face. The face she'd known and trusted since she was a little girl. "I'm not lying. I'm asking you to respect my privacy. Whether or not you trust me is your decision."

Jil sighed and put her chin in her hand. Her throat felt thick. "It's so hard to believe I'm never going to see her again. And that I really hardly know her."

"Of course you do."

"Our whole life is a smokescreen, Padraig…" Her voice broke and tears overflowed down her face.

"No." Padraig lifted her chin. "That isn't true."

"She lied to me."

"Yes, she did. Because she loved you. Because she didn't want to have to explain everything she left behind. Let her have her way. You were her only chance at being a mother. This was her doing her best."

CHAPTER THIRTY-EIGHT

Jess met Jil at the front door as soon as she walked up to the porch, suitcase in hand. "You have a visitor. She's been waiting over an hour."

Jil squeezed Jess's arm. "Morgan texted me. Said you were at the station?"

Jess looked down. "We'll talk about it later."

Jil nodded and moved past her into the kitchen. "Karrie. What are you doing here?"

She looked up, her forehead creased with concern. "My dad called this morning."

Jil's toes tingled like someone had dropped ice water on her feet. She sat down opposite her. "Has he said anything to the police?"

"No. Not yet. I asked him to let me talk with you first."

Jil forced herself to breathe normally, to slow her heartbeat. "Okay. What is it?"

Karrie drummed her fingers on the table, her face serious. "He had ruled out carbon monoxide poisoning because there was no evidence of that at the scene, but he did mention another possibility. He said he'd only ever seen something like this once before in his career. And he can't even be certain it's the same thing, but he'd once seen a case about a particular cancer drug interacting with an inhalant to produce the type of effect Elise had. That's why he'd looked harder at cyanide poisoning, but ruled that out. Still, it looks sort of like—"

"A toxin?"

Karrie nodded. "It's a rare occurrence, but that is the only thing that fits."

"So she was poisoned." Jil leaned back in the chair, surprised to feel Jess solidly behind her. Jess's hand squeezed her shoulder, and she put her hand over top of it.

"But why? And how?" She turned to Karrie. "What is this inhalant, exactly?"

Karrie frowned. "It's not that hard to find, really. Janitors and hospitals use diluted versions all the time in their industrial cleaning products."

"But undiluted it's lethal."

"To someone in Elise's condition, on the drugs she was taking…" Karrie looked up, her eyes troubled. "Absolutely."

Jil's mind raced back to the bottle of cleaner she'd found in the garbage. *Mix with nine parts water…*

Who could have used it on her?

She looked up at Jess, who frowned back at her questioningly.

Only one person made sense.

But why the hell would he want Elise dead?

Jil watched from the top window as Ben pulled into the driveway and idled in his truck for a few moments. He took off his hat and approached the door.

Jil opened it before he could knock. She noticed that his eyes looked sunken and hollow—like he hadn't slept for weeks.

He followed her to the kitchen. When he saw St. Clair, his face blanched even whiter.

"You're going to arrest me for giving her that cleaner?" his Adam's apple bobbed.

St. Clair leaned against the counter. "Why don't you just tell me what happened?"

Ben took several deep breaths as he twisted his painter's cap around and around.

"Why don't you sit down, Ben?" Jil said gently. She pulled a chair out for him and he sat down slowly, staying at the edge. "When did you last speak to her?" she asked.

"Elise called me the night before she died. Asked me to come first thing in the morning to talk about repairs to the house for the spring. But she didn't answer the door when I knocked, and I...I had a real bad feeling. I knew she was sick, eh, so I knocked again, then tried the front door."

"She didn't come down?"

He shook his head. "I went in. Found her in the bathroom upstairs. Looked like she'd fallen, but then I thought, why would she be in the shower with her clothes on?"

Jil leaned against the counter. She felt sick. "Then what happened?"

"I saw a bottle of the cleaner she'd asked for on the floor beside her. Figured she must have been using it and got a little woozy. Hit her head. Except that I didn't see any blood."

That's because she didn't fall. She hot-boxed the shower and waited.

St. Clair gave her a quizzical look. How much was showing on her face?

"What did you do next?" St. Clair asked.

"Well..." Ben's face flushed a deep scarlet, and he twisted his cap around again. "It seemed...it seemed indecent, you know, to leave her in the shower of all places. It wasn't...right, somehow. I picked her up. She wasn't stiff or anything. I heard bodies are supposed to be stiff, but she wasn't. She wasn't cold. But she was so light. I didn't realize..."

"You carried her to her bed?" St. Clair finished.

"I did. I put her blanket on her and left her there."

"You didn't call the police?"

Ben shook his head. "I didn't know how to answer the questions they were gonna ask me. Since it was me who'd left that cleaner there. I figured it would be better to leave her so someone else found her. Looking like she'd died in bed and all that."

Relief hit Jil like a cold mist down her back.

Padraig had found her in bed. He'd thought he was telling her the truth.

"You're going to arrest me now?" Ben's knees shook visibly as he tried to stand, but St. Clair shook her head. "No, Mr. Hennessy, I'm not going to arrest you. You've made things complicated, but you obviously didn't mean anything criminal."

Ben's chin trembled. "She was such a decent woman, Detective. You know? I just…I wanted…"

Jil patted his shoulder, blinking hard. "It's okay, Ben. We understand."

After he'd left, Jil turned to St. Clair, who sighed deeply and shook her head, leaning against the counter. "I'm sorry about this," she muttered. "I feel really bad about it. Especially…"

"I'm pretty sure you were just following the evidence."

"Yeah. Falsified evidence."

Jil touched her arm. "Cup of coffee, Detective?" She could almost feel St. Clair's professional posture dropping away.

"Call me Laine. You've earned it."

Jil smiled, despite herself. "Okay, Laine. Do you prefer tea?"

She raised one eyebrow and laughed a little. "I do, actually."

"Right then. Why don't you sit down?"

Laine sat down gingerly at the kitchen table and crossed her legs. By the time the kettle boiled, she'd relaxed enough to accept the steaming cup Jil handed her. Amazing how Elise's house enfolded so many different people into simple common rituals.

Laine shook her red curls back over her white collar. "Somehow, I just don't feel like going back to the precinct right now."

"I can see why you'd need a break. Can't be easy."

Laine sighed, blowing air onto the surface of her tea. "No kidding."

Jil tucked her legs up onto the chair, surprised at how stiff she felt. Her body craved some real rest. But there were still a few issues to resolve. "So, can you tell me about Nic?"

Laine exhaled a long breath. "I honestly don't know what's going to happen to him. He's in pretty big trouble."

"How did you find out what he'd done?"

"You mean, purposely tampered with evidence to protect a known art forger? Or fabricated evidence against you to have Mrs. Fitzgerald's body exhumed?" She rolled her eyes. "We'll notice an obstruction pattern here. He's going to be reprimanded. He deserves it."

Jil couldn't argue. She bit her lip.

"He's a good friend of mine too," Laine said softly.

"Which makes it worse, doesn't it?"

She looked up, almost sharply. "He let his personal demons get in the way of the job. And that can't happen."

"So has he really been arrested?"

"Detained. Questioned. Not formally charged yet. That would come from internal affairs." She tilted her head back, as if worried she'd said too much.

"What if I put in a bid to ask them to drop it?" Jil said.

Laine stared at her. "Why would you do that?"

Jil poured milk slowly into her clear mug, watching the dark tea cloud—the light lines swirling and blending until it was all the color of blond hardwood. "I know how hard it is to find out someone you loved isn't the person you thought. I'm not saying I agree with his methods. Clearly. But I understand why he did it."

❖

At 8:59, Jil got out of the car and approached the door to the post office. Her fingers were tingling. What if it was empty? Worse—what if it held more secrets? She didn't think she could take any more.

The slow-moving postal worker gave her a watery smile as he slid back the deadbolt on the door. Jil waited impatiently for him to move away from the door, then dashed inside…and stared at the box for a full thirty seconds before approaching.

Luckily, nobody else was there to observe this.

Finally, she twisted the key into the slot and pulled back the door. Inside lay a thick brown envelope.

This. This is what she'd been waiting for. She felt the outline of something hard as she tucked the envelope under her arm and retraced her steps to the car.

The Fabergé brooch spilled into her hand. She bounced it in her palm, the weight of the precious stones hefty, the surface rough.

This had been here the whole time.

Her hands had gone cold and she struggled to open the letter. What did Elise have to say for herself?

What *could* she possibly say that would make a difference?

There, in Elise's beautiful script: just three lines.

For safekeeping, darling, in case you ever need it. And you'll know when you do.
With all my love and deepest affection.
Elise.

She read it twice, three times. Folded it and slipped it into the front lapel of her black jacket. Then she sat down on the concrete fountain and slipped the ring onto her finger—on the right side, where it wouldn't have to be replaced. Just in case.

When had she gotten so sentimental?

She took out the letter again and read it one more time. *With all my love and deepest affection.* For the first time in weeks, she felt like she could breathe. Really breathe. She inhaled, and felt her stomach expand, her lungs fill.

Her mind replayed the conversation she'd memorized, finding new meaning.

You're never to make contact with her. And if she finds you—"
"How would she find me?"
"You might be surprised."
He sighed heavily. "If she finds me there's not much I can do about it."

"I need more than that, Duncan."

He chuckled. Another rustle, like he was digging into a pocket or a small bag. "Here. Pin it on yourself. Take it as my promise."

The butterfly signaled freedom. Elise had traded a priceless painting for Duncan's promise that he would never interfere with her life. Would never reveal to Jil all the secrets he knew would destroy her memories.

The nasty voice—that niggling distrust in the back of her head that doubted—was silenced.

Elise had loved her.

No matter what else she'd done in her life—how many compromises she'd had to make to reconcile the past she'd been born into with the future she wanted—she'd loved Jil in the best way she could.

That had to be enough.

❖

Jil pulled the rented car into the roundabout at the airport. "Checked in virtually?"

Mila looked at her with a wry smile. "I can't believe you're doing this for me."

"Well, you can thank Padraig more than me. He's the one who set this up."

"But still. You could have stopped him if you'd wanted to. What you did for Nic was enough. You could have stopped there."

"I don't pretend to agree with everything," Jil said. "But I know you didn't hurt Elise. And I know that staying here will put you in danger with Duncan. At least now you'll have a chance to start over."

"Yeah."

"Where will you go?"

Mila winked. "You don't think I should tell you really, do you?"

Jil laughed. "If it were me, I'd go to Europe. So many countries, so little need for passports."

"You are a pretty good detective, I have to say."

She rolled her eyes. "After I found out about Elise and Duncan, I started contemplating running a produce stand. And when I found out Elise and Padraig had been colluding about me since I was a teenager, I seriously almost quit."

Mila turned so she was looking Jil in the eye. "You trust people who lie to you. That doesn't make you a bad detective, you know. It makes you a loyal daughter."

Jil popped the trunk to let Mila grab her carry-on. Her words replayed in the empty space she left behind after she slammed the door.

It had been a long time since she'd been anyone's daughter. But she supposed if she had to fit herself into a box for either Padraig or Elise, that's where she'd best be shelved.

How many homes had she lived in, with foster mothers who weren't mothers at all? Sharing melamine plates and front-door cubbies, using toothbrushes that were suspiciously damp when she picked them up?

And then suddenly there was Elise's warm kitchen.

Elise, who'd never had a child before—let alone a teenager with such a past.

All the way home, she let the memories of their life together play through her mind. Things she hadn't wanted to remember, or allowed herself to feel, just in case it had all turned out to be a lie.

But there were some things you couldn't lie about, and Elise loving her had been the truth.

She cruised by their old house, where a For Sale sign hung swinging by the old birch tree. Someone else could find happiness here, and she'd be happy for them.

Her life was back at her loft, with Jess.

❖

Jil stood outside the door to her loft for a few extra moments, just savoring the feeling of coming home to someone. It was a feeling she hadn't expected to have, let alone miss.

As she opened the fire door, the warm smell of cinnamon flooded over her head. Jess turned around from the counter where she was putting something hot on the cooling rack. "Hey, you're home."

Bread. Cinnamon bread.

Jil swallowed hard, past the lump in her throat.

When she wrapped Jess in her arms, she made a silent promise to whoever might be listening that she'd never let her go again.

Jess held her for a long time, then finally, they broke away.

"I have one question left." Jess leaned back against the counter.

Jil mirrored her movements, finding a spot against the island. "I know. I have the same question."

"About the Monet?"

Jil pursed her lips. "God, she was full of secrets, wasn't she?"

Jess sighed. "Maybe it's better that we don't know. Innocent by reason of ignorance, right?"

"What I wouldn't give for just one more hour with her." Jil sighed. Tears welled up in her eyes and she let them fall freely—a sudden storm that would pass if she just let it come.

Jess laid a hand on her arm. "I hardly think you'd waste the time…"

"No, that's really the first thing I'd ask her." Jil laughed through her tears. "Elise, tell me that story about how you stole a Monet?"

And what else haven't you told me?

About the Author

Stevie Mikayne writes fiction with a literary edge, combining her obsession with traditional literature with a love of dynamic characters and strong language. She is currently pursuing a PhD in creative writing from Lancaster University in the UK. Her first mystery novel, *UnCatholic Conduct*, was short-listed for a Lambda Literary Award.

When she met a woman who could make the perfect cup of tea, create a window seat under the stairs, and build a library with a ladder, she knew she'd better marry her before someone else did. They live in Ottawa, Canada, with their young daughter.

Books Available from Bold Strokes Books

Illicit Artifacts by Stevie Mikayne. Her foster mother's death cracked open a secret world Jil never wanted to see…and now she has to pick up the stolen pieces. (978-1-62639-4-728)

Pathfinder by Gun Brooke. Heading for their new homeworld, *Exodus's* chief engineer Adina Vantressa and nurse Briar Lindemay carry game-changing secrets that may well cause them to lose everything when disaster strikes. (978-1-62639-4-445)

Prescription for Love by Radclyffe. Dr. Flannery Rivers finds herself attracted to the new ER chief, city girl Abigail Remy, and the incendiary mix of city and country, fire and ice, tradition and change is combustible. (978-1-62639-5-701)

Ready or Not by Melissa Brayden. Uptight Mallory Spencer finds relinquishing control to bartender Hope Sanders too tall an order in fast-paced New York City. (978-1-62639-4-438)

Summer Passion by MJ Williamz. Women loving women is forbidden in 1946 Hollywood, yet Jean and Maggie strive to keep their love alive and away from prying eyes. (978-1-62639-5-404)

The Princess and the Prix by Nell Stark. "Ugly duckling" Princess Alix of Monaco was resigned to loneliness until she met racecar driver Thalia d'Angelis. (978-1-62639-4-742)

Winter's Harbor by Aurora Rey. Lia Brooks isn't looking for love in Provincetown, but when she discovers chocolate croissants and pastry chef Alex McKinnon, her winter retreat quickly starts heating up. (978-1-62639-4-988)

The Time Before Now by Missouri Vaun. Vivian flees a disastrous affair, embarking on an epic, transformative journey to escape her past, until destiny introduces her to Ida, who helps her rediscover trust, love, and hope. (978-1-62639-446-9)

Twisted Whispers by Sheri Lewis Wohl. Betrayal, lies, and secrets—whispers of a friend lost to darkness. Can a reluctant psychic set things right or will an evil soul destroy those she loves? (978-1-62639-439-1)

The Courage to Try by C.A. Popovich. Finding love is worth getting past the fear of trying. (978-1-62639-528-2)

Break Point by Yolanda Wallace. In a world readying for war, can love find a way? (978-1-62639-568-8)

Countdown by Julie Cannon. Can two strong-willed, powerful women overcome their differences to save the lives of seven others and begin a life they never imagined together? (978-1-62639-471-1)

Keep Hold by Michelle Grubb. Claire knew some things should be left alone and some rules should never be broken, but the most forbidden, well, they are the most tempting. (978-1-62639-502-2)

Deadly Medicine by Jaime Maddox. Dr. Ward Thrasher's life is in turmoil. Her partner Jess left her, and her job puts her in the path of a murderous physician who has Jess in his sights. (978-1-62639-424-7)

New Beginnings by KC Richardson. Can the connection and attraction between Jordan Roberts and Kirsten Murphy be enough for Jordan to trust Kirsten with her heart? (978-1-62639-450-6)

Officer Down by Erin Dutton. Can two women who've made careers out of being there for others in crisis find the strength to need each other? (978-1-62639-423-0)

Reasonable Doubt by Carsen Taite. Just when Sarah and Ellery think they've left dangerous careers behind, a new case sets them—and their hearts—on a collision course. (978-1-62639-442-1)

Tarnished Gold by Ann Aptaker. Cantor Gold must outsmart the Law, outrun New York's dockside gangsters, outplay a shady art dealer, his lover, and a beautiful curator, and stay out of a killer's gun sights. (978-1-62639-426-1)

The Renegade by Amy Dunne. Post-apocalyptic survivors Alex and Evelyn secretly find love while held captive by a deranged cult, but when their relationship is discovered, they must fight for their freedom—or die trying. (978-1-62639-427-8)

Thrall by Barbara Ann Wright. Four women in a warrior society must work together to lift an insidious curse while caught between their own desires, the will of their peoples, and an ancient evil. (978-1-62639-437-7)

White Horse in Winter by Franci McMahon. Love between two women collides with the inner poison of a closeted horse trainer in the green hills of Vermont. (978-1-62639-429-2)

Autumn Spring by Shelley Thrasher. Can Bree and Linda, two women in the autumn of their lives, put their hearts first and find the love they've never dared seize? (978-1-62639-365-3)

The Chameleon's Tale by Andrea Bramhall. Two old friends must work through a web of lies and deceit to find themselves again, but in the search they discover far more than they ever went looking for. (978-1-62639-363-9)

Side Effects by VK Powell. Detective Jordan Bishop and Dr. Neela Sahjani must decide if it's easier to trust someone with your heart or your life as they face threatening protestors, corrupt politicians, and their increasing attraction. (978-1-62639-364-6)

Warm November by Kathleen Knowles. What do you do if the one woman you want is the only one you can't have? (978-1-62639-366-0)

In Every Cloud by Tina Michele. When Bree finally leaves her shattered life behind, is she strong enough to salvage the remaining pieces of her heart and find the place where it truly fits? (978-1-62639-413-1)

Rise of the Gorgon by Tanai Walker. When independent Internet journalist Elle Pharell goes to Kuwait to investigate a veteran's mysterious suicide, she hires Cassandra Hunt, an interpreter with a covert agenda. (978-1-62639-367-7)

Crossed by Meredith Doench. Agent Luce Hansen returns home to catch a killer and risks everything to revisit the unsolved murder of her first girlfriend and confront the demons of her youth. (978-1-62639-361-5)

Making a Comeback by Julie Blair. Music and love take center stage when jazz pianist Liz Randall tries to make a comeback with the help of her reclusive, blind neighbor, Jac Winters. (978-1-62639-357-8)

Soul Unique by Gun Brooke. Self-proclaimed cynic Greer Landon falls for Hayden Rowe's paintings and the young woman shortly after, but will Hayden, who lives with Asperger syndrome, trust her and reciprocate her feelings? (978-1-62639-358-5)

The Price of Honor by Radclyffe. Honor and duty are not always black and white—and when self-styled patriots take up arms against the government, the price of honor may be a life. (978-1-62639-359-2)

Mounting Evidence by Karis Walsh. Lieutenant Abigail Hargrove and her mounted police unit need to solve a murder and protect wetland biologist Kira Lovell during the Washington State Fair. (978-1-62639-343-1)

Threads of the Heart by Jeannie Levig. Maggie and Addison Rae-McInnis share a love and a life, but are the threads that bind them together strong enough to withstand Addison's restlessness and the seductive Victoria Fontaine? (978-1-62639-410-0)

Sheltered Love by MJ Williamz. Boone Fairway and Grey Dawson—two women touched by abuse—overcome their pasts to find happiness in each other. (978-1-62639-362-2)

Death's Doorway by Crin Claxton. Helping the dead can be deadly: Tony may be listening to the dead, but she needs to learn to listen to the living. (978-1-62639-354-7)

Searching for Celia by Elizabeth Ridley. As American spy novelist Dayle Salvesen investigates the mysterious disappearance of her ex-lover, Celia, in London, she begins questioning how well she knew Celia—and how well she knows herself. (978-1-62639-356-1).

Hardwired by C.P. Rowlands. Award-winning teacher Clary Stone and Leefe Ellis, manager of the homeless shelter for small children, stand together in a part of Clary's hometown that she never knew existed. (978-1-62639-351-6)

The Muse by Meghan O'Brien. Erotica author Kate McMannis struggles with writer's block until a gorgeous muse entices her into a world of fantasy sex and inadvertent romance. (978-1-62639-223-6)

No Good Reason by Cari Hunter. A violent kidnapping in a Peak District village pushes Detective Sanne Jensen and lifelong friend Dr. Meg Fielding closer, just as it threatens to tear everything apart. (978-1-62639-352-3)

The 45th Parallel by Lisa Girolami. Burying her mother isn't the worst thing that can happen to Val Montague when she returns to the woodsy but peculiar town of Hemlock, Oregon. (978-1-62639-342-4)

Romance by the Book by Jo Victor. If Cam didn't keep disrupting her life, maybe Alex could uncover the secret of a century-old love story, and solve the greatest mystery of all—her own heart. (978-1-62639-353-0)

A Royal Romance by Jenny Frame. In a country where class still divides, can love topple the last social taboo and allow Queen Georgina and Beatrice Elliot, a working-class girl, their happy ever after? (978-1-62639-360-8)

Bouncing by Jaime Maddox. Basketball coach Alex Dalton has been bouncing from woman to woman because no one ever held her interest, until she meets her new assistant, Britain Dodge. (978-1-62639-344-8)

All Things Rise by Missouri Vaun. Cole rescues a striking pilot who crash-lands near her family's farm, setting in motion a chain of events that will forever alter the course of her life. (978-1-62639-346-2)